The '68 Camaro Between Kenickie and Me

PACIFICA ACADEMY DRAMA SERIES
BOOK TWO

CHRISTINE MILES

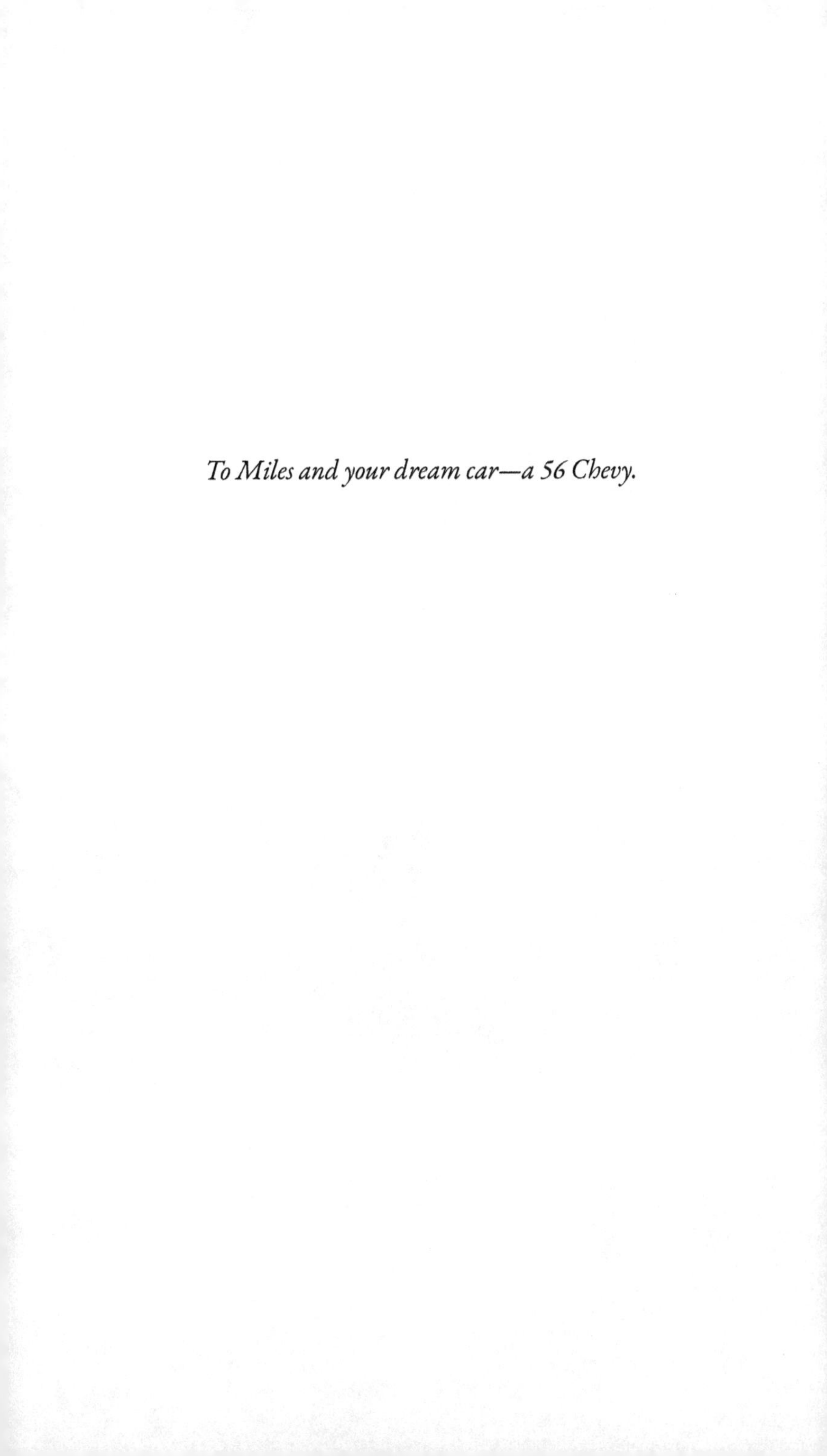

To Miles and your dream car—a 56 Chevy.

Books by Christine Miles

Adult Contemporary Romance

Timing is Everything Series

Last Time We Loved (Book One)

First Time We Laughed (Book Two)

The Time We Met (Book Three)

This Time It's Forever (Book Four)

Smart is Seriously Sexy Series

Off-the-Charts Chemistry (Book One)

Passion Under the Microscope (Coming Winter 2024)

Young Adult

Pacifica Academy Drama Series

Me, Shakespeare and the Anti-Love Club (Book One)

The '68 Camaro Between Kenickie and Me (Book Two)

Teddy Brewster's Hold On Me (Book Three)

Silver Bells for Me and (Saint) Nicolas (Book Four)

You and Me Dancing to Gershwin (Book Five)

Summer in Winter Wonderland (A Cozy Mystery)

Chapter One

Mrs. Meridian stared at me and my mother, her worn out face set in dissatisfaction. "Mrs. Carlisle, I called this meeting today because I'm very concerned."

I caught my mother's beauty queen smile slip. The former Miss Hawaii had probably chosen to wear her black, female-power Chanel suit and Chanel No. 5 perfume for this meeting.

"Natalie hasn't turned in a single hour of her twenty-five hours of community service for this school year. And it's March."

My mother glanced at me.

I met her how-could-you-embarrass-me-like-this smile without a blink. Because this was so not a big deal. But Mrs. Meridian, being in charge of the Pacifica Academy student body's required community service, had to make it a big deal.

My mother ripped her eyes from mine. "Her dad and I assumed she was taking care of this." She shot me another how-could-you look. "She usually works in his office during summer break, but last summer she was gone with her grand-parents."

And the road trip with them had been totally worth it.

"Natalie, as part of this school's curriculum," Mrs. Meridian said, talking to me as if I were a little kid, "you can't, technically, pass the year without your community service hours."

"I know that, Mrs. Meridian," I answered as politely as I could manage. "The school year just...got away from me." I looked at my mother. "I'll work in Dad's office until I've earned the hours. What's the big deal?"

"The 'big deal,'" Mrs. Meridian continued, "is that your hours are due in less than two months."

My mother frowned at her. "Why are we just now meeting about this?"

Mrs. Meridian's nose turned upward. "I've sent three e-mails to your school account."

The same account I had access to so I could check my grades.

"I never heard from you or Mr. Carlisle, which is why I scheduled this meeting."

Mrs. Meridian again punished me with her stare.

I pretended great interest in her massive collection of red and gold San Francisco 49ers crap filling the bookcase behind her desk.

"Oh, Natalie." My mother released an exasperated groan. "You didn't."

I shrugged. "I didn't think the e-mails were important." Not a complete lie. The school sent stuff to my parents all the time because they made such big, yearly, gift donations.

My mother faced me, her dark eyes hard. "We'll talk about the e-mails later. But in light of what I'm hearing and your unacceptable behavior, working in your dad's office is not an option."

Wait...what?

She glanced at Mrs. Meridian. "I'm sure you know I'm involved with many charities. She can work with me until her hours are finished. Will that suffice?"

Oh, my God. Absolutely not. Because working with her would turn into a form of punishment. For *embarrassing* her.

"Of course, Mrs. Carlisle. But I do have a couple of other suggestions if—"

"What are they?" Anything had to be better than my mother.

"Well, the school works closely with a couple of nonprofits and they always need help. Or if you'd like to earn your hours on campus, Mr. Lowry has started working on set construction for the spring musical, *Grease*."

The drama kids? That could be a different kind of torture than working with my mother. Being around kids who lived and breathed theater?

I frowned at my lap.

"He told me he's short on help with the start of spring sports, and there's much to build and paint." She leaned back in her chair. "I'll be sending an e-mail to parents about him needing help and this being a way for students to finish their hours. Or start and finish them."

My mother focused on me again. "I think it's nice Mrs. Meridian has offered two other options as a way for you to fix this mess you've created. You need to make a decision right now. I have a luncheon to get to and need to speak with Mrs. Meridian privately before I leave."

Their conversation would include her signature smile, apologies, and another "gift donation" to the school. But as much as I hated to admit it, she was right. I'd gotten myself into this and had a choice to make. Spend twenty-five hours with her and watch people worship her, or spend it at another nonprofit and doing something boring. Like filing. I couldn't believe it, but working on the set seemed like the best choice. I'd also be really working so the time would go by faster.

"Natalie, we're waiting. What are you going to do?"

"Help Mr. Lowry." I had heard the technical theater teacher was pretty cool, which meant he *had* to be better than my mother.

"Okay." Mrs. Meridian leaned forward. "You'll start this Saturday. The hours are eight to noon every Saturday morning until the twenty-first of April. And that does include two Saturdays over spring break."

My eyes widened. "Saturday mornings?" *And* two spring break Saturdays?

Her satisfied smile became innocent. "Did I fail to mention Mr. Lowry and his crew work Saturday mornings? They can't work after school. That's when play rehearsals take place."

I knew that, too. I just hadn't made the connection.

"And there's so much to do, Mr. Lowry can't stop for those two Saturdays."

I stared at Mrs. Meridian. *Score one for the old bat.*

"You'll get your community service sheet from Mrs. Oliveri every Friday," she continued. "Mr. Lowry will sign off on it every Saturday and give it to me. Understood?"

"She understands," my mother answered for me. "Please wait for me out there."

I stood, grabbed my backpack and marched from Mrs. Meridian's office. Every Saturday morning for four hours. I did the math and my steps faltered when I reached the school office's quiet main area. Seven Saturdays.

A tall boy with sandy-blond hair, who I recognized as a fellow junior, walked in and headed straight for Mrs. Oliveri. She sat behind the front desk.

"I need to talk to Mrs. Meridian really quick about my community service," he said.

She was obviously on the hunt for students and their hours.

I dropped my backpack near the closest chair and flopped down.

"She's with someone, but should be done soon," Mrs. Oliveri said as the phone rang.

Eight o'clock for the next seven Saturdays. There went my Friday night social life.

The boy looked at me. He smiled and it seemed a bit wicked. But in a teasing way.

I glared at him and started playing with the hem of my god-awful navy-blue cardigan sweater that completed the girl's school uniform of a khaki skort and white polo shirt.

The boy stuck his hands in the pockets of his khaki pants, headed toward me, and, for some reason, sat in the seat beside me. Though there were two empty chairs across from us. And I noticed, with him now so close, he smelled good. Body wash made for guys good.

"Natalie Carlisle's in the office. You don't look too happy to be here. What'd you do?" he asked. With way too much interest and excitement.

I lifted my head, turned right and our eyes connected.

Mrs. Oliveri was still on the phone, so I quietly said, "I told some nosy boy to mind his own fucking business."

His blue eyes flashed with humor. "Did it work?" he asked, also in a low voice. "Did the nosy boy mind his own fucking business?"

"Who are you and why are you talking to me?" I snapped.

The humor in his eyes dimmed. "Ouch. You do go for the jugular, Queen Carlisle."

Why did he call me that? And why wouldn't he leave me alone?

His wicked smile came back. "I'm Giles Corey."

I sensed he was screwing with me and a twinge of embarrassment hit since I couldn't challenge him.

My mother breezed into the office. "Natalie, walk me to the doors."

As I slung my backpack over my right shoulder, Mrs. Oliveri said, "Shane, you can head back to see Mrs. Meridian."

I halted at hearing his real name. Shane. Shane...who?

He unfolded his long, lean body from the chair. "Good luck with that," he mumbled while angling his head slightly toward my unhappy parent.

I walked toward my mother and met her stony expression with one of my own.

She stopped us at the main entrance and exit doors. "Please stand up straight."

I clenched my teeth, then straightened my shoulders and tightened my middle.

"Because of all this trouble and embarrassment you've caused, you're grounded."

At least I could count on her for crap like this.

"Nothing social until further notice. I'm calling your grandparents right now to let them know, since you'll be with them until your dad and I get back from our trips." She directed her Gucci, high-heeled feet through the doors.

I dropped my shoulders and nearly choked on my anger as she disappeared from view.

The beauty queen had mastered breezing into my life when there was a problem and breezing out once she'd handed over the signed check.

So unbelievably typical.

* * *

Ella and Quinn, my best friends since middle school, stared at me across the cafeteria table. I'd just finished telling them what happened with my mother, Mrs. Meridian, and my community service hours.

"You chose working on that set. And Saturday mornings," Ella Walker stated after she finished her bite of sliced apple dipped in thick caramel. She arched her right eyebrow. Her light-brown skin and dark, curly hair made her razor-sharp hazel eyes stand out. "What the hell were you thinking? Those kids are the most ridiculous ones in this school."

"Not true." This from Quinn Abbott, the "nice one."

At least, that's what Ella and I called her since we were the "darkness" of our friendship.

Quinn reminded me of a short, curvier version of the Disney princess Sleeping Beauty. If she'd been a real person. Quinn barely hit five-foot-two in heels. Ella and I looked like giants standing next to her.

"There are some really cool kids in theater," Quinn stated. "I'm sure it'll be fine."

"I know that, Q." But I only knew one person in theater and she acted in the plays. "Meridian didn't mention the Saturday mornings until after I chose. It was really only working on the set, or with my mother and people who worship her. It's not a big deal."

Then again, I'd be working with kids I didn't know and who wanted to be there. And who knew what the hell they were doing. They were probably morning people, too.

I moaned. "El, you're right. It'll totally suck."

"Go back to Meridian and tell her you've changed your mind," Ella said.

I pictured my mother and her satisfied, triumphant smile. "No way. I'll suck it up. It's only seven weeks. By the way, I'm also grounded."

Ella smirked. "That's never stopped you before."

"Yeah, but she was really pissed this time. She'll make my

grandparents stick to it. At least I'll be with them for a while. My parents are traveling."

Which meant I could be imperfect me, wearing T-shirts, old jeans, even older comfy hoodies, and keeping my long, black, heavy hair pulled into a messy knot or ponytail. My hair was a blessing and curse, and courtesy of my mother's Hawaiian genes.

I forked my third bite of salad and the boy from the office —Shane—sauntered into the cafeteria and caught my eyes. He headed for the opposite side of the noisy, crowded room.

His teasing, bright blue eyes appeared in my head. As did his wicked smile. A smile that made you want to be in on the wickedness. But today that smile had been at my expense.

"Quinn, do you know anything about a boy in our class named Shane?"

She gave me her are-you-kidding-me look. "He and Maddie Harrington have been going out since the Snowflake Formal. He's in theater with her. He's really good, too."

Of course. Maybe the weird name he'd given me had been one of his characters? What irritated me most was I hadn't been able to make that smile leave his...cute face...by showing him I knew his name.

Quinn frowned. "But they're totally not getting along right now. Probably because Maddie won't stop bitching about him getting Kenickie and her getting Marty instead of Rizzo. In *Grease*? I wish she'd get over it. The cast list was posted over a month ago." She squinted at me. "Why are *you* asking me about him?"

Ella squinted at me, too, their confusion justified. I, like them, was never curious about any of the boys in this school, especially a drama boy.

"He came into the office when I was in there and was an ass. I told him to fuck off."

"And that's why we love you." Ella laughed. "I've taught you well."

"He's always been nice to me." Quinn shrugged. "But this reminds me I want to set you up with Chad's new roommate." Chad being her boyfriend, a student at San Francisco State.

I shook my head. "For the zillionth time, I'm not interested. I'm also grounded. Even if I were interested, I couldn't go out on a date."

"Fine. But I wish you'd get over that jerk, Tanner, and move on. Nat, it was months ago."

"I *so* agree," Ella added.

I frowned. "I am over Tanner. I haven't thought about him in forever."

"Then why are you still in that club?"

I ignored Ella's ongoing attitude toward our school's first Anti-Love Club that started at the beginning of the school year. She didn't get it since she'd never been dumped or liked someone who didn't like her. But I loved the club that had nothing to do with being anti-love.

"Look, I like being single. So stop trying to set me up." Because most boys, even college boys, were nothing more than Neanderthals stuck in bodies ruled more by hormones than common sense. And *genuine* respect for girls. There were few boys in this school I could stand being around for more than five minutes.

In the few minutes I'd been around Drama Boy, he was definitely not one of them.

Chapter Two

"Okay, everyone," Warren said in his presidential voice. "The first thing we need to do today is vote on our newest possible name for the club."

We'd been working on coming up with a new name since anti-love didn't fit what we'd created. The club had turned into more of a support group. Kids came in, usually because of boy or girl problems, then left when they got over it. Or got back together with the person. The only original members were me, Warren, and Lexi. But we did have two girls who'd been with us since the fall. And today we had some kids from last week's meeting, where Warren had suggested the Moving Up and Forward Club and the Let's Stick Together Club.

"I said last week I hated those names."

Warren narrowed his brown eyes, his face scrunched up in his version of stink eye. Because of his easygoing personality, I'd connected with him, our only senior, the best. He tolerated my bitchy, and I tolerated his I'm-the-president-and-in-charge attitude. I'd also listened to him talk a lot about his long-time crush on Drew Chang, also a senior, who liked girls.

"You've hated all the names we've come up with," Erin mumbled. "But have never come up with your own ideas."

I ignored her since I'd been trying to like the freckle-faced freshman with red hair. But Erin, for some reason, really wanted a boyfriend. From this school. Striking out with boys was the main reason she'd been in the club since November.

"I don't think the names are that bad," Lexi, a fellow junior, said while playing with a lock of her long blonde hair. "So I vote for the Moving Up and Forward Club."

Of course. Lexi's constant niceness sometimes drove me crazy.

"I do, too," Erin strongly stated.

"If those are the *best* we can do, I agree," Alisha, another freshman, replied.

Her flawless ebony face and tiny figure didn't match her sometimes feisty personality. But this part of her caused us to get along just fine. And she, like me and Lexi, decided months ago she didn't need a boy to be happy.

Warren started to say something, but a knock on Ms. Simmons's door interrupted him.

I frowned at seeing Mr. Yates. Warren and I had him for American Government, an honors class for juniors and seniors.

"Hi, Ms. Simmons. Have you talked to them yet?"

The English teacher and our club's advisor got up from her chair behind her desk. She placed her reading glasses on her head. Her serious expression, combined with Mr. Yates's question, made the energy in her classroom shift to awkward as everyone became silent.

"No. I was waiting until they finished voting on a new name for the club." Her serious expression deepened. "But you can talk to them now."

Warren and I eyed each other, then looked back at Ms. Simmons and Mr. Yates.

Something not good was about to happen.

Mr. Yates, who looked at least one decade beyond retirement, walked into the classroom and crossed his arms over his chest. "Getting a new name for this club might be a waste of time after today. As the student council advisor, I've been getting complaints in the council's suggestion box about this club."

Wait...what?

I glanced at Warren, who lifted his shoulders and shook his head.

I straightened. And then, as vice president of the club, opened my mouth to ask who'd been complaining, but Mr. Yates held up his hand.

"Anonymous complaints. And even if they weren't, I wouldn't be able to tell you."

I closed my mouth so hard my teeth clicked.

Where and from who was all this coming from?

"Well, what are they saying about the club? About us?" Warren whined. "Mr. Yates, we're not doing anything wrong. We're supporting each other."

"Warren, that's not the feedback I'm getting. What I am getting is members complain about other students in this school."

Silence again filled the classroom. Because it was, depending on the day, sort of true. But what the hell? We had a what-happens-in-the-club-stays-in-the-club pact. We made sure all new members knew it, too. It couldn't be former members behind the complaints.

"I'm also getting that you talk about things, meaning personal relationships, that have nothing to do with being an academically successful student at this school."

My temper cracked. "How is supporting your classmates not helping them be successful in this—school?" I'd almost dropped an F-bomb in front of two teachers.

I reigned in my irritation and frustration. I didn't need detention on top of everything else. I'd be grounded the rest of the school year.

"Ms. Simmons did explain the supportive side of this club."

I slid my eyes to Ms. Simmons, but her narrowed eyes were centered on Mr. Yates.

"But I'm not convinced," he continued. "Based on what I'm getting, it sounds like an unhealthy environment has been created in here. So this is your only warning. If I keep getting complaints, I'll have to shut down this club." He nodded at Ms. Simmons and left.

I sat back in my desk and started to shake from my anger. And the total unfairness.

None of us, or our club, had done a thing to deserve this.

Ms. Simmons walked to the front of her classroom. "I want you to know he caught me off guard earlier today with all of this. And I'm on your side. The club's side. But I think if you want to keep this club going, you'll have to change some things. Starting with the name."

"We're trying, Ms. Simmons," Lexi said. "And Mr. Yates knows that now."

"Well, I don't think it's fair he wants to shut *us* down after getting some complaints. What about our side of it?" Alisha grumbled.

"Exactly," I muttered. "Thank you, Alisha."

Warren sighed. "I think we're going to have to present our side of it to him and prove the haters are wrong. Can we do that, Ms. Simmons?"

She smiled. "I think that's completely fair."

I pictured former, original members Jade and Nate, who probably never would've gotten together as a couple if not for the club. I also pictured Paige, a freshman and another former member from the club's beginning, who'd left because she'd developed the confidence to move on to a new boy. They were still together, too.

"There isn't a past member who hasn't benefitted from being in the club. Complaining about other students or not." It was hard not to roll my eyes after saying that. "We're just venting. Which we have every right to do. The point is we are supporting and building each other up. And I know we can prove it, Ms. Simmons."

She nodded. "Good. But you better get to work. Because he's going to be a tough sell."

* * *

Gramps parked in a spot outside of a massive building called Easton West Classic Car Restoration, located in an industrial part of South San Francisco. He'd picked me up and surprised me by heading here. He'd also refused to answer my questions about why we weren't going to Sausalito where he and Grams lived. The place I called my *real* home.

"Gramps, what are we doing here?" I asked as I looked all around us.

That's when I spotted a yellow 67 Pontiac GTO in perfect condition parked near us.

"An early birthday present. Your mom's probably going to be even more upset when she finds out about this, but I couldn't help the timing."

I faced Gramps and smiled for the first time since Mr. Yates ruined our meeting. "My present? Already?" My seventeenth birthday fell during spring break, the last week of March. My crabby mood started to lift. "And who cares what she says."

He frowned. "It's really a very belated sixteenth birthday present. Maybe that'll ease your mom's displeasure when she finds out. I'm not sure I'm happy about the timing of this, either." He gave me a long, hard look through his glasses. "But they arrived a couple days early with it."

I knew I should feel ashamed. When my grandparents gave me their disappointed looks, I usually did feel bad. But I couldn't stop myself from shaking with anticipation. If it was the gift I could clearly imagine, nothing—not my mother or community service or Mr. Yates—would burst my belated sixteenth birthday present bubble.

"Gabe Easton, the owner, was nice enough to let them drop it off here." He grinned. "This is the place that restored my Chevy several years ago. And your grandma wanted to be here, too, but it's her volunteer day at the library. Are you ready? Gabe's waiting for us."

I scrambled from the SUV since I now knew for a fact why we were here.

The lousiness of yesterday and the club meeting evaporated as we walked up to a tall man standing outside the office portion of the building. He seemed a little older than my dad, with his graying light-brown hair and goatee.

He and Gramps shook hands and smiled at each other.

"How's the Chevy treating you?" he asked Gramps.

"Take her out as often as I can. Gabe, this is my granddaughter, Natalie."

His warm, wide smile reached his blue eyes. "It's very nice to meet you. Your grandpa says he's turned you into a classic muscle car enthusiast."

I returned his smile and nodded.

I'd always be a grandpa's and, to some extent, daddy's girl instead of a mommy's girl.

"So how does the car look?" Gramps asked.

Excitement tore through me, and a giggle escaped as I bounced in place.

"It's in decent shape. We've already got it in the shop."

We followed him past the office entrance and right to the first enormous, open garage door. And there sat my dream car. It just didn't look the way I imagined, being a crappy yellow-beige. But it was still the most beautiful 68 Chevy Camaro SS 396 I had ever seen.

I squealed. Loud enough for everyone in the shop to hear, and I so didn't care. I threw my arms around Gramps. He returned my hug, turning it into more of a bear hug. We released one another, and I sprinted into the shop toward my car.

I stood beside the driver's side and admired her overall beauty. I then placed my right hand on the roof, slowly slid my hand left and stopped at the windshield. I finished my greeting after sliding my hand over the hood. And I sighed.

I planned on having so much fun in this car. Far from my mother and the Carlisle name.

"Where's the key?" I had to hear the engine. And find out what she could do with me behind the wheel.

Gramps walked up to me, his smile slipping. "The engine, which is original, needs work."

My mouth fell open. "I can't drive it?"

"No, honey. I'm sorry. It also needs new suspension, breaks, tires..." His voice trailed off since I knew he saw my shoulders slumping with each thing needing to be fixed. "According to the former owner, it's been sitting for a long time because he never came up with the money to restore it. I can't have you driving this without knowing it's safe." He put his arm around my shoulder to give me a sideways squeeze.

"That's where we come in," Mr. Easton said. He joined us at the car. "Once we get done, she'll be better than she was in sixty-eight, brand new. But it will take time."

The restoration would take closer to forever, but I had no choice but to grumble, "Okay." And just because I couldn't drive my beautiful Camaro didn't mean I couldn't sit inside of her.

I withdrew from Gramps and, giggling, opened the driver's side door. At that moment, a powerful car tore down the street in front of the shop. A street that would be perfect for drag racing since this industrial area was pretty secluded. And at night the area would be empty.

The car's tires screeched to a halt, and I smiled. A few seconds later two younger guys in a black, pristine 70 Chevelle slowly drove by—my smile disappeared when I caught a good glimpse of the passenger. Nosy Drama Boy. Shane.

I glanced at Mr. Easton. His hair was a bit darker, but same height. Same blue eyes.

Drama Boy was *this* man's son?

The driver parked the Chevelle in a nearby space. The two, laughing loud and hard, hauled themselves from the car.

Mr. Easton wasn't laughing or smiling as the two ambled toward us. But their humor vanished when they saw us. Drama Boy did a double take when our eyes caught. His surprise clearly mirrored mine.

The other guy, with darker hair but the same blue eyes, said, "Sorry. But he dared me to get it up to eighty before we reached the shop."

"I don't know if you remember my son, Gabe Jr.?" Mr. Easton said to Gramps.

Gramps nodded and said, "Well, did you get it up to eighty?"

His question eased the tension, and Easton Junior smiled. "I was going over ninety."

I fought a smile as they laughed.

"This here's my youngest son, Shane."

"Nice to meet you," Gramps said, and Drama Boy gave him a quick, friendly smile.

"This is Joe Carlisle. Remember the 56 Chevy we restored about seven years ago?"

Gabe Jr. nodded at his dad's question. He appeared to be in his early to mid-twenties and must've been working in the shop, even back then. His much younger brother, being my age, would've been around ten years old, which explained why he didn't nod.

"Shane, you and Natalie have to know each other from school," his dad continued.

Gramps looked at me. "I forgot about that."

I pushed my surprise aside, leaned forward, and asked, "Or is it Giles Corey?"

His face brightened with humor.

In that instant, and not in the school office while pissed off at my mother, I recognized him from a couple school plays. He'd been in *Romeo and Juliet* last semester, and I was pretty sure he'd been in *The Wizard of Oz* a year ago. But I'd have to check my yearbook on that one.

"You remembered," Drama Boy said with a touch of sarcasm. "I'm really touched."

"Giles? Wasn't that one of your characters a couple years ago?" his brother asked.

Drama Boy's eyes never left mine. "Yeah. It's a joke between us."

I glared at him, then focused on Mr. Easton. "Can we start talking about my Camaro?"

"Yes," Gramps said. "She has definite ideas for it."

Mr. Easton and Gabe Jr. smiled. The other Easton didn't smile.

"This Camaro is *your* car?"

Something about the way Drama Boy said that made me say, "Yes. I also know your brother drives a 70 Chevelle. And the yellow car out there is a 67 Pontiac GTO."

Drama Boy's shock transformed into something resembling respect.

I'd accomplished exactly what I wanted.

His brother laughed. "The GTO belongs to one of our fabricators. I'm also the shop foreman." He held out his hand, and I returned his firm handshake. "The three of us can talk in the conference room." He released my hand and looked at his brother. "Check in with Carl after you get changed. I think he'll need some help with the Fairlane."

Drama Boy nodded and, after a swift glance at me, started to leave. And it occurred to me he, of all people, knew this private, tomboy, classic muscle car junkie side of me I didn't want *anyone* else to know.

I didn't need my classmates judging me more than they already did.

"Wait a minute." I tried on a friendly smile. "Can I talk to you for a sec?"

Drama Boy stopped, and it took him a few seconds but he nodded.

Gramps, Mr. Easton, and Gabe Jr. headed back outside.

I pushed a lock of hair behind my ear. "Could you not tell anyone at school about this?"

He frowned. "Tell them what? That you talked to me outside of school?"

I returned his frown. "No. About this. The car stuff. It's no one's business."

His expression changed into confusion. "Okay. I'm great at keeping secrets. And you've...surprised me." He then gave me his wicked smile. "You're also cute when you're nervous." He turned and walked deeper into the shop.

I narrowed my eyes as I watched him veer left, toward a hallway, then he was gone.

Why the hell had he called me "cute" when he didn't like me anymore than I liked him?

"Natalie?" Gramps called out. "Let's go. We've got a lot to talk about."

I turned toward them and suppressed my irritation. And the image of Drama Boy's irritating smile. I had way more important things to focus on right now. Like my dream car.

Chapter Three

I stared out the passenger-side window at the school.

I'd chosen to work on the set. And if I'd known Mrs. Meridian would push it to the point of calling my mother in for a meeting, I would've started my hours at my dad's office weeks ago.

But why did the hours have to be done on Mrs. Meridian's schedule?

"Natalie, you have no one to blame but yourself for this. Stop pouting." Gramps sighed. "Behave yourself and I'll see you at twelve."

I opened the door, dragged myself out, and closed the door behind me, a little hard. I flinched. Whenever I rode in his 56 Chevy I gave it respect. But today I couldn't hide my bitchy.

I stood by the curb, a few feet from the steps leading to the school's double doors, as Gramps drove away in his beautiful metallic-blue car.

I shivered from the chilly air, despite standing in the sun, fighting through the city's typical salty, marine haze I could also smell and see. The sun might win today, and though I wanted to still be in my cozy bed, Alta Plaza Park was only a few blocks away. So the idea of stretching out on the grass and listening to music for four hours started to pull me away. But common sense hit. A no-show would worsen this entire community service situation. I couldn't risk my academic future. And Gramps controlled my Camaro's restoration that would take next to forever based on the work we talked about with Mr. Easton and his oldest, not annoying son.

I faced the school and took a deep breath, but the air came out in a burst of agitation.

I just had to get through the next four hours.

I started to walk up the steps when I noticed a guy approaching on a bicycle. He slowed down, then stopped beyond the steps. The young guy straddled the bike between his long legs and shook his head. He had on black sunglasses, old jeans, and a hoodie sweatshirt.

He unfastened his helmet. "That's such a badass ride." He gave me a wicked smile.

I rolled my eyes.

Why was Drama Boy suddenly everywhere I went?

"We have a picture of your grandpa's car, and other restorations, hanging in our lobby. It's one of my favorites." He pushed his bike out from underneath him to stand beside it and walked toward me. "But it's surprising. I figured Carlisles would be into foreign cars."

His assumption about my family made my crabby mood hit boiling point. Even though my mother did drive a BMW SUV. "And I never would've guessed a drama boy would know anything about hot rods. Are you sure you're related to the Easton family?"

"Drama boy?" He grinned. "That must mean you know I'm in the plays. You remembered my last name, too." He raised his eyebrows. "This must be an off week for you."

Why couldn't he get over the fact I hadn't known his name? Why did he even care?

He leaned toward me, and I breathed in.

"But we do have a connection now. Your secret?" He straightened. "I think it's cool you're into old cars. But I'm wondering what else the kids at school don't know about you."

I gave him my if-looks-could-kill-he'd-be-turned-into-dust stare, which made his smile grow. "I'm so happy you approve. And you can stop your wondering about me at any time."

"Too late for that, Sunshine." He broke our stare to pick up his bike. "This has been loads of fun, but I have community service hours to earn."

Oh, this couldn't be happening.

"Did you say you're here for community service, too?"

"So that's why you're here on a Saturday morning."

He carried his bike up the stairs. He set it down by the doors, reached into his back pocket, and pulled out his student I.D. Our I.D.'s doubled as key cards. Our way of getting into the building since the doors were always locked.

He glanced at me. "This is why you were in the office the other day."

I glared at his back as I walked up the stairs. "Why are you here? Aren't the stars of the shows too perfect and wonderful for working on the set?"

He smiled. That smile. "You know I'm in the plays *and* think I'm a star?"

Before I could fling a reply hard enough to knock him off his pedestal, the inside door opened and—my eyes widened. Because it was Paige, a former member of the club. Her round face brightened in her own surprise when she saw me.

Drama Boy picked up his bike, which forced me to take a few steps to my left. Once he and his bike were out of the way, Paige opened the outside door for us.

"I thought I saw someone out here and turned around. Hey, Shane. And Natalie? What are you doing here?" She stood aside and held the door open for him.

"The same reason you are, I'm sure."

She looked so happy. And confident. At the club's start, she'd resembled a scared, wounded rabbit, always looking like someone would pounce on her for breathing too hard. She had her dark-blonde hair pulled back in two French braids, and had on an old pair of jeans with paint splattered on them.

I'd been smart enough to wear my hair up, and jeans, black Converse, and a T-shirt under my zip-up hoodie. But my clothes weren't worn out from manual labor like hers.

"You're here to work on the set?" Paige followed me into the school.

"It shocked me, too," Drama Boy threw over his shoulder. He headed left with his bike toward the Theater Department and auditorium. "See you in there, Sunshine."

I looked at Paige. "What's his deal? Is he always Mr. I'm-So-Cool-Because-I'm-In-Drama Guy?"

She gave me a cautious smile. "He is really cool and nice. I promise." She threw her arms around me. "I feel like I haven't talked to you in forever." She pulled away. "I miss you guys. And the club. It's so freakin' cool you're going to be working on the set."

At least one of us thought that. And her enthusiastic words about the club and all of us stopped me from telling her what happened at Friday's meeting; figuring out the what next with the club something else I'd rather be focused on at this moment.

"We should head to the auditorium. I'm sure Mr. Lowry already has kids working."

I so didn't want to be here, but seeing Paige made me *not* want to run from the building.

The feeling disappeared, though, when Mr. Lowry,

looking his gray, ponytailed, hippy-ish self, thought it would be a super idea to introduce me to everyone as we stood, steps away from set construction, in a circle on the stage. There were around twenty kids. I could tell, by their laughter and excited chattering with Mr. Lowry and each other, every kid wanted to be here. The shocked, almost snide looks some of them gave me made it clear I wasn't wanted. Worse, I recognized some faces but didn't know their names.

"So, what can you do?" Mr. Lowry asked me.

My eyes swept over the construction site filled with wood, dust, tools, some of which looked a little scary and dangerous, and other building items. I'd hammered nails into walls to hang pictures, but that's where my "construction" knowledge began and ended.

What the hell had I gotten myself into? But then I remembered Mrs. Meridian saying something about painting. I didn't see any paint out, but it seemed they'd recently started building the set. That thought led me to the car. Greased Lightning.

I opened my mouth, then a nearby girl muttered, "I'm sure she's really good at getting people to do things for her."

My back became rigid when muffled laughter from another girl followed her comment.

Bitchy Natalie, the side of me most of my classmates knew, wanted to face her and dare her to say that to me when her friends weren't around. But I caught Paige's encouraging smile.

I managed to keep my temper in check as I said to Mr. Lowry, "I can paint whatever you need me to. I can also help build the car."

"Great," he replied. "I'll have Shane get you going on painting some props today."

Of course it had to be him.

"We're nowhere near Greased Lightning yet. We haven't

figured out how we're even going to construct a…" He shook his head. "I'm drawing a blank on the type of car—"

"It's a 48 Ford Deluxe convertible," I heard myself say.

I felt everyone's eyes and froze. Out of shock I'd answered without thinking. I'd also spoken at the same time as another kid on this stage. He stood across from me in our circle.

Our eyes locked, and he gave me his stupid, irritating smile.

These next seven weeks were going to be the longest of my life.

* * *

So have you made anyone cry yet?

I laughed quietly at Ella's text. My phone sat in front of me on the stage floor.

I was near the back of the stage, sitting cross-legged in front of ten medium-sized, narrow cardboard boxes stacked and glued two high and five across. Mr. Lowry told me to make the boxes look like lockers. Easy enough.

Nat's smart enough not to make enemies on her first day.

I smiled at Quinn's text and tapped out with my left hand, because I held the paintbrush in my right, *Thanks, Q. But this one girl's pissing me off. Don't know her name.*

The girl who'd made the snide comment. I'd caught her nasty looks throughout the morning. I'd just been working on these boxes since Drama Boy showed me where the paint and paint brushes were stored. He'd then walked away and never came back. Totally fine with me.

Yeah, I smelled like paint, but I liked this easy, quiet job. And everyone had a job, the big one being putting together a massive backdrop, the outside of Rydell High. At least, that's what I'd overheard and heard through Paige, who had checked on me. Even now, the sounds of high-pitched drilling and hammering filled the stage area. As did the nonstop talking and laughter.

What does she look like?

Then came Ella's reply, *Does she need to be reminded of who you are?*

I, as casually as possible, turned my head left and found her talking, that looked more like flirting, with Drama Boy. I rolled my eyes, then she caught me watching her.

And if nasty looks really could turn people into dust, I'd be floating in the air.

I yanked my hard gaze from hers and replied, *I don't know what her problem is. She has brown, curly hair. She's short and heavy. Horrible laugh.*

I'd heard her cackling while she talked-flirted with another boy.

Paige dropped beside me. "Those are looking good."

I'd just finished painting the boxes gray, but had to wait until the paint dried to start making them look like actual lockers.

Quinn's reply popped up in our thread. *I think her name's Theresa? If it's who I think, she was new this year. Senior.*

Paige would know for sure.

Before I could ask, she said, "How did you know what kind of car Greased Lightning is?" She giggled. "Are you a closet *Grease* fanatic? Or were you the girl, after the first time you saw the movie, who fell in love with Danny Zuko?"

It sounded like Paige had been that girl. I'd seen the movie twice. Maybe. And because of the cool cars. The only scenes I'd liked were the "Greased Lightning" number and when the two guys were racing.

"Paige, do I really seem like a closet *Grease* fanatic?"

"Well, you knew the car and you're suddenly working on the musical..." She shrugged. "If you don't like this show, why are you working on the set?"

I wanted to say because it beat working with my narcissistic, judgmental mother for seven weeks. But I said another truth. "Required community service."

"We're here for that, too, but we want to be here. Why would you pick something you don't want to be doing? Sounds kinda like torture."

"That's a great question, Paige," came a familiar voice from above us.

I angled my head up. "Is eavesdropping a part of your nosiness?"

I sensed Paige's eyes bouncing from me to Drama Boy.

"And I thought Greased Lightning had brought us closer." He shook his head in phony disappointment. "But seriously. You need to start cleaning up. It's almost noon."

Silence followed him as he walked away.

"What's with you two?" Paige mumbled.

I rose from my cross-legged seat on the stage. "Mutual dislike."

Shane Easton could choke on all his classic cars knowledge. But he did need to keep his mouth shut about me. Or I'd make sure he never smiled that smile again.

Paige stood and brushed off her backside. "Oh, heads up," she said quietly as some kids walked by us, "if anyone tells you to lick the paintbrush to see if it's clean, it's a joke."

Obviously naïve little Paige had fallen for it.

"Who told you to lick the paintbrush? Was it Drama—Shane?"

"No!" she answered. "He'd never do something like that. He's the one who told me about it. I think he was trying to give me a heads up, but it was too late."

Okay. Maybe he wasn't a complete ass.

"It was the girl who made the snotty comment about you earlier. Theresa Flanagan. I heard she's the one who started it, too. Something she did at her old school."

I rolled my eyes. "How nice of her. Just stay away from her, Paige."

Call me when you get home. I wanna hear how it went.

I started to reply to Quinn's text when I heard a girl loudly say, "Mr. Lowry, *Natalie* is on her phone even though we haven't been dismissed."

I raised my head and looked in the girl's direction. *Theresa. Flanagan.*

"She's actually been on it all morning."

I felt numerous eyes as I took a deep breath and slipped my phone into my hoodie's pocket. I released the air and remembered what Ella had texted.

"Natalie, school cell phone rules apply during this time," Mr. Lowry said.

I dragged my eyes from Satan's minion to Mr. Lowry, giving me a kind smile.

"That wasn't made clear to you this morning. Just remember it for next time."

I tried to return his smile and nodded. Then everyone, who'd been listening to this exchange, went back to chatting while cleaning up. And a laughing Theresa joined her friends.

Maybe she needed to learn she didn't want to go into battle with bitchy Natalie Carlisle.

Chapter Four

I walked into school Monday morning knowing who I needed to talk to about the Anti-Love Club. I also wanted to ask her about a certain member of the set crew.

I wove my way between kids walking to their first classes. Many kids were in groups, talking and laughing. Many were still at their lockers. Which is right where I found Kassidy and with her boyfriend, J.R. He leaned against the locker next to hers. They were facing each other, talking, then laughed. And a prick of jealousy made me stop. Someone swerved around me. But my eyes never left them. They looked intimate. Like being a couple was effortless. They'd even broken up and reconnected over a play, and still made togetherness look so easy.

I shook my head.

I liked being single. I also really liked Kassidy and missed having her in the club. She didn't take anyone's crap, either.

I walked up, and she smiled so brightly I thought I might need my sunglasses.

"Hey, you," she said. "What's up?"

He stayed quiet.

After he'd, in a fit of stubbornness and irritation with Kassidy, joined the club in October, I'd never warmed up to him. Even after they got back together. He'd only stayed in the club long enough to help some geeky freshman kid ask a girl to Snowflake Formal. Which had worked.

But I still liked to give him shit he could also dish out.

"I really need to talk to you." I glanced at him. "Alone."

His hazel eyes rolled upward. "It's great to see you, Natalie. I'd almost forgotten how friendly you aren't."

"I've missed you, too," I said with equal sarcasm.

He clasped the end of Kassidy's long, dark braid and tugged it gently. "I'll see you later."

Based on their blinding smiles for each other, I figured it was his way of giving her a kiss in the school's crowded hallway, and I again felt that prick of jealousy. Until he turned and fell into step beside Maddie Harrington walking with Drama Boy. Her boyfriend.

Maddie waved in our direction, but it seemed more for Kassidy who returned her wave.

Drama Boy flashed that dumb smile of his, then winked.

I glared in response and muttered, "He's so obnoxious."

Kassidy's smile vanished. "Natalie, you and Justin need to get to know each other. I swear you'd like him. He really isn't like most of the boys in this school."

"I'm not talking about your Romeo." I eyed Drama Boy walking confidently down the hallway with Maddie and J.R. "Shane Easton."

She laughed. "What on earth are you talking about? Shane's the best."

Why did everyone in this school think he was Mr. Wonderful?

"How do you even know him?"

A fair question since I'd never, with the exception of her,

hung out with the drama kids. Well, until I started community service. And as much as I liked and trusted Kassidy, we weren't the kind of friends who shared secrets.

I kept my answer simple. "Working on the set of *Grease*."

Her mouth inched open.

"It's how I'm getting my community service hours. And that's all I'm going to say about it. Now for the real reason I need to talk to you. The club's in trouble."

I told her what happened on Friday and added I planned on sitting with Warren and Lexi at lunch today to talk about next steps. Quinn and Ella—mostly Ella—would have to deal with it.

"I wonder who's complaining about the club all of a sudden." She zipped up her backpack. "And it's not fair Mr. Yates can shut it down without hearing both sides."

"So that means you'll help us defeat Mr. Yates? And our haters?"

"Absolutely. I know Meg will help, too." She slammed her locker door shut. "Consider us back in the club until we get this figured out."

Meg being her best friend and co-founder of the club. But she'd gotten back together with her boyfriend, Owen, a few weeks before Kassidy and J.R.

We headed for our first period classes.

"I have one more thing I need to talk about." I wanted to know about my enemy before going into battle with her. "Tell me what you know about a senior named Theresa Flanagan."

* * *

I went for my seat behind Warren and beside Quinn in American Government. The mood in here was mainly somber; Mr. Yates's class not the best way to start the school week or day. All he did was lecture, which made his fifty-minute class feel like fifty hours.

Warren turned in his seat to face me. "What's wrong? You look more upset than usual."

Only because what Kassidy told me about Theresa made me feel a bit sorry for her and rethink going into battle.

"Is it about what happened Friday?" he asked.

Quinn put down her phone. "What happened Friday?"

I didn't want to go into the details with Quinn, even though she'd always been more supportive of me being in the club than Ella.

"Mr. Yates has it in for the club right now. But he won't win." I looked at Warren. "The good news is I talked to Kassidy, and she and Meg are going to help us."

He smiled. "That is good news. Good thinking, Madam Veep."

I smiled back and it grew while I pulled my phone from my sweater pocket. "The other good news is I got a car Friday afternoon and have pictures of it."

Warren laughed.

Quinn shrieked, causing everyone in the classroom to look at her, then stopped to stare at me. "You get in trouble for blowing off community service for almost the whole school year and get a *car*? How did that happen?"

"It's a very belated sixteenth birthday present." I brought up one of several pictures I'd taken on my phone. "Gramps couldn't help the timing. I waited to tell you until today so I could show you a picture and tell you all about how perfect my car will look."

Warren leaned over his chair's back for a better angle as Quinn stretched across her desk's side. I held my phone out enough for them, and only them, to see the pic.

"Will look?" Quinn glanced at the pic, then at me. "What is that?"

My smile slipped. "Q, it's my dream car. I have pictures of this car in my room—well, not *this* car. But it'll look like the pictures I have. We're having it restored."

"Your grandpa bought you a car that has to be fixed first?" She leaned back in her seat. "Why didn't he buy you one that was already fixed?"

I wanted to say because the restoration made the car *mine*. But Quinn and Ella didn't get this side of me. Their first cars would be foreign. Probably from Germany, too.

My mother, the beauty queen, didn't get this side of me, either.

Warren stared at me. "You and that car aren't going together in my head."

"She's always been into old, ugly cars." Quinn went back to her phone. "But don't tell anyone. It's a big secret."

My jaw tightened as I closed out the picture and dropped my phone in my lap.

"Ella's going to die when she sees it." Quinn shook her head. "Nat, you could have any car you wanted. But you pick one that looks like it's falling apart? You're so weird sometimes."

Why had I even bothered to show her the pic?

"Well, I think it's an inspired choice for a first car."

I sent Warren a grateful smile. At least he, on some level, tried to understand.

"I'm mad I didn't know this about you." He gave me a sharp look. "But I'm still looking forward to riding in it. Someday."

I couldn't wait to test the posted speed limit in my dream car. Someday.

Warren faced forward when Mr. Yates approached the Smart Board.

I pulled out my textbook, spiral notebook, and pen.

My phone buzzed. Ella had texted me and included Quinn.

Why didn't you ask for a real car? That runs?

Quinn muffled a laugh.

I forced myself to ignore her and Ella's text.

This generation of cars were more car than anything they would get. Trying to explain that to them would be a huge waste of time. And was it really their fault they didn't get it? I grew up appreciating classic muscle cars and hot rods. They didn't.

I slipped my phone into my sweater pocket and started doodling my beautiful Camaro.

* * *

Ella sat in her seat beside me in English. "I've decided I'm going to be the next president of student council."

I stared at her. "What the hell are you talking about?"

She had never expressed any interest in student council. Her single contribution to school as of today had been joining the activities committee. They were in charge of planning all the big school events, like the dances and prom. She'd lasted for two meetings because nobody allowed her to be in charge.

"And why the sudden interest in student government?"

Her eyes flashed with irritation. "Since I found out there's *never* been a female president in this school. It's ridiculous. And how perfect is the timing? With my dad running for mayor this year? You and Quinn are going to help me win, too. And vote for me, of course."

We were...what?

She couldn't be serious. And it's not like I didn't have enough going on.

It seemed admirable she wanted to be the first female president of our student council. Maybe her dad wanting to be the city's next mayor *had* influenced this. But she, like me, knew nothing about student government. I didn't exactly feel any kindness toward student council right now, either. Specifically, its teacher-advisor.

"El, do you even know what goes on in student council? And we don't know anything about campaigning."

She raised her right eyebrow. "How hard could being in student council be? From what I can tell, all they do is plan school spirit days and school-wide fundraisers for charities. And work with student activities on the dances." She smiled. "Piece of cake. All you two have to do is help me with my campaign posters. And hand out buttons. I've already come up with my slogan."

She leaned across her desk and motioned for me to do the same. But when she caught a few kids sitting near us, listening, her eyes hardened. "Does it look like I'm talking to you?"

Two kids focused on their notebooks and one turned in their seat to talk to another kid.

I mentally cringed at how nasty her question had sounded.

"Vote Ella Walker," she said, as if nothing had happened. "The girl who will *walk* P.A. in the right direction." She laughed. "Perfect, right? I know I'm going to win. Just like my dad."

We sat back in our chairs as Ms. Simmons stood behind her podium.

I returned her confident smile, though I didn't think she understood what she was getting herself into.

Ms. Simmons picked up where we'd left off Friday in our poetry unit, and I absently retrieved my book and notebook from my backpack.

Ella would also, most likely, be running against students involved in student council for the last three years. If she got elected, something about her win wouldn't seem fair.

Guilt settled itself around me since Ella was one of my best friends. But helping her campaign for president made me feel like I would be cheating on my club, which needed me more than Ella did. Because I knew we could—somehow, someway—change Mr. Yates's mind.

* * *

All around our cafeteria table were loud conversations and bursts of laughter. A huge difference from the seriousness filling the circle between the five of us. And not one of us had touched our lunches yet.

Kassidy looked at me, Warren, and Lexi. "The first thing we need to talk about is the club's name. I thought you guys were going to change it back in November. What happened?"

Warren glanced at Lexi, and they focused on me.

I rolled my eyes. Because this was so not my fault.

"We've been trying to come up with a different name, but our Madam Veep has been *less* than cooperative," Warren stated.

"How is it my fault the names you guys came up with sucked? The Let's Stick Together Club? Are you kidding me?"

Meg winced. "Yeah, I have to agree with Natalie. That does pretty much suck."

"Thank you."

"Then you come up with a suggestion," Warren snapped. "I can't do it all by myself."

Kassidy picked up her baggie of green grapes and waved it between Warren and me. Which made us smile. But we were never snarky with each other.

I said as a peace offering, "I think the new name needs to come from what the club is really about. Because it's not about anti-love and broken hearts. That's the surface stuff. What brings kids into the club."

They became silent and stared at me.

My face warmed, an unusual reaction for me, and I added, "It's just a suggestion."

"It's perfect," Meg said, and not hiding the surprise in her voice.

"And a *fantastic* place to start. Warren? Lexi?" Kassidy's eyes bounced between them.

They replied by each giving me a tight, sideways hug. Something that warmed me all over, too. My friends, namely Ella, weren't huggers.

Warren gasped. "I have an idea on how we can get the new name. And show Mr. Yates what the club has to offer kids in this school. But we'll need to come up with some questions."

I frowned. "Why? What for?"

"We're going to conduct," he dramatically stated, "a poll."

Okay. I didn't hate his idea. At the same time, I didn't feel overly confident we'd get the answers we deserved and needed, and all because of Mr. Yates's warning.

Chapter Five

I lifted my eyes from my poetry homework and glanced at the framed photo on my desk.

I smiled and picked up the frame, which held a picture of what my Camaro would eventually look like, painted a color I called San Francisco Bay blue. My car would also have white pin striping that started just before where the two doors opened and would run up to the front end. Both stripes would then merge into a thick white border to frame the don't-screw-with-me headlights of the 68 Camaro. And the leather interior, with bucket seats up front, would match the car's color.

I looked up at the black fabric bulletin board above my desk. The board held polaroids of me with my friends, my dog, Chloe, and a few more pictures of perfect-condition 68 Camaros.

My smile grew at the thought of tearing down the freeway in my dream car. Especially on a day like today when I wanted to get away from everything.

I really didn't have the time or interest in helping Ella run for president. And did she even need my help? She'd probably get elected for wanting to be the first female president of student council. And because of her dad. Not because she truly cared about "walking P.A. in the right direction." But maybe she'd surprise me once she started running against kids who did care? And I did like Warren's poll idea, but resentment with Mr. Yates and the complainers stirred inside me at the fact they'd put us—the club—in such a defensive position.

I closed my eyes and pictured myself in my car, with the windows rolled down, my hair blowing around my head, and driving south. North wasn't far enough from this city. But as I headed south in my imagination, Easton West Classic Car Restoration, located in *South* San Francisco, reminded me of how far away I was from freedom. That made the strong image fizzle and die. Then Drama Boy's smile and wink drifted into my mind.

I opened my eyes and frowned.

Where had that come from? Thinking about my car at his family's shop?

But as I was about to squash the image it hit me—I hadn't researched him yet.

I set the frame back in its place, stood, and went straight for my yearbooks on my bookcase headboard. My bedroom in my grandparents' warm, spacious house was cozy. But between my bulletin board, other favorite photos hanging on the walls, including a poster-sized sketch of a 68 Camaro Gramps bought me that I hung over my bed, I'd take this room over my legal bedroom. In a cold penthouse in Nob Hill I hated.

I pulled out my most recent yearbook and sat on my bed's edge. When I opened the book, I saw the *Romeo and Juliet* program. I went to the page with the cast list and smiled at my accurate memory. Drama Boy had played Romeo's cousin, Benvolio.

I put the program aside and found the two pages dedicated to last year's musical, *The Wizard of Oz*. My smile doubled in size when I spotted him, as the Tin Man, in a picture on stage while arm-in-arm with the three other main characters. The Tin Man seemed like a big part for a sophomore. And he'd gotten Kenickie this year. Which meant he *must* be good.

My curiosity led me to find his class picture and I couldn't help but notice his eyes reminded me of my Camaro's future color. He was pretty hot. In a sandy-blond, wholesome, teen heartthrob...drama boy kind of way. But I knew, from how he and his brother tore up to the shop in the Chevelle, he had some bad boy in him. Easton Junior did say his brother dared him to get the car up to eighty before they reached the shop.

The two very different sides of Drama Boy weren't making sense.

I heard a soft knock from my doorway and looked left.

"Sorry, sweetheart. I didn't mean to startle you. Dinner's almost ready." Grams pointed at my yearbook. "That doesn't look like homework."

I closed the thick book with a *pop!* I then stood and dropped it on my bed.

I heard the approaching *tap, tap, tap* of Chloe's paws on the hardwood stairs and floors before she trotted into my bedroom. She launched herself onto my bed, and I scooped her into my arms. She was a feisty black, white, and tan Basenji my grandparents gave me when I turned thirteen. I'd taken one look at her sweet, puppy face and fallen in love.

"Just got sidetracked for a few minutes," I said around Chloe licking my chin. I'd really lost my mind for a few minutes. Drama Boy had taken up too much of my time. I smiled at her. "Your hair looks nice."

Every eight weeks she had her short, silver hair trimmed. The style never changed, but Gramps and I always noticed.

"Thanks." Her smile slowly changed to a frown. "Your mom called. The trip to L.A. for the groundbreaking has been postponed."

After Gramps retired a few years ago, he handed over his real-estate development company to my dad. The company being the reason my parents traveled so much.

"They'll be back tomorrow," Grams added.

I groaned.

"I talked her into letting you stay the rest of the week, but you'll be back with them Friday afternoon."

"*This* is my home." It came out bitchier than I intended, and I instantly felt bad when her mouth tightened.

"Natalie, please don't start."

I nodded and said, "I'm sorry." I meant my apology, too, but I hated leaving them, this house, and especially my Chloe.

My mother didn't like animals, particularly ones with fur. I had almost nothing in common with the beauty queen. At least my dad loved old cars, too.

"Thank you." Grams's smile returned. "I'll see you upstairs."

I hugged Chloe tighter to me, which made her squirm, but I refused to release her. Though I had through Thursday with her, I never knew when I'd see her again after I left here.

* * *

I stood in the school office, tapping my foot as I waited for Mrs. Oliveri to come back, and heard from behind me, "Hey there, Sunshine."

I rolled my eyes as Drama Boy stopped beside me at the counter that separated the waiting area from the actual office portion.

I eyed him. "Would you stop calling me that?"

Humor filled his ridiculously pretty blue eyes. "Sure. When I see you smile. But then I might not recognize you."

I tore my eyes from his.

Where the hell was Mrs. Oliveri? I needed to get to my

club meeting. My mother told me I could only have until 3:30 *because I'm still grounded*.

"What are you in for this time?" he asked. "Scaring freshmen with your *super* awesome personality?"

I whipped my head in his direction.

Okay. He was definitely hot. And always smelled really good. But none of that made up for the fact he was an annoying, nosy, smartass.

"Not today. I'm here for my community service log. Are you always *super* nosy?"

He laughed. "Yeah. It's a gift. And I'm here for mine, too. Isn't it funny how community service keeps bringing us together."

"Try irritating," I muttered. "And, unlike you, I never asked why you're in here."

"Okay." He faced me. "So do you have certain days and times you play nice? Like maybe I should try you on Tuesdays and Wednesdays at, I don't know, three o'clock?"

"I'm always nice." I leaned forward. "To people I like."

Unbelievably, his humor disappeared and hurt flashed across his face. But up until this second he'd taken as much as he dished out.

I looked away.

"You don't even know me," he quietly said. "And, unlike you, I get to know people first before deciding if I like them or not."

His statements yanked my conscience. Because, outside of his family's business and being active in theater, I didn't know him. At all. But that didn't stop my snide side from returning and I faced him. "I know more than you think I do, *Benvolio*."

He stared at me for a few seconds, then started laughing.

I crossed my arms. "What's so funny?"

Mrs. Oliveri finally appeared at her desk.

"You keep surprising me."

"Community service logs?" she asked.

He nodded, his laughter reduced to his wicked smile. Which pissed me off—again—since that smile of his was again at my expense.

She handed over our logs, and I, as nicely as possible, pulled it from her fingers. "Thank you," I said before whirling from the counter.

"*See you tomorrow morning, Sunshine,*" he sang—and really well—to my back.

I continued my march from the office without a backward glance. I also cursed myself with every stair step I took for noticing he could sing.

Chapter Six

I walked into Ms. Simmons's classroom and stopped. All thoughts of Shane Easton, and the fact I'd let a high school drama boy get to me, vanished at seeing almost every original Anti-Love Club member staring at me. Their faces were full of excitement.

I raised my eyebrows. Not just at seeing them, but noticing they, with the exception of me, Warren, Lexi, Alisha and Erin, were the only ones at the meeting. So not normal, either.

Ms. Simmons smiled at me and lifted her shoulders.

"Isn't this awesome?" Lexi practically squealed.

I approached them. There were nine of us in the classroom; Warren the only boy.

"Yeah, but what the—" I stopped myself again from blurting out *that* bad word in front of a teacher. "It's great to see all of you. Really. But what's going on? And where's everyone else?"

Warren's smile slipped. "We think Mr. Yates scared them off."

Lexi frowned. "That's the not-so awesome part."

My intense dislike for Mr. Yates tripled in strength.

I dropped my backpack and community service log, then sat at a desk beside Warren.

Despite my irritation with Mr. Yates, I smiled at seeing Jade and Paige. I knew Kassidy and Meg would be here.

"Meg and I decided we needed all the help we could get right now," Kassidy stated.

Jade squared her shoulders. "Kass is right. There's definite strength in numbers. And Nate wanted to be here, but he's really busy with baseball. He did say he'll help if he can."

Paige smiled. "I've missed this club. You guys. So when Meg caught me after school the other day, I totally jumped at the chance to come back and help."

"I caught everyone up while we were waiting for you," Warren said. "What took you so long, Madam Veep?"

"Dealing with community service." And an infuriating, too-cute-for-his-own-good drama boy who, for some reason, loved laughing at me. Which made him nothing more than an ass.

Why the hell was I even still thinking about him?

I forced him from my mind. "It's great you guys are here. But nine isn't exactly a strong number. And what if those cowards who abandoned us refuse to take our poll? Or give rotten answers because they're cowards?" Yeah, I'd spoken harshly. But I'd also said the truth.

"That kind of attitude isn't going to get us anywhere," Erin said under her breath.

"I agree." Meg, sitting to my right, placed her arm around my shoulders and gave me a squeeze. "Nat, we're all upset about this. But we have to stay focused."

"Well, I would so love to know who's complaining about us." Alisha crossed her arms. "It's okay for other students to do it, but not us? That's *screwed* up."

"I have to admit I'm curious about that, too." Lexi

absently twirled a lock of her hair around her index finger. "I can't imagine who could be doing such a thing."

"Guys, we'll probably never—not ever—find that out. What matters most is getting the answers to our poll before spring break. And..." Kassidy's voice trailed off as she looked at Warren, grinning like the Joker from Batman.

My instincts went into high alert.

"Warren caught me before the meeting," she continued. "He has another, very unique idea on how we can prove to Mr. Yates this is a great group. And it could work. But everyone has to commit, or it won't make a real impact."

Warren, still wearing his Joker grin, slapped a flyer on his desk. In bold, blue, all capitalized letters were the words—my eyes widened.

Oh, shit.

"Lip sync competition?" Meg faintly said.

Silence followed and everyone looked at each other, their eyes wide like mine.

I faced Warren. "No. Absolutely not."

"I heard about this." Lexi picked up the flyer. "Student council is doing the lip sync competition next month instead of their usual, end-of-year talent show."

I would've felt relieved since the talent show usually featured too many kids with no talent. But I couldn't believe where Warren and Kassidy were going with this.

They couldn't be serious about us being in the competition.

"You want us to participate in *this*?" Alisha pointed at the flyer.

Warren nodded. "I already have ideas for songs, too."

I burst into laughter. Our president had clearly lost his mind.

Paige's face turned pasty. "I want to help you guys. But there's no way I can get on a stage and perform. In front of the entire school." She glanced at Kassidy. "I'm not like you."

"Me, either." Meg shook her head. "Running in a cross-country meet is one thing, but this is *totally* different. And how would this help the club?"

"Exactly," I said. "Most of the kids who participate will get up there and act stupid."

Warren ignored my bitchy and said, "Participants are allowed up to two-and-a-half minutes for their performances."

Meg, Paige, and Erin moaned as I growled, "*Warren.*"

"I'm not totally against this." Jade's shoulders dipped. "But that sounds like a long time."

"More like forever," Erin whispered, her pastiness matching Paige's.

"Would you listen?" Warren shot me a dark look, snatched the flyer from Lexi, and pointed to a bullet point. "There's first through third place, and students *and* teachers vote. But participants can't vote. They don't want us voting for ourselves." He leaned forward. "Think about it. If we get the poll answers we need, change the name, and nail this competition, how could we not change Mr. Yates's mind?" Warren smiled. "I know this will work."

I shook my head while keeping my narrowed eyes trained on our insane president.

Kassidy looked at Paige and Erin and Meg. "I know two-and-a-half minutes sounds like forever. But I swear once you're up on the stage it'll seem like seconds. And you have to remember we'll be up there together."

Paige and Erin's faces relaxed. But only by a fraction.

Lexi smiled. "I love it! I'm in."

I somehow stopped myself from rolling my eyes.

"Okay. Me, too." Jade giggled. "Nate's going to flip when I tell him what we're doing."

No. This could *not* be happening.

"Well, if we're going to do this crazy thing, and nail it, we'll have to lip sync *and* dance."

I sat up at Alisha's comment. Because I'd heard enough. "I'm so not doing that. And I hate this idea." Lip syncing while dancing in front of the entire student body, and the teachers, sounded like a special place in hell I had no interest in visiting.

"Big surprise there," Erin muttered.

I crossed my arms and leaned forward. "You just said you didn't like the idea of being on stage for that long."

"But I didn't say I hated the idea," she snapped back.

"Is everything okay back there?" Ms. Simmons's raised voice settled around us.

I continued glaring at Erin until she broke our eye contact.

Warren turned and smiled. "Just a difference of opinion. We're fine." He faced forward. "Like Kass said, we all have to commit. Right now, I have four yays. So, what's it gonna be?"

"Please, Meggie? We *can* do this."

Meg sent Kassidy a long, hard stare. And the longer she stayed silent told me she'd choose stage fright over this insane plan. But then she released a tiny smile.

My shoulders drooped.

"I can't believe I'm about to say this," Meg mumbled, "but...okay. I just hope stage fright doesn't kill me."

Kassidy and Lexi threw their arms around her.

Now Warren only needed—

"Same here." Erin straightened. "But I'm willing to risk it for the club. I'm in, too."

"What do we have to lose?" Alisha shrugged. "Could be fun. But it's going to take *soooo* much rehearsing."

Was I the only sane person here? And that left Paige and...me.

"Everyone has to agree before we can talk about that. So Paige?" Warren asked.

I sent her a wide-eyed, pleading look.

Surely shy little Paige would stick to her first reaction?

She hesitated, then said, "I know the stage fright will kill me. But you guys were so great to me in the fall I can't say no."

Shit.

Everyone but me clapped. Before all excited eyes settled on me.

"Madame Veep, we can't do this without you," Warren said in a sing-song voice.

"We don't want to do this without you, either," Kassidy added.

I looked at each one of them.

I knew what I wanted to say, but couldn't make the emphatic *no* come out now that everyone but me had agreed to this plan. Lip syncing and dancing were so not my thing. And in front of the entire school? What would Ella and Quinn think? I cringed thinking about it. But everyone here was counting on me. With the exception of Erin, and sometimes Lexi, I liked all of them, too. I couldn't let them down. Especially since four former members had come back to help. My conscience would never let it go.

So I did the only thing I could. I sighed, rolled my eyes and asked, "When are you guys planning on starting rehearsals? Because I'm grounded right now."

Laughter and more clapping filled the classroom.

"But who's going to teach us to dance? And together while lip syncing?" My question sounded snarky, but it felt fair since no one had brought that up.

"I can do it," Lexi murmured. "I've been in dance since I was six."

Silence fell, and I scanned everyone's faces. Based on their expressions, no one else had known this about Lexi. And a bit of warmth spread through me knowing I wasn't the only one with a private side.

"Aren't you full of surprises. And *fabulousness.*"

I focused on Warren whose Joker grin had returned.

"How come you've never mentioned this before?" Jade asked.

"It's for fun. Not a big deal." She started playing with that same lock of hair. "But I know enough to give us a chance in the competition."

"That's all we need," Warren answered. "And I get telling boyfriends, but I wanna keep this quiet for as long as we can. Better chance of blowing minds in a month. So boyfriends are a part of what happens in the club stays in the club. Anything else?"

Our silence being Warren's answer.

"Okay. Now we can talk about music."

As I listened to everyone throw out suggestions of Top 40 pop songs I wouldn't listen to if my life were being threatened, I wanted to take back saying yes to this competition.

We were definitely going to have a huge problem agreeing on a song.

Chapter Seven

I followed the sound of my mother's voice into the sunlit kitchen. I didn't hear my dad's voice, which meant she had to be on the phone.

The squeaky-clean room smelled of lemon and bleach. Between the smell and every surface shining under the sunlight streaming through the windows, it felt like I'd walked into a Mr. Clean commercial. My mother had this place cleaned every other week, whether they were in town or not. Even my bedroom, on the other side of the kitchen, smelled like lemon. I'd gone to bed with a headache because of the smell and woken up with it.

I so needed aspirin and coffee before I started day two of community service. But when I saw her sitting on the red padded bench beside the dining-room windows that had a spectacular view of the building next door, I stopped.

She was yakking away on her cell while still in her night-gown and matching robe.

I rolled my eyes and continued walking toward her.

She glanced sideways, then stared at me like the equally shiny hardwood floors had suddenly given birth to me.

"Why aren't you ready?" I heard the edge in my voice, and based on the way her mouth hardened she didn't appreciate it. But I could've cared less. "I have community service this morning." *Because you had to save face with Mrs. Meridian.*

She said into her phone, "Can I call you back? My daughter needs me."

I wanted to laugh, but I crossed my arms. "*Just* to take me to school."

She ended her call, set her phone down, and looked me up and down. "I forgot. But it's just something else you can hold against me. It also explains why you're dressed like that." She scanned me again. "Did you at least wash your face and brush your teeth? And please stand up straight."

I straightened and muttered, "Yes. I did."

So what if I had on an older pair of skinny jeans, my worn Pacifica Academy hoodie and had my hair pulled up in a knot? I didn't look that bad. And what the hell did the beauty queen know about manual labor?

"We need to go. Now. I want to stop at Starbucks—"

"You'll have to drive yourself since I'm nowhere near ready."

My mouth fell open.

She couldn't be serious. Parking around the school could be a real bitch since it didn't have an actual lot. I also had another problem. "You know I'm terrible at parallel parking." In fact, I despised it. Even though Gramps had spent an embarrassing amount of time teaching me—and not in the Chevy—the tricks to parallel parking in tight city spots. "Why can't Dad take me?" He didn't give a crap about how he looked this early in the morning.

"He's at work. Stop being dramatic."

Of course my workaholic dad was at his office on a Saturday morning.

So much for my Starbucks. I didn't have time to deal with

trying to find parking there, too. I'd have to choke down aspirin with a bottle of water.

She eased off the bench and went for her tan Coach purse sitting on top of the gleaming dining-room table. "This will be good practice for you since it's part of living in the city." She reached into her purse, withdrew her BMW key and held it out for me to take. "You'll be fine. And I've always been able to find parking on Clay. But you are to come straight home when you're done for the day."

I snatched the key from her perfectly French-manicured fingertips. "Fine."

I whirled from her and marched in the direction of my bedroom. Now I needed to bring my purse. And if her precious Beemer SUV ended up scarred because of my terrible parallel parking skills, she'd have no one to blame but herself.

* * *

I stared at my finished masterpiece and smiled. It had turned out pretty good, considering I'd never painted ten cardboard boxes to look like lockers.

Several kids were still working on the Rydell High backdrop. I'd felt the constant drilling in my brain since I walked in here with a minute to spare. Today I'd noticed a few kids wearing headphones. They had to be listening to music and were, like me, working on props by themselves. And maybe Mr. Lowry made an exception to the no-phone rule if we asked? I'd have to ask Paige the next time I saw her. She, for some reason, wasn't here today.

I would've been jealous, if not for the fact being here gave me an excuse not to be at "home" with my mother.

A burst of familiar laughter from behind me caused me to slightly turn.

Drama Boy had been nearby since the day started and

working with another boy on what would be the Rydell High scoreboard. He worked hard for someone who had a big part in the musical. But he did have a real and pretty cool job when not at school. His job at his family's shop explained his confidence working on the big set pieces, like the scoreboard. Everyone liked him, too, and went to him with questions if Mr. Lowry was busy with something else.

"Are you finally finished with that?"

I closed my eyes, counted to three, then angled my head up to look at Theresa.

She had her curly hair pulled into pigtails. The hairstyle made her round, pale face look wider. She also looked ten years old and back in fifth grade.

"Yes," I answered as politely as I could. I then reminded myself of the Theresa Flanagan highlights Kassidy gave me on Monday.

Parents going through a nasty divorce. Forced to leave her school and friends, and move here with her dad and her dad's much younger boyfriend. The cause of the nasty divorce.

"Good." She pointed at a picnic bench, which looked as old as the city of San Francisco, sitting off to our right. "Mr. Lowry wants that painted next. Just the table part. In red. As in Rydell High's school colors?"

Theresa had a right to be hurt and pissed off. But it didn't give her the right to come into a new school and take it out on everyone who crossed her path—I suddenly remembered Drama Boy's remark in the office. About me "scaring freshmen with my *super* awesome personality."

I didn't exactly have a reputation for being the friendliest girl in school. Especially being best friends with Ella. But I'd never thought of myself as a cruel bully like Theresa. Or Ella.

I forced myself to ignore Theresa's condescending tone and asked, "Why isn't Mr. Lowry telling me this?" Which really meant, who the hell put you in charge?

"He's busy talking with Mrs. Chaplin. He asked me to do it, but I'm still helping with the backdrop and you now have nothing to do." She tilted her head to the right. "Try to be quick. The rest of it will have to be painted, too. *Before* the show runs next month." She turned and bounced back to where they were working on the backdrop.

My sympathy for Miss Theresa Flanagan started to evaporate. And too busy my ass. More like too busy socializing with her friends.

I sighed and stood.

Theresa wasn't worth jeopardizing passing junior year.

I had begun painting the table Rydell red when I heard, "Natalie, what are you doing?"

I looked at Mr. Lowry and straightened. "Painting the picnic table?" I stupidly replied. But dread began to build in my stomach, causing it to tighten, as frustration took over his normally relaxed face.

"Why are you painting it red? It's supposed to be brown."

I placed the paintbrush on an unpainted part of the table and angled my chin up.

That conniving bitch.

"Theresa told me to paint it red." I was so not taking the fall for this.

He turned left. "Theresa, can you come here?"

His booming voice reached across the stage and caused students' heads to snap up. Including Drama Boy's.

My face burned, but at the same time I wanted to lunge for her throat as she skipped over with an angelic expression. But I saw hints of evil hanging around her large, spooky green eyes.

"Why is Natalie painting this? And red? I specifically told you brown."

Her eyes became larger, and I couldn't fight my smirk.

"I only asked her to paint it because I was still helping with the backdrop. And she had nothing to do since she was done with the lockers." Theresa looked at me and added, "But I never told her to paint the table red."

My mouth inched open. But I couldn't get any words out. They were stuck in my throat.

"I guess she wasn't listening."

I tightened my hands into fists. "You told me to paint it red." My body, shaking from anger, made my voice shaky.

I must've sounded on the verge of tears, because Mr. Lowry tried smiling at me. But I could tell he didn't know who to believe.

Theresa shrugged. "Mr. Lowry, I have no idea *what* she's—"

"It's fine. I'm just glad I caught you before you finished," he said directly to me. "I think the brown is dark enough to cover the red. But it might take two coats."

I nodded my reply.

He gave us a long, skeptical stare before walking away.

Theresa tried to do the same thing, but I blocked her path. I also somehow stopped myself from taking the can of red paint and throwing it in her smug face.

"You better stay the hell away from me the next five weeks."

"You don't scare me." She leaned forward. "Especially since everyone knows the only reason you're here is because daddy and mommy couldn't *buy* you out of community service."

Oh, she did not say that to me.

I took a step closer. "What did you just say?"

A warm hand clasped my fisted right hand and tugged me back a couple steps. But I kept my eyes locked on Theresa.

"Take it easy, Natalie. And Theresa, you need to get back to doing whatever it is you do around here."

"Shane, are you actually defending her?" She glared at me. "And she started it."

I stepped toward her, determined to finish it, but Shane's grip on my hand stopped me. He stepped backward, pulling me away from Theresa, who stalked off in the opposite direction.

I turned and started taking deep breaths.

"You seem like a girl who would have a mean right cross."

I heard the smile in Shane's voice, but continued breathing deeply. If he hadn't interfered, everyone would've seen me right cross her face. I'd probably also be facing expulsion.

"Not that I would've blamed you for knocking her out. I heard what she said to you."

I looked up, our eyes met, and I saw compassion. And a little bit of anger? No. Him feeling anger about what happened didn't make any sense.

I shook my head and broke our eye contact. "You feel the same way she does."

"Okay. That *was* the case. But now I know better and I'm sorry."

I glanced at him.

Did he really apologize?

"I'm sure she did say to paint it red. A few other kids have had trouble with her, too."

I nodded, though hearing that didn't make me feel better.

"If you didn't care, you wouldn't have worked so hard on those lockers." He smiled. "They turned out great."

My posture began to relax as my breathing returned to normal.

At least someone around here appreciated what I'd done.

"Thanks." Thinking about him stopping me from flattening Theresa, I added, "And thanks for what you did."

Maybe he wasn't so bad after all.

"I have an older sister who doesn't take anyone's crap,

either. I've had to calm her down a few times." He laughed. "You two would get along great."

I'd get along with his...who?

"If you need me to stop your right cross again, I'll be over there." He, giving me that smile, pointed to where he'd been working on the scoreboard. "And between you and me, I think the table should stay red."

Chapter Eight

I stood outside the Beemer's driver's side door, but I couldn't find the energy to get in and drive back to that place and her. Especially after this shitty morning.

My phone kept illuminating with chats from Ella and Quinn. They were already planning Ella's campaign and posters, even though the student council race didn't begin until after spring break. And my club members were still trying to come up with songs we could agree on.

I shoved my phone into my hoodie pocket and reached for the door handle. Then I spotted Drama—Shane—walking by with his bike. He had his gray helmet on, and when I lowered my eyes, I noticed the flat back tire.

"It looks like you're having a crap day, too."

He kept walking. "Caught a nail on my way here. It happens."

Watching him walk his bike down the sidewalk, and remembering what he'd done for me earlier, I wanted to help *him*. He also looked kind've pathetic in a cute, helpless boy way with his unfastened bike helmet on his head. And helping him would postpone going "home."

I stepped forward. "Hey, do you want a ride?"

He stopped and looked over his shoulder at me. He also had his sunglasses on, so I couldn't really see his face. But I could still tell my question surprised him.

"Where'd that come from?"

Okay. I deserved his confusion and question.

"I just thought, after what you did for me, I could give you and your bike a ride home." I, remembering his apology from earlier and my treatment of him, quietly added, "It's also a way of saying I'm sorry for being such a...bitch to you." I crossed my arms. "But if you don't want a ride, the phrase is *no thank you*."

He faced me. "Easy, Sunshine. I didn't recognize you playing nice." He smiled. That smile. "You know that's twice in one morning, right?"

I tilted my head left. "Kenickie, do you want a ride or not?"

He hesitated, then said, "Well, since you've gone out of your way to learn my character's name and sort've asked nicely, why not."

I met him at the Beemer's rear and opened the back door. My mother kept nothing in the back except her emergency kit, but I'd still have to put the backseats down.

"But why are you suddenly being nice to me?" he asked.

I opened the driver's side passenger door and forced the backseat down. And it occurred to me these seats had never been down. "I told you why. And I could say the same thing to you."

"I don't think I've been mean to you."

I eyed him. "No. You've just made fun of and laughed at me."

"I've mostly teased you," he replied, picking up his bike. "Because you're too serious."

I let that go, and within a few minutes we were in the Beemer.

He belted himself in, and I noticed *him* for the first time as he examined the car.

He'd taken off his helmet, which had flattened the top of his hair. His height made him seem a little out of place in the compact SUV. And his lean body looked more than good in snug jeans and a black T-shirt. He had nice arms, too. No obnoxious bulging biceps. Just the right amount of definition. Probably from working on cars. And the school shows. He had to spend a lot of time outside since his arms and face were a perfect shade of sunshine gold.

He turned my way, and I looked forward and started the car.

Had I really just checked out a high school drama boy?

"This is a pretty nice car. But it can't be your grandpa's."

I smirked at him knowing a 56 Chevy man wouldn't drive a Beemer SUV.

"It belongs to the real Queen Carlisle." I gave him a hard stare, then put the car in reverse to back up a bit. "She forgot I had to be here this morning. Where do you live?"

"Sorry about that name, too. And Fillmore and Jackson. Not too far from here."

I nodded at his second apology and directions, and carefully pulled out of the space.

When we reached the stop sign, I braked and waited for another car. But then stayed there, though I could turn. And I knew where I *really* wanted to go, to turn around this crap-ass day. My mother told me to come right "home," but she didn't remember we were done at noon. And it's not like she kept track of the Beemer's mileage.

"Are you waiting for the stop sign to turn green?"

I looked at him, Shane being the key to my brief escape from reality. "Are you busy?"

He looked around the car, at himself, then at me. "Define busy."

I rolled my eyes. "I'll try a different question. Can you get us into your family's shop?"

I think he squinted at me before releasing a long, low whistle. "I'm not sure how to answer that since me and my bike are at your mercy right now."

"Would you be serious?"

"Only if you repeat very slowly...Kidnapping. Is. A. Crime."

I sat back. "I'm not going anywhere until you—"

A quick, high-pitched beep from behind us caused me to jump and he laughed.

I drove through the intersection, pulled up alongside a parked car, and put the Beemer in park. "Now, I'm not going anywhere until you stop being a smartass."

He sighed. "Okay, Sunshine. I get it. You've had a bad morning and want to go see your car. And no, I don't have anything going on now and can get us into the shop. Some of the guys might be in there working today. Including my brother."

I faced forward. "Let's get the hell out of here."

"But they already tore your car apart. All you're going to see is the chassis."

Better to see my car's base frame than nothing at all.

"We don't fuck around at Easton West Classic Car Restoration."

The serious way he said it made me smile. "Is that posted in the shop somewhere?"

His mouth opened before he said, "I suggested it, but my dad said no—did you make a joke? And *smile?*"

I pressed my lips together to fight my laughter at his genuinely shocked expression.

I shook my head since we needed to leave. Now. "I don't care. We're still going."

He shrugged. "Okay. But I have to be home by five."

I put the Beemer in drive, checked for oncoming cars, then headed straight.

He relaxed into the passenger seat and rolled his head in my direction. "Thanks for the apology. And I'm still calling you Sunshine."

"Lucky me." I was getting used to it, though. "So is five your curfew? Or do you have a hot date with Maddie—" Did I really say that?

I cringed at my ridiculousness and chanced a glance at him.

His usual good humor had vanished, and he stared out his window.

One of my questions bothered him, but why? The first had been a joke and those two had been dating—I then remembered what Quinn had said about Shane and Maddie that day of my meeting with Mrs. Meridian and my mother. Something about them not getting along because of *Grease* and the cast list. Seemed a little weird they'd still be fighting over something that happened so long ago, but it's not like their relationship was my business. And why did I care?

"I was joking with you," I said as we approached a stoplight.

"I know." He turned and gave me that smile. "You're apologizing, saying thank you, smiling, almost laughing, and joking around. I'm tempted to check your forehead for a fever."

Shane checking my forehead for a fever might not be a bad idea.

* * *

In the few minutes we were deep inside the shop, I'd spotted a 55 Ford Fairlane, a 61 Pontiac Ventura, a 53 Chevy convertible, and a 69 Plymouth Barracuda. All in various states of restoration; all paint long since stripped.

The shop smelled of paint and ground metal and guys. Not disgusting B.O. Just soap and hard work. We were also alone. If anybody had been in here working, they were gone.

"There are some really cool cars in here," I said as I followed him.

"The 'Cuda's going to be a force from the car gods. The owner wants to drag race it."

I smiled, the silence surrounding us and these amazing cars soothed my mood. My neck and shoulder muscles relaxed, and I no longer had a headache. Being even more honest with myself, Shane had helped my mood, too, by going along with this spontaneous trip.

"The chassis isn't too far from where your car was a week ago," he said.

My smile grew as excitement fluttered inside me.

I followed him deeper into the shop until we reached our destination near those same enormous doors. But today I noticed a car parked nearby and underneath a protective cover.

I stopped beside him, right next to my Camaro's chassis. "So where's the rest of it?"

"The body's in sandblasting. And they sent the engine out. We don't do that work here." He looked at me. "I heard from my brother you want to keep the original engine. If you can."

I nodded, though surprise hit me at hearing he'd talked to his brother about my car. "I want to keep as much original as I can." I glanced at him. "Why screw with perfect unless you absolutely have to? And a three-ninety-six is fast enough for me."

His eyes warmed. "Wow. A high school girl into old cars *and* who can talk engines." He grinned. "That's really cool."

A little spark ignited inside me at his compliments, but I tried to ignore it as I stepped over the frame and sat in the narrow opening. Then I closed my eyes and pictured my seat, the steering wheel, new dashboard and car radio console, the shifter, passenger seat and, in seconds, I saw myself in my finished dream car; the image so powerful I could smell the brand-new leather upholstery and hear my favorite Linkin Park song blasting from the speakers.

"What are you doing?"

"Sitting in my car." More like sitting in my Camaro that represented freedom.

I felt Shane sit down next to me, outside the frame, and I opened my eyes. He stared at me with a combo of confusion and appreciation. Kind of like last Friday when I'd been here with Gramps. And like last Friday it made my defenses shoot up and surround me.

"Why are you looking at me like that? Don't even think about laughing at me."

"I'm not going to laugh at you, Sunshine. I'm still trying to...figure you out."

"I told you to stop doing that." But the kindness in his eyes and voice made the spark grow stronger. And warmer. Which so wasn't a good thing.

"And I told you it's too late for that, so hear me out."

I waited, barely breathing.

"At school you're this girl who walks around, never smiling, and looking straight ahead. Ignoring everything around you. And you don't like anybody but your friends talking to you."

I guess I deserved all that, too, but it didn't stop me from asking, "How have you noticed all that about me?"

He focused on the floor. "You're impossible to miss."

"Why? Because I'm a Carlisle?"

"No. It has nothing to do with your last name." He cleared his throat. "I mean, you're tall and have you looked in the mirror?" He turned stop-sign red. "Everyone knows your mom was a beauty queen and you look a lot like her."

I fought a smile at his embarrassment as I stared at my car's frame.

It's not the first time I'd heard that. In fact, I usually hated hearing it. So she'd been a big-time beauty queen a million years ago. It's not like she won Miss America. But the spark's warmth spread inside me since I now knew why he'd called me "cute" last week.

"Awkward moment's passing," he mumbled, his face returning to golden brown.

The giggle escaped before I could stop it.

He whipped his head in my direction. "This is what I mean. The Natalie Carlisle sitting here inside her 68 Camaro chassis, and smiling and laughing, doesn't match up with school Natalie. What's wrong with being this Natalie all the time?"

I sighed, and my smile became a frown. "Because *this* Natalie is personal. And I like it that way. What's wrong with that?"

"I don't think *this* Natalie is as personal as you think. You're in the club Kassidy started."

I stared at him. "How do you know I'm in the club?" Seriously, how did he know so much about me?

"I'm friends with Kassidy who's friends with you."

Okay. Fair enough. But it still surprised me he'd noticed these things.

"And everyone knows why she started it. So some guy must've hurt you."

I shrugged. "I'm over it." Not a lie. And what else could I say? It's not like I'd go into the details with him.

"Then why are you still in the club?"

I straightened since he'd just scratched a sore spot. "Because the club's about more than that. It's a good thing. I don't care what anyone at school says about it. Or that Mr. Yates would love to shut us down."

He frowned. "Why does he want to shut you down?"

I rolled my eyes. "He told us we're getting complaints from other kids."

"Well, I'm not bashing your club, Sunshine. I'm pointing out a lot of kids at school might already know there's more to you than being a—" He looked away.

For some reason, being known as a bitch around school suddenly bothered me and my defensive armor came back. "What about you? Drama boy and muscle car boy aren't going together in my head right now."

"Okay. But this place isn't a secret. We've gotten families from school as customers." He leaned toward me to the point our shoulders touched, and the warmth reached higher. Almost to my chest. "The *drama boy* side of me is for fun," he continued. "And because I like to make people laugh. But I only get roles like that in the musicals."

I smiled. "I remember Kenickie being an asshole."

He laughed and leaned away from me, and the warmth stopped before reaching my chest. Which was *so* a good thing. My insides were acting like I'd never been around a really cute boy, and I mentally shook off my ridiculousness. But the spark—

"He is. At first," he replied with a playful smile. "And what a lot of people don't know is in the stage version, 'Greased Lighting' is Kenickie's big number. *Not* Danny Zuko's."

"You're right, Kenickie," I said, grateful for him interrupting my thoughts. "I didn't know that." I paused, searching for something else to say. Because I also liked this too much. Talking to him. And I asked, "So, no big dreams of making it to Broadway?"

"Nope."

I looked around the shop. "Will you be in charge of all this someday?"

"No." He stood. "I have to show you something. Because you'll get it." He held out his right hand, which I grasped, and he helped me up.

I guess that meant we were done talking.

I suppressed the disappointment trying to fill me up.

He, still holding my hand, led me to the car under the protective cover. Only when we reached the car did he release my hand. But not before giving it a quick squeeze.

"Are you ready to have your mind blown?"

I couldn't help but laugh and nod.

"Laugh number two?" He started to pull off the cover. "Maybe you need to kidnap me and bring us here again next Saturday."

Though it was beyond wrong, something about me "kidnapping" him next Saturday and him squeezing my hand excited me. But then he jerked the cover off, and I focused on the car.

I blinked before looking at Shane, grinning and watching me. I then looked back at the perfectly restored, black muscle car with shiny chrome strips. "That's a 70 AMX." Also known as one of the rarest, fastest classic muscle cars out there. "I've only seen one of these. And I went to almost every classic car show between here and Vegas with my grandparents last summer."

Also known as the best vacation of my life.

"So I now know for a fact that's where you get this from. You must be close to them."

"I am. This belongs to a customer?" I couldn't take my eyes off the spotless car.

"No. It's my dad's *real* car. He keeps it stored here because me, him, and my mom moved into a condo after my sister left for college."

Of course his dad owned this muscle car.

I bit my lower lip before asking, "Is it as fast as I've heard it is?"

Our eyes snapped together.

"Fuck yeah."

I gave him my wicked smile and he gave me his. Then my phone started ringing. Our moment ended when I dragged my eyes from his to pull my phone from my hoodie pocket.

My smile became a scowl. I stopped myself from growling at the caller. My *mother*.

"I have to get home. But thanks for doing this." I turned from him and added, "I had fun."

"Okay...hold on a sec. I need to get the cover back on."

I should've helped him. But anger with my mother had paralyzed me.

So much for her memory loss.

Once he'd re-covered the AMX, we started walking. Until he grabbed my right hand.

"Wait. Give me your number."

I stared at him as he pulled his phone from his jeans pocket. "Why? What for?"

What reason could he have for wanting to exchange numbers?

"Because I officially consider us friends. And I had fun, too."

The spark inside me turned into a jolt at hearing him say he'd also had fun.

I fought my returning smile as he added, "And as your friend who spends a lot of time here, I can send you pics of your car's progress. I know you'd love that."

I would love that. Before allowing myself to think too much, I rattled off my number.

He smiled once he had my number in his phone and sent me a text.

He'd typed *Kenickie*, followed by the emoji wearing sunglasses.

I stopped fighting my smile. But I still shouldn't have let myself get sucked into this world I loved. With him. Though this had been *so* much fun.

I'd clearly lost my common sense the second I saw him walking his bike with a flat tire.

Chapter Nine

"I knew that car was going to be nothing but trouble when your father told us about it," my mother said to my dad.

I continued staring at my bedroom ceiling from my propped up seat on my bed.

My mother had wasted no time ripping into me the second I'd walked in the door.

My dad sighed, then said, "Lani, the car was a gift from my parents."

"A completely inappropriate gift. She's barely seventeen and doesn't need a car like that. And where are we going to park that thing once it's finished? It's certainly not taking my spot in the building's garage."

Score one for the Beemer.

I so wanted to ask them if I needed to be here for this "discussion," but stayed silent. My mother's head was one smartass comment away from nuclear-level explosion. Something I didn't want to deal with. It also wouldn't be fair to my dad, trying to defend me and his parents.

Because he got it.

"We're months and months away from that. And Dad said they'd store the car."

"I'll also be at college." *Far away from here. And you.*

I sensed her glacial stare as she said, "Does that Sean's parents know you two snuck off to South San Francisco? In *my* car?"

"His name is Shane." I rolled my head to look her straight in the eyes. "Shane. Easton. Yes, they know we went down there. His family owns the shop."

He'd texted his dad on our way to the shop to let him know what we were doing. And his dad hadn't given a crap. It also pissed me off she couldn't be bothered to remember his name. It's not like he had a hard name to remember—guilt made my breath hitch in my chest.

I'd been the same way with his name not too long ago.

The thought of being anything like my mother caused my stomach to twist.

She broke our hostile stare and turned hers on my dad. "Because of this stunt, she's now lost her driving privileges. Indefinitely. Make sure you tell your parents that, too."

My dad responded with a frustrated sigh.

I went back to staring at the ceiling. But my bitchy side wanted to remind her about getting me to community service.

"You're in a whole lot of trouble right now," she continued. "I think it would be best if you stayed with your grandparents over spring break while we're gone for the ground breaking in L.A. You also need to be here for community service."

Wait...what?

I sat up straight and looked almost desperately at my dad, and he faced my mother.

Yeah, she drove me crazy, but I still liked the spring break trips. I didn't have school, spent real time with my dad, and my birthday fell during the break. Another reason for the trips.

"You're going without me? During my—" My voice cracked. From fury and hurt that slashed my heart and reached my core. The hurt then filled and burned my eyes. But I would never let the beauty queen see me cry.

I concentrated on my anger and barely heard my dad's voice.

"Don't you think you're overreacting? And the community service has been handled."

"Richard, she took off with some boy we don't even know to South San Francisco, in my car, without permission. Knowing she was grounded. And why she is grounded? Because of the trouble and embarrassment she caused us with the community service."

I trembled from fury. And the fact at this moment I hated my mother.

Her hard eyes settled on me. "Maybe it'll give you some time to think about the bad choices you've been making lately. Please don't come to dinner looking like you do now." She gestured toward my community service clothes, then turned on her sandaled feet and left.

I scooted down my bed, turned onto my right side and buried my head under a pillow.

Maybe my choices hadn't been great. But why did she have to make me sound and feel like a junior criminal? Between the grounding, loss of driving, and losing the spring break trip, it would feel like she'd sentenced me to jail. And how would I help the club? Help Ella with her campaign? I officially had no life outside of school, home, and stupid community service.

My dad's weight sunk my bed's right side. A second later he lifted the pillow off of my head. His brown eyes softened, but he also looked frustrated. Stuck between being a supportive husband to her and dad to me. He spent a lot of time there.

Another round of guilt caught my breath.

"I understand you're excited about your car, but she has every right to be upset about her car. And you are grounded." He shook his head. "But I don't like the thought of leaving you behind on your birthday. I'll talk to her about the trip once she's calmed down."

I nodded, even though an enormous part of me didn't want to go anymore. Not even for my birthday. And not if it meant dealing with *her* for an entire week.

"Fine. You're right," I roughly said. "But she makes it sound like I took off with some thug and drove to Mexico. Shane's nice. A hard worker. Everyone likes him. His family seems really nice, too." Shane didn't deserve to be talked about as if he were less than a zero.

My dad cracked a smile, which I liked to see. He rarely smiled. My mother ran our last name while he ran the business. His job seemed to take away his sense of humor. When he did smile, though, he appeared younger. More handsome, too.

"It sounds like you like Shane. And his family is nice."

"Dad, we're just friends." But only as of today. The fact he'd met Shane's family at some point made me ask, "How do you know his family?"

"I met them when they finished your grandpa's Chevy." He laughed. Something else he rarely did. "Your Camaro's in the best restoration shop on this side of the country. How'd it look?" he almost whispered.

I smiled. My first since being at the shop with Shane. "It's a chassis right now."

"Not surprising. And probably not worth the trouble seeing it caused?"

I responded with a slight shrug. I'd gotten myself in more trouble, but I'd loved seeing that much of my car.

"Did you happen to see any other cars they're working on?"

I nodded, and my anger and hurt eased at this close and rare time with my dad.

I sat up, crossed my legs and grabbed the pillow he'd taken off my head.

Shane yanking the cover off the shiny, black AMX appeared in my mind, as did his wicked smile, and I said, "You and Gramps would've loved being in there." I hugged the pillow. "But I have to tell you about Mr. Easton's *real* car."

* * *

I had finished loading up my backpack when Ella and Quinn surrounded me.

"What the *hell* happened to you this weekend?" Ella asked.

"We were worried," Quinn tried in a kinder voice. "You're always on your phone. I even tried calling you, but it went to your voicemail."

I shut my locker door. "My mom took my phone away Saturday afternoon."

They fell silent, and I turned to face them.

The noise in the hallway sounded louder than usual for a Monday morning. All around us kids talked and laughed with the excitement of this being our last week before spring break. I usually felt the excitement, but this time I couldn't get there. Not after I spent the rest of my weekend in my bedroom and kept myself busy with homework. The only times I left were for food and to get myself something to drink. Definitely like being in jail.

"She just gave it back to me this morning when she

dropped me off." After a rotten, tense ride to school. "I haven't even turned it on yet."

Ella laughed. "What'd you do this time to piss her off?"

I'd expected the question, but telling them about Saturday wasn't close to an option. I couldn't imagine their reaction to me "kidnapping" Shane and spending so much time with him. They'd crucify me. Especially since I'd made it clear I thought of him as nothing more than a stupid high school boy. He also happened to be with a girl Quinn considered a friend.

Our time together had been innocent. Nothing more than friendly despite his flirty comments here and there. But I'd liked it. Way too much.

"What's up with you?" Quinn snapped her fingers in my face.

I blinked her into focus.

"I know your mom drives you nuts. But you usually stay out of her way, so she'll stay out of yours. And now you're probably still grounded, right?"

I nodded and reached into my sweater pocket for my phone. I needed to get it turned on and everything I'd missed cleared out. I also didn't know how to answer Quinn's first question.

"So when will you not be grounded? You're supposed to help me start preparing for my campaign," Ella whined. "And I'll be gone the whole break. I'm going to New York City."

My frown deepened as I went into my phone to clear the texts from Quinn and Ella, and a series of chats from them, Warren, and other club members. They were still trying to agree on a song. But I could catch up with Warren later. I had no idea what I would say to him, though, since my grounding would totally interfere with the lip sync competition plan.

I glanced at Ella and said the only thing I could. "I don't know, El. I saw enough chats from you and Quinn Saturday morning that it looks like you'll be fine without my help. After break I'll help you post flyers around here and hand stuff out."

I'd spoken sharply, and she returned my frown. But what the hell did she want from me?

"We were also thinking," Quinn said, "about doing a routine for the competition."

Oh, shit.

"Something to go along with her campaign. Nat, you have to be part of it."

"Yes. You do." Ella all but bit out her words.

How the hell could this be happening? Was *everybody* in school planning on being in this lip sync competition? And what about my commitment to the club? Quinn might understand, but Ella would probably blow a gasket at me being in the competition with them instead of her. It's not like I could be in both routines. And knowing Ella Walker as well as I did, she'd make me choose. Them or her.

"Natalie, you're my best friend and I need you right now. So kiss your mom's ass, your dad's ass, or beg if you have to. Just get yourself not grounded." Ella spun from us and stalked down the crowded hallway.

My temper simmered inside me and my eyes met Quinn's. "Did she really just say all that to me? And, what, does she think I got grounded on purpose?"

"Nat, she wants to win. Can you blame her? It's for a good reason."

I didn't feel so sure about that, but kept my opinion to myself.

How would I tell her—them—I couldn't do the competition with them because I'd already committed to being in it with my club? And how were they even going to pull a routine together in time with Ella gone for the entire break? A question so strong I asked Quinn.

"We weren't going to plan something really hard," she

answered. "I'll be gone, too, and we know you always go somewhere."

I released a bitter laugh. "Not if my mother has anything to say about it." I turned from her, done with this conversation, and bumped right into Maddie.

I stepped back and my face flushed.

Her big brown eyes seemed sad. I also saw some irritation, and my heartbeat accelerated.

Had Shane told her about Saturday afternoon?

"Did you two have another fight?" Quinn quietly asked her.

"Yeah," Maddie muttered. "That's all we seem to do."

I somehow stopped myself from breathing a sigh of relief. A part of me did feel bad since she looked and sounded upset by whatever happened with Shane. But it appeared to have nothing to do with Saturday afternoon. And why did I keep making a big deal out of nothing?

"We're spending way too much time together because of *Grease,* and I'm over it." She lifted her chin. "But I'm actually here because I need to borrow your notes for our chemistry midterm. He went through it so fast on Friday I missed some things."

Quinn nodded and went into her backpack.

Maddie glanced at me. "Hey, Natalie. I heard that Theresa girl gave you a hard time on Saturday." She huffed. "She must be crazy messing with you."

I tried smiling, but my image around here felt like another weight added to my heaviness. And how had Maddie even heard about what happened? Then again, it's not like Theresa and I had been alone on the stage.

Quinn stepped close to me. "What's she talking about?"

I so didn't want to get into the story and said, "It was nothing, Q. She's pissed off at the world. I'm going to class. See you in there." I gave Maddie a half smile and turned.

I needed to get away from them and get to class so I could talk to Warren about all the crappy song suggestions before Quinn walked into the room.

I was determined to put off Ella's bitchy ultimatum for as long as possible.

Chapter Ten

I stared at the poll Warren slipped me after American Government. A poll he'd worked on with Kassidy because "Our club's Veep fell completely off the grid over the weekend." He'd also given me crap about getting my phone taken away and still being grounded. The pressure from him and Ella and Quinn why I decided to hide in the silent library with my lunch and the poll.

I picked up my pen and concentrated on the questions they'd created.

1.) When did you join the club and are you still a member?

Okay. Easy enough. I quickly wrote my answer.

2.) Why did you join the club?

Because a dickhead college boy dumped me for a girl who would sleep with him and stay up all night, partying. But I couldn't write that and went with: *I was mad about a bad break-up and the club was a safe place to let it all go. And remember I <u>don't</u> need a boy to be happy.*

3.) If you're still in the club, what's kept you as a member?

I went with the first two words that popped in my mind—friendship and support.

I focused on what I'd written. No, I hadn't warmed up to some members, but when it came to the others, especially the original members, I'd always felt free of their judgment. Something I couldn't admit to giving all of them. I'd given Jade way too much crap about the school dances and still didn't get Lexi's super niceness. I hadn't given the one freshman kid and Erin a chance at all. But if we were going to succeed in proving the haters wrong, I had to be a different Natalie. The one from Saturday afternoon, and before the shit storm at "home."

I added a sentence about the members being judgment free and I could be myself with them. What I'd written hung onto me for a few seconds, then I went to question four. Which I skipped since the question asked for reasons why a member left the club.

5.) List two things you love about being in the club.

I started to answer this last, easy question when my phone buzzed. I had it on my lap, totally against school rules, but I got tired of its bulky weight in my sweater pocket. And our school librarian rarely worked in the back part of the library.

I picked my phone up and froze when I saw who texted me.

Pop quiz, Sunshine. What car was known as the poor man's Porsche?

I looked up and all around me, as if I expected Shane to have magically found me in the library and be hiding behind a nearby bookshelf. But, of course, he was nowhere in sight. Which meant he had to be at lunch in the cafeteria and sitting with...who?

I looked back at my phone and re-read Kenickie's message. I'd added him as a contact using his newest character's name. I guess it had become a joke between us. And there didn't seem to be anything flirty about his text. Just a challenge. No harm in taking him up on it.

I texted back, *The Corvair. Not much of a pop quiz.*

I set my phone back in my lap and continued answering my last question. I had finished writing I loved our weekly meetings because it gave us a chance to talk, vent, and help each other if needed when my phone buzzed again.

Now that I know who I'm up against, I'll come up with a better second quiz.

I smiled as I typed, *I'm only going to play if I can quiz you, too.*

I sat back in my chair and waited. Then my thoughts drifted to Maddie and what she'd said this morning. About the fighting with Shane and her being "over it." I had no idea what she'd meant by that. But I had to assume it meant they *weren't* sitting together right now. Still, I began regretting my second, probably too flirty text. Maddie seemed nice enough. Her comments about Theresa rubbed me the wrong way, but she hadn't said them to be hurtful.

My phone buzzed and lit up with his reply *Consider it on. But where are you?*

He must've looked for me in the cafeteria. And the same jolt from Saturday started in my chest and spread down and throughout my stomach. Then everything inside started crackling. All the way to my toes.

I tried to shake it off and typed, *I'm in the library. Still so nosy.*

But the crackling felt awesome. And so very wrong. Because we were *just* friends.

I needed to focus and finish question five, and wrote how I loved our activities—

It's a gift. Tough time when you got home Saturday?

I released a soft groan.

Why did he have to be nice? And cute? And though I

wouldn't go into all of that drama in a text, I had a feeling he truly wanted to know what happened. Our drive back had been silent and tense. Our drive to the shop had just been silent.

I replied, *It was fine. Thanks for asking.*

I then came up with a question and tapped out, *What year did the Camaro come out?*

Super easy question for him, but the challenge had officially begun.

As I waited for his reply, I finished my sentence about how our club activities were like being in sports or other clubs. They were about supporting each other and building confidence. I then listed wearing our old club shirts to the fall dance as one example.

You're a bad liar. What's 1967? And I should've known you'd ask me a Chevy question.

I laughed quietly.

He could make me laugh and when I least expected it. A rare thing for me.

That makes us tied, Sunshine. For now.

The crackling inside my body returned. I'd never reacted to any boy like this and oh...shit. I was stupidly crushing hard on an off-limits high school boy.

* * *

After school I spotted Warren about to leave out the front doors and caught up with him.

"Here." I handed over my poll. "Now what?"

We walked over to stand outside the busy school office. There were several kids at Mrs. Oliveri's desk and some parents. Kids were leaving through the main doors in groups, too.

"Once we get everyone else's, we'll have to look at all the

responses. And put it all together for Mr. Yates. I told everyone to have them back to me by Thursday. That reminds me," he added as he stepped out of the way for two kids who looked like freshmen, "Ms. Simmons told me we couldn't meet on Friday. Because of spring break." He leaned toward me. "I think she just wants to get out of here right at three."

"Can you blame her?"

He straightened and sighed. "I suppose not. But all of us *are* meeting this week. At lunch Thursday. Spread the word. We've got to get our song picked and figure out rehearsing." He stared long and hard at me. "What are we going to do about you, Miss Grounded for Life?"

Good question. And what about Ella and Quinn?

I looked left to avoid his stare. And my eyes landed on Shane and another boy—the same boy who'd been working with him on the scoreboard at community service—walking down the stairs. But Shane wore a deep frown as he talked with his friend.

Before they cleared the last step, Shane glanced over and our eyes collided.

I tried to ignore the crackling—more like Fourth of July scale fireworks—but I couldn't.

His face softened a bit and he sort've smiled, but his unhappiness showed. He didn't look anything like the joking and relaxed boy from Saturday. Because of another fight with Maddie?

"*Hello*? What are you—oh, hey guys."

Warren's voice made me jump, and I broke my eye contact with Shane. I still saw them give us quick smiles before turning in the direction of the auditorium.

"So what are we going to do about you?" Warren asked again.

I shoved my curiosity and Shane from my mind, and focused on Warren's question. "I don't know. I'll try talking to my grandparents since I don't think I'll be going anywhere for the break." But the guilt from saying that to Warren and not my best friend caught my conscience and I added, "Don't get your hopes up."

"Just tell them how important this is and we need you."

They needed me. Ella and Quinn needed me. I kept getting ridiculous crush attacks on Kenickie, and was being sabotaged by a *crazy* senior at community service.

What kind of mess had I gotten myself into?

Chapter Eleven

s I headed to the cafeteria for lunch, my phone buzzed and I knew who texted me. I, smiling, stopped steps from the cafeteria's entrance and pulled out my phone.

Quiz 2, Sunshine. And it's a good one. What was the first muscle car?

I leaned against the wall. This question seemed too easy. It made me question my answer since he seemed to think he stumped me. But I knew my classic muscle cars.

I tapped out, *The 64 Pontiac GTO. Is that the best you can do, Kenickie?*

I inched my way toward the entrance before I hit send. He had to be in the cafeteria, and I couldn't ignore the strong urge to see his reaction when he received my text. I also had to see for myself what was up with him and Maddie, this being the second lunchtime he'd texted me.

I, as casually as possible, peeked around the corner to see into the crowded, noisy cafeteria. I knew he sat on the far right side with...other drama kids. He sat at the table's end with Drew, Warren's crush, and two other boys, one being his friend I saw him with yesterday and from community service. I also saw a senior—Bree?—and a couple of girls I didn't know. But I didn't see Maddie with them.

I scanned the cafeteria and—I frowned.

She was with Sloane, and her best friend Brandy, several tables away from Shane's table. Sloane being Mrs. Chaplin's—the choir teacher and musical director—rotten daughter. I'd never had Mrs. Chaplin, but I hated her and her daughter. They'd tried to get Kassidy kicked out of *Romeo and Juliet*. But Kassidy won the battle. And Brandy, like Sloane the musical star, walked around this school as if she were a queen, being our star, varsity girl's volleyball player.

Maddie and Shane had to be more than fighting right now. But them actually breaking up would've been all over this school. So weird.

I shook my head and looked back down at my phone.

Playing a silly trivia game. That's all Shane and I were doing.

I sent the message and quickly glanced up. It took a second, but when my reply hit his phone he instantly put down his sandwich and swiped his phone off of the table.

"Nat, what are you doing?"

I whirled toward Quinn, looking at me like a sane person who'd just realized her best friend might be insane. "I was..." How could I explain this? Because I probably did look insane.

"Are you texting Ella? She'll be here in a few."

I shoved my phone back in my sweater pocket.

She walked into the cafeteria, and I followed her. I somehow found the strength not to look in his direction. Especially since I suspected his eyes were on me.

We sat down at our usual table, and my phone buzzed with his answer.

I noticed Warren and Lexi sitting with Kassidy, Meg, Jade and their boyfriends not too far away. I sent them a little wave, which they returned. They were all talking, laughing, and I tried to ignore the pull toward them.

My phone buzzed again, and I jerked my eyes from them and eased it from my pocket while Quinn emptied her lunch bag. I held my phone down and used the table as cover.

Good answer. But the right one is the 49 Oldsmobile Rocket 88.

So it had been a trick question.

I read his second message.

Does that mean I get the point? And stop looking so serious.

I fought a smile as I typed, *No. Trick questions aren't fair. I'm checking your answer. And serious is my thing.*

What I texted caused me to glance over at my club members. Still talking and laughing.

"Aren't you going to eat?" Quinn asked.

I dropped my phone in my lap and opened my lunch bag. Chicken Caesar salad with purple grapes. My lunch options were limited since my mother only kept healthy food around.

"What's with you lately? You seem so distracted."

I rolled my eyes. One way of showing Quinn I felt fine. Though I didn't feel fine. At all. "Q, stop asking me that. I'm grounded from life, but everything else is the same."

Not a total lie, but I couldn't shake the guilt. I still had no idea how to tell her and Ella about being in the competition with the club. And they, and everyone else in this school, could never know about the texting with Shane. My phone then buzzed. Like he could read my mind.

Someone's a sore loser. And serious doesn't have to be your thing. Got a question for me?

"Is that Ella? Where the hell is she? I'm going to text her."

I smiled at his text and ignored Quinn.

I came up with a question but knew it would be easy for him. If we were going to play this game for a while, and keep score, I needed to sharpen my classic muscle car knowledge.

Thanks, Dr. Kenickie. What does GTO stand for?

I really wanted to ask him about Maddie. But were their problems any of my business? And Quinn might know, but I sure as hell couldn't ask her without being interrogated.

I took a few bites of my crunchy salad. Then, while Quinn texted Ella, I slowly turned my head right and leaned back to see if I could see him from my seat. I barely saw him and only because he was lounging back in his chair with his phone down like I had mine, and texting me.

"She should be here in a sec. What are you looking at?"

I faced forward and continued eating my salad.

Quinn gave me the same look when she caught me at the entrance. And I couldn't blame her one bit since I had lost my mind.

His answer hit, and I picked up my phone.

What's known as Get Tickets Often?

The giggles rippled out of me. Then I remembered Quinn sitting across from me.

She frowned. "Who are you texting? Because I've *never* heard you laugh like that."

Ella suddenly appeared, dropped her lunch bag on the table, and sat beside Quinn.

"Sorry. Campaign stuff. And my biggest competition will be our VP, Tyler. But I can beat him. I know the lip sync competition will push me ahead. My dad told me to find his *weakness*. And a nerd like Tyler will never do something like that." She laughed.

And something about the sound turned my insides to ice.

Ella opened her lunch bag. "What'd I miss?"

I saw that. You need to laugh more.

Which meant he was watching me, too.

"Natalie has to be texting some guy she hasn't told us about," Quinn answered. "You should've heard her laugh before you got here."

Excitement I shouldn't be feeling replaced the ice from hearing Ella's laugh right as another text from him popped up.

Real answer. What's Gran Turismo Omologato? Is that the best you can do, Sunshine?

"What the hell? Who did you meet?" Ella asked.

I had no choice but to end this and deal with my best friends.

I texted, *I'm just getting started. I'll get you in round three.*

I closed out of text messaging and sat up. Time to start lying out my ass. "There's no guy. And when would I have met one? Grounded, remember?"

"Then who made you laugh like that?" Quinn whined.

"Just someone in the club," I said, remembering how happy they looked.

"Right," Ella muttered. "I know who's in that club."

Irritation with her never-ending bitchiness toward the club, this stupid conversation, and my guilt caused me snap, "You don't know them at all, Ella."

Her hazel eyes narrowed. Quinn simply stared at me.

My phone buzzed, but I forced myself not to grab it. I couldn't look away from them.

Ella's mouth eased into a tight smile. "I was joking. Calm down."

Now she was lying.

"Let's talk about something else," Quinn said. "Like the routine? I have some ideas."

Ella faced Quinn. "Good. I have some, too. We need to get this figured out."

I had to tell them the truth. But the tension between us stopped the words from coming out. What I needed to say would make things so much worse, and I couldn't deal with *another* mess right now.

I sat back in my chair and eyed my phone. I had to know

what he'd texted. Hopefully something funny and just for me. Like his earlier text.

I picked up my phone and pressed the home button.

I can't wait.

Not funny and probably too flirty. But it did make me smile.

Chapter Twelve

I should've been studying for my math midterm, but I had muscle car history on my mind. Shane had been right about the 49 Oldsmobile Rocket 88; the GTO cited as the first muscle car of the 1960s.

The more I racked my brain for a great question, I realized I may not be able to stump him since he'd grown up in that world. But I couldn't let it stop me from trying. Even if I had to do more research. It's not like we'd made any real rules with this game.

I heard a knock from my doorway and there stood my mother, still wearing one of her many designer power suits. She always wore them on days she met with her various charities.

To keep her off my back, I'd changed into a new pair of skinny jeans, a long, thin, black sweater and kept my hair hanging loose. But I so wanted to pull it up and off my neck.

"Can I talk to you for a few minutes?" she asked.

I nodded, and she walked into my room. She seemed calm. A good sign she hadn't come in here to start anything. She'd kept her distance since Saturday, which had been fine with me.

She sat on my bed's edge, something she rarely did, and my muscles tensed. I didn't trust her "playing nice" side, because underneath it was where her disappointment with me existed.

"I've had some time to think the last few days and talk to your dad," she said. "He told me about the boy you were with and his family. I'm...sorry I rushed to the wrong conclusion about him. I've also reconsidered you joining us on the trip to L.A."

I remained silent, though I did feel surprised, mostly by her apology about Shane. I also never thought my dad would change her mind. I should've been happy he did, but on Saturday I'd really felt the strong desire *not* to go with them. And seventeen wasn't exactly a big birthday.

"We do always go on a trip for your birthday. We're leaving Friday afternoon so you don't miss school. But you're to *look* and be on your best behavior since it's also a work trip."

Look and be on my best behavior. I wanted to ask her when I'd ever looked or acted badly on one of our trips. Okay, so this one would include my dad's work. Still, she made me feel like a juvenile delinquent.

I picked up a pillow and hugged it to my chest.

She stood and headed for my doorway.

I sifted through everything going on in my life. The club, the competition, the community service, even—no. He so couldn't be a part of this decision. For many obvious reasons. But the thought of being imperfect me at my *real* home in Sausalito with my grandparents and Chloe for a week, far from my mother, became the stronger desire.

"What if I'm okay with not going with you two?"

She faced me. "*Natalie.*"

My defenses, always simmering below my surface, bubbled over. "If I go with you guys, I'll miss two Saturdays of community service. That's eight hours I don't want to make up at the last minute. Hours are due the first week of May." All true statements, too.

She eyed me, almost cautiously. "This is really the reason you don't want to go?"

"Yes." Totally a lie, but I didn't feel guilty about it.

She stayed silent a few seconds, watching me, probably looking for signs of deceit, before saying, "Alright. It's your choice. I'll talk to your dad when he gets home, and we'll call your grandparents." She turned to leave, but stopped. "I appreciate your honesty. And maturity."

Her version of compliments. Still better than being treated like a junior criminal.

Because she seemed to be in a reasonable mood, and remembering my promise to Warren about getting out of my grounding, I asked, "Will I still be grounded over the break?"

She opened her mouth, and I looked away and waited for the dreaded yes. But it never came. I then peeked at her and my heart accelerated with hope. She seemed to be giving my question serious thought.

"As a way to reward your maturity, and as a birthday present, you'll no longer be grounded starting Friday after school. Normal curfew rules. We'll tell your grandparents, too."

I squeezed my pillow tighter to my chest. If I had a different kind of relationship with my mother, I'd jump off my bed and throw my arms around her as my thank you.

"But no driving. That still stands."

I nodded and said, "Thanks."

"You're welcome." She gave me a hesitant smile. "That sweater looks nice on you."

I shrugged my thanks to that compliment since I only dressed like this at "home" for her, and she left without another word. I then grabbed my phone. I had to text...who?

I usually texted Ella and Quinn with news like this. But I

really wanted to text Warren and my other club members. Maybe snap a photo of me opening my bedroom window and post it to Snapchat with the caption FREEDOM. They would probably know what it meant. At the same time, I didn't want Ella and Quinn to know. I still couldn't deal with the lip sync competition conversation. And did they even have to know? They would be gone all next week. I could always tell them my mother took away my jail sentence after the break.

When I thought about them being gone, relief filled me up. Relief without guilt. It probably made me a terrible friend, but I couldn't help what I felt.

I opened text messaging and saw his last message at the very top.

I can't wait.

I opened our thread and scrolled through the messages from yesterday and today. I smiled again at a couple of his replies, but focused on a certain thing he'd said.

Serious doesn't have to be your thing.

Maybe something inside me *was* changing.

I had no idea what to call our texting. It seemed way stronger than simple friendship. A connection full of sparks that could power the kinds of cars we kept texting about.

Did he feel the same way? He'd been the one who started the game. And what about Maddie? They were clearly having problems, which started before our texting. I didn't really have anything to feel guilty about. Except flirting back. And liking him and the flirting and the texting too much. But I also knew if they broke up tomorrow, nothing could happen between us. We'd have to stay friends. Because we'd be socially annihilated, more me than him. Ella and Quinn would never understand, and I'd probably be labeled the rich bitch who'd stolen the good drama boy away from the perfect drama girl.

Not a fair label. A label that made me grit my teeth. But

the thought of ending our silly trivia game made me feel empty. Like I'd miss out on something extraordinary.

Right or wrong, I liked—loved—that I could be me with Shane Easton.

* * *

I stood outside my open locker and shielded my phone from other kids at their lockers.

I'd found a question online last night, and though he and Maddie weren't getting along at all, I first needed to ask him something I should've on Monday.

So I have a quiz for you. But...should we be doing this?

I, trembling at what his response might be, set my phone down on the shelf in my locker.

I'd started unloading my backpack to make room for the books I needed this morning when my phone vibrated and lit up with his response.

I hesitated before picking my phone back up.

Why not? Are you having fun?

I sighed and my trembling settled down.

Of course, he'd answered my question with questions of his own.

I replied, *Yeah. I'm having a lot of fun. You?*

I finished loading up my bag and his reply appeared in our thread.

Yeah. So ask me your question. You left me hanging yesterday.

And I guess those were my answers.

Fine. If he didn't think our trivia texting was a big deal, I wouldn't, either.

I re-read his message, then looked all around to see if I could catch a glimpse of him in the hallway. But I didn't see him, which meant he had to already be in class.

I remembered the question I found while I should've been studying my math notes.

Since you know so much about Oldsmobile muscle cars, what does 442 stand for?

The number being their line of popular and powerful cars back then. I had a feeling he'd know this one, too, but it would take him time to tap out his answer.

I headed for class and his too-fast reply hit.

Do I really have to type all that out?

I bit my lower lip as a way to fight my ridiculous, crush sick smile.

So lazy, Kenickie.

When I reached American Government, I paused outside the classroom. I couldn't walk in there smiling and texting Shane with Quinn and Warren inside. Their questions would totally ruin this moment.

Class is starting, Sunshine.

How convenient. And you'll owe me an answer.

I straightened and pressed my lips together to get rid of my smile. Time to be *that* Natalie.

Chapter Thirteen

re you in the library again?

A I frowned at Ella's text as everyone settled around me in desks with their lunches at our normal place in the back of Ms. Simmons's classroom.

I kept my phone down and paused before replying. I intentionally didn't tell her and Quinn about our lunch meeting today.

Yes. Studying. Why?

"Thanks for letting us meet in here for lunch," Warren said to Ms. Simmons. "The cafeteria is way too noisy and we have a lot to talk about before the break."

She smiled. "You're welcome. How's the poll you told me about?"

"I got all of them back," he said to her and us. "Just gotta go through the answers and put it all together so we can show it to Mr. Yates. I was thinking the Friday after the break?"

I nodded my okay with everyone else, and my phone buzzed with Ella's reply.

What the hell, Natalie. We wanted to talk about our idea for the routine.

I rolled my eyes, because I so didn't want to deal with Ella and her routine. I still couldn't understand how they'd be able to put something good together with them being gone the entire break. School started back the first Monday of April; the competition less than two weeks later.

I had to tell them to find someone else. I'd blame it on my mother and being grounded. They were also my best friends and wouldn't stay mad at me forever about this. Or would they?

I closed out text messaging and dropped my phone in my lap.

"Next question," Warren said. "Is anyone going to be gone for the break?"

"Dad and his girlfriend have to work." This from Kassidy. "But Justin will be here. And he really can't go anywhere because of soccer."

"Same with Nate and baseball," Jade added. "My parents wanted to go somewhere but I talked them out of it." She giggled. "Everything with Nate still feels so new. I can't leave him."

Bitchy Natalie would've rolled her eyes at hearing this. But this Natalie, sitting here with her club members, totally understood. Even though I liked a boy I shouldn't like.

"My sister's coming home from school. With her *newest* boyfriend," Meg said. "But I might go to Stinson Beach for a couple days with Owen and his family."

My phone buzzed with another text. I stared at his message.

Okay, Sunshine. I'm back. And with a question.

I hadn't heard from him since yesterday morning. Also known as the main reason for my crappy mood. I'd, like a total moron, checked my phone a bazillion times and for nothing. I'd also spent way too much time wondering if it had anything to do with Maddie since they still weren't sitting together at lunch. But I guess not.

The hurt from him disappearing for so long—something I had no business feeling—caused my snarky, *I'm not answering. On the grounds you never answered my question.*

"*Natalie?*"

I looked up to see eight pairs of eyes watching me.

Warren gave me his stink eye, then said, "You're always gone during the break, right?"

"Not this time. And I have good news." I smiled. "I won't be grounded as of Friday after school." Warren gave me a sideways hug. Everyone else smiled and clapped. But fear of this somehow getting back to Ella and Quinn made me ask, "Can we keep it between us? Please?"

Warren, Kassidy, and Meg exchanged confused frowns, but then slowly nodded and shrugged along with everyone else.

Yeah, sorry about that. Yesterday was not a good day.

Well, crap. I guess I shouldn't have been pissy with him. But what could've happened? More drama with Maddie?

"What happens in the club stays in the club," Lexi said.

I yanked my eyes from my phone to send her and everyone a thank you smile.

"I'm not going anywhere, either," Lexi mumbled. "Which is fine with me since my parents are driving me crazy." She shook her head. "So it sounds like everyone is going to be here next week?"

I asked him, *Is everything okay?*

I caught Paige, Alisha, and Erin nod after I sent my text.

"Fabulous," Warren said. "Now, let's talk about the competition. I signed us up as 'Warren and Friends.'"

It will be. And I know I owe you an answer.

So what are you waiting for, Kenickie?

"I have good news, too." Lexi leaned forward. "My aunt is

my dance teacher and her studio is here in the city. I told her about the competition and asked her if we could use her studio to rehearse when she's not using it. And she said yes."

Relief and surprise in the form of laughter filled our tight circle.

Where we would rehearse hadn't even crossed my mind. Getting to the rehearsals from Sausalito would be a challenge since I couldn't drive myself. Hopefully my grandparents wouldn't mind taking me if I explained everything to them. And begged.

"Wow, Lexi. That was awesome of you." Jade laughed. "This will be so much fun."

There was a quick knock at Ms. Simmons's door. I turned —my eyes grew and my mouth opened as J.R., Owen, and *Shane* walked into the room.

What the hell was he doing here? He couldn't be here because of me. Or was he—

"Hey, can we talk to you guys for a sec?" J.R. asked.

I tried not to look at Shane, but his wicked smile had magnetic strength. It seemed only for me, and the sparks between us fired my insides.

Oh, this really wasn't good. At all.

"How long is it going to take?" Warren asked. "We have a lot to talk about."

I dragged my eyes from Shane to focus on J.R. and Owen.

"We wanted to tell you we got the last spot for the competition."

J.R. spoke so fast I wasn't sure I heard him right. No one else looked certain, either.

"You three," Meg slowly said, "are going to be in the competition? Together?"

They nodded, and Meg burst into laughter.

But Kassidy, not laughing or smiling and looking straight at her boyfriend, said, "You're going to compete against us? Why on earth would you do something like that?"

"Kass, it's not what you think." J.R. stepped forward. "We were going to surprise all of you and be a part of your group. But Mr. Yates told us Mrs. Chaplin and Mr. Lowry don't want more than ten kids on stage. Something about protecting the *Grease* set and props."

Okay. I had to admit what he said sounded pretty sweet. And everyone else's expressions, including Kassidy's, softened. But why would Shane want to be a part of this? Us?

"We still wanted to be in the competition," Owen added. "To support you. Shane heard us talking in class about it and now the three of us are in it."

Silence followed.

What *could* we say to that? They seemed so genuine. And it looked like Kassidy and Meg wanted to leap over the desks and throw their arms around J.R. and Owen. But Owen's explanation didn't explain why Shane had decided to be in the competition with them. Then again, it's not like he wasn't used to performing in front of the entire school. Of course he'd be up for being in this competition.

I peeked at him and our eyes caught. He smiled, but this one held more affection.

And there came another round of sparks.

I bit my lower lip to stop *my* smile and looked away.

"Owen, this is really, really sweet," Meg said. "But you can't dance."

I laughed along with everyone else. I think I even heard Ms. Simmons laugh.

"I know," he mumbled, then shrugged. "But I still want to do this."

"I can teach you a few things." Shane spoke for the first time. "Between me and J.R., I think we can stop you from tripping over your feet and falling off the stage."

More laughter filled the room.

"Actually," Warren stated, "something like that could really work to our advantage."

There were moans, and Meg threw her apple at him, which he barely caught.

"I'm with Meg." Erin rested her chin on her right fist and gazed at the three boys. "You guys are *soooo* sweet."

Bitchy Natalie would've rolled her eyes at that, too. But we had to stick together.

She was also right.

"So you're not mad?" J.R. asked Kassidy while giving her a crooked smile.

She, all but glowing, shook her head. She then focused on Shane. "But you are absolutely *not* to make all of you look that good."

He gave her a quick nod.

"Now get out of here." Warren shooed them off. "We've got planning to do."

J.R. and Owen turned to leave, but Shane walked right to me.

"I have to tell her something first."

My pulse accelerated when he leaned down. Our heads were inches apart. And of course he smelled like his yummy body wash. It probably had a silly name. Like Ocean Hottie.

I felt all eyes on us as he said, "Four, four, two. Four-barrel carburetor, four-speed transmission, and dual exhaust." He gave me that smile and straightened. "See ya guys later."

He passed J.R. and Owen who, like everyone else, stared at me—us—with wide eyes.

My face burned under their scrutiny.

Had Shane lost his mind?

"*What* did he say to you?" Alisha asked once the boys left.

"It sounded like another language," Lexi said as she twirled a strand of her hair with two fingers. "But the way he said it was kinda...hot."

Paige looked at me. "I thought you two hated each other."

I stared at my desk, while wanting to fan the heat from my face.

Had he really just done that?

Warren nudged me. "What was that all about, Madame Veep?"

"Nothing." I laughed and managed to pull yet another lie right out of my ass. "It has to do with *Grease*." I rolled my eyes. "And the car, Greased Lighting. So not a big deal."

Everyone but two members accepted my answer and shrugged it off. The eye rolling I'm sure helped. But Kassidy and Warren's eyes were still filled with questions. And suspicion.

I sighed and said, "Look, lunch is going to be over soon. We haven't even started talking about a song or a rehearsing schedule."

As I hoped, what I said took the attention off of me. But Shane would hear about this.

"She's right." Kassidy yanked her eyes off me. "We need to get focused."

"Since we haven't been able to agree on songs," Warren declared, "I decided to pull rank and choose for us." He glanced at all of us and seemed to be daring us to challenge him.

I stayed quiet since we did need to get this figured out.

"I've chosen a Panic! At the Disco song."

Okay. I liked that band.

"So listen to my idea. Because I really think we'll be unbeatable."

Chapter Fourteen

I had almost made it to the stairs when I heard two familiar voices call my name.

I stopped and took a deep breath before turning to face Ella and Quinn.

"Are you avoiding us?" Ella asked, her voice edgy with irritation.

Yes, I wanted to say. *I'm avoiding you and the lies I can't stop telling.* "No. I just need to be outside when my mom gets here." Sort've not a lie.

"We missed you at lunch," Quinn tried. "We've got the song and routine figured out. We need to talk to you about it." She laughed. "There's no way we can't win."

Her words might as well have been a noose around my neck. I had to tell them. Especially now that we had our song and a rehearsing schedule. Working around everyone's plans for the break, we'd decided to start rehearsing Tuesday and Thursday of next week. But Lexi still had to okay it with her aunt. And I'd left the meeting feeling Warren might be right. That *we* would be unbeatable.

My phone buzzed inside my sweater pocket. I knew who it

had to be since I'd avoided answering the trivia question he'd texted at the end of lunch. Shane's attention, for that brief moment before he, J.R. and Owen left the classroom, had been way too obvious.

I'd deal with him later. First, I had to get out of this. So I reached for some truth. "Guys," I said as I pushed a lock of hair behind my right ear, "I don't want to let you down. But you should do the routine yourselves or find someone else."

Quinn's face fell with disappointment.

Ella's, on the other hand, hardened. "Did you even try talking to your mom about your stupid grounding?"

I, looking her straight in the eyes, said, "Yes. And she wouldn't budge. She's really pissed at me right now." It was scary how good I'd gotten at this lying thing.

Quinn's disappointment changed to sympathy. "Is she still making you stay here for the break? Even though it's your birthday?"

I nodded at my other lie.

Ella, still giving me her angry bitch face, crossed her arms. "That's great, Nat. You choose now to start being some kind of rebel. We planned the routine for *three* people."

My temper snapped. "Ella, I'm sorry. What else do you want me to say? I didn't get grounded to screw up your campaign. I was grounded, first. Remember?"

A tense silence settled inside our small circle. All around us students walked by. The noise level in the school's hallways seemed at full volume with spring break one day away.

My phone buzzed again. I wanted to run from here to some place quiet and text him back. He, with the exception of my club members, being the only other person at school who made me feel normal. Happy. And at this second, I didn't care if my feelings were wrong.

Ella's face transformed into something resembling

compassion. But her eyes were still hard. "You're right. It's not your fault you can't help me out right now."

Something about her words stung. Probably guilt that I could help her. If I wanted.

Ella glanced at Quinn. "No big deal. We'll find someone else." She slid her eyes back to me. "I won't be at school tomorrow. But follow me on Snapchat while I'm in New York." She blew us a kiss, and darted around me and down the stairs.

Quinn reached out and squeezed my right hand. "We'll find someone else, she'll win, and she'll get over it."

I didn't respond since I didn't feel her confidence.

"I won't be at school tomorrow, either," she continued. "But I'll check in with you while we're gone. I'll see you on Snapchat, too."

She headed back in the direction of her locker, and I sluggishly went down the stairs.

I thought I'd feel better telling them what little truth I had, but the guilt wouldn't let me go. I'd have to tell them the complete truth once we were back from the break.

Warren said he wanted to keep our involvement in the competition secret for as long as possible. I trusted my club members to keep quiet. But what if J.R. or Owen or now Shane let something slip to their friends? Even if by accident? What about Nate and Paige's boyfriend? Hopefully they'd all been sworn to secrecy. I couldn't imagine the consequences if Ella found out before I'd had a chance to say anything. Her fury would rival an F5 tornado. And would she forgive me and get over it?

At least I had over a week to prepare myself for that shitty conversation.

I walked outside and sidestepped fellow students talking in groups and waiting to be picked up. I then gave the pick-up zone a half-assed glance. When I didn't see my mother's

SUV, I walked farther from the entrance and took out my phone.

I read his first recent message, *I'm still waiting for my answer, Sunshine.* I then read the second one, *Are you pissed at me?*

I replied, *A little. You could've texted your answer.*

He had to be at *Grease* rehearsal, and I closed out of text messaging to continue watching for my mother. So it surprised me when he quickly responded.

Okay. Fine. But I liked seeing you in there, smiling. And laughing.

I didn't know how to reply. Except smile at my phone and at the sparks I couldn't stop.

I promise we're not doing anything wrong.

Because he and Maddie were still fighting? And the trivia questions weren't a huge deal. But our texting had turned into something more than trivia and neither of us wanted to stop.

Where did that leave us?

I slowly scrolled up to find the question he'd texted way earlier.

A classic cars quiz. What were three of the worst cars ever made?

I heard a quick honk and looked up to find my mother waiting for me in the pick-up zone.

I walked toward her car while finally answering his question.

Good quiz, Kenickie. The Pinto, Vega, and Cricket.

"Why were you standing all the way over there?" she asked the second I opened the passenger-side door.

I threw my backpack on the floor, climbed in and shut the door. Pretty hard, too, since my defenses went into overdrive. "I needed to get away from all the craziness. Everyone's excited about spring break."

She pulled away from the curb. Her huffy silence meant

I'd offended her with my tone. But why did almost everything she said to me have to be a criticism?

His reply popped up.

Thanks. But you keep surprising me. And I like it.

Oh, I really had gotten myself into so much trouble.

* * *

I slouched down in my seat behind Warren and pulled out my phone.

Because so many kids were absent the Friday before a break, a lot of teachers ran movies, including Mr. Yates. He'd put on some boring documentary about presidents and government. Other kids sitting toward the back like me had their phones out, too, and I didn't feel bad with my choice to shoot Shane a text. I never would've been able to do this if Quinn were here.

I wanted to ask him something and it had nothing to do with classic cars.

So are you going anywhere for the break?

I really wanted to know if he would be around for community service. I already knew Paige would be there. And probably Theresa Flanagan who I'd seen around, but mostly the back of her frizzy head. A good thing for both of us.

Nope. We haven't gone anywhere since my brother was a senior.

I smiled. The fact he'd texted back so fast meant he must be trapped in a classroom and "watching" something boring, as well.

Where are you going? Somewhere cool that'll make me jealous?

I peeked at Mr. Yates, concentrating on the documentary, then texted, *Just really cool Sausalito. Staying with my grandparents since my parents will be gone.*

I then started to wonder about Maddie's plans, and my smile faded. If they...made up...he'd probably spend a lot of time with her. Unless he had to work at the shop.

They're going somewhere without you? That seems messed up.

My choice. But it'll be weird. First year I won't be with them on my birthday.

I hit send, then cringed. Why I had told him such personal stuff? I'd never even brought up my parents being gone for my birthday with Ella and Quinn. But they thought I had to stay here as punishment.

They're leaving you on your birthday, too? When is it?

It's not a big deal. I like staying with my grandparents. The 28th.

Mr. Yates suddenly turned to scan the classroom, and I shoved my phone between my legs. I saw, from the corners of my eyes, other kids copy my actions. I then pretended to be watching the documentary.

He scanned the room once more and turned toward the Smart Board.

So does that mean you aren't kidnapping me tomorrow?

My shoulders shook from silent laughter.

Not this week, Kenickie.

I'd caught the attention of a couple kids sitting near me, but Mr. Yates hadn't noticed. And I went back to pretending to watch the documentary while I waited for his reply.

That sucks. I was looking forward to being kidnapped again by you.

I, smiling, shook my head at his obvious flirting.

Guess you'll have to find someone else to kidnap you.

Again, Maddie's face appeared in my mind. They'd spent the entire week apart and now he seemed to be *really* acting single.

Wouldn't be the same, Sunshine.

I had to ask him about Maddie. Right now. Because no matter what he said, their fighting, and how hard I tried to go around it, I felt one muscle car away from being the *other* girl.

I have to go. Movie's over. But this was fun. Way better than trivia.

Okay. I'd try talking to him tomorrow right after community service. In person might even be better. I wanted to see his reaction to my questions. Look into his perfect San Francisco Bay blue eyes for the truth about his relationship with Maddie.

Chapter Fifteen

I checked my phone again to see the time while Paige painted her side of the picnic table. She'd offered to help after I told her what happened with Theresa a week ago. Almost 8:30 and Shane still hadn't shown up.

I wanted to shoot him a quick text. But fear I'd seem more like an overly concerned girlfriend than just a friend stopped me. Though I couldn't help feeling concerned. He'd never been late or not shown up. At least, not since I'd started being here. And he'd made it clear during our texting yesterday morning he'd be here today.

I glanced at the auditorium doors, for what had to be the millionth time, expecting to see him walk inside. Nothing.

"Who are you looking for?" Paige asked.

I whipped my head forward and slipped my phone back into my sweatshirt pocket. "No one. Just noticing how much has gotten done the last couple weeks."

I felt her eyes as I picked up my brush and continued painting the table brown.

Because of the break, Mr. Lowry had half the amount of students this morning. Unfortunately, Theresa *had* shown up.

She and her minion-friend I had no interest in knowing were working with some students on the main Rydell High backdrop. They were sketching out what would eventually be painted. No drilling today. The silence, with the exception of students talking and laughing, being a nice change. Shane's friend worked on the scoreboard alone, and I eyed the auditorium doors. Again. I then faced the table and focused on getting it done. I officially hated brown paint.

When we were finished painting, Paige and I headed toward the girl's dressing room to rinse off our brushes, and Theresa and her minion-friend emerged.

Theresa and I exchanged withering stares before she glanced at Paige. "Don't forget to lick the paintbrush, sweetie." Their cackling filled the quiet space.

Paige stared at the backstage floor like she wanted it to open beneath her feet.

I stepped toward Theresa, feeling like we'd picked up where we left off last week. Only now, I didn't have Shane to stop me from doing or saying something nasty.

"Maybe that's funny for people who are spawned from Satan, but it's not funny here."

Her creepy green eyes narrowed into slits. "It's called a joke, princess. Do you know what that is? Or do you need me to give you the definition?"

Her condescending tone caused me to take another step closer. And, what, my family's money meant I didn't have a brain?

Remembering her family situation, and what she'd done and said to me last week, I couldn't stop myself from unleashing bitchy Natalie. "Why don't you get on your broomstick, *sweetie*, and go back to wherever you came from. I'm sure your evil monkeys are missing you. And no one at this school will notice you're gone."

Her minion-friend stared at me, mouth open, as Theresa's

eyes darkened and became round. With rage. And some fear. Which meant my last sentence had hit a sore spot.

"Girls, what's the problem now?" Mr. Lowry's exasperated voice a knife slicing through the thick tension before he appeared at my left side. He subjected all of us to a hard stare. He then pointed at Theresa and the minion. "Get back to work on the backdrop." As they spun away, he said, "Natalie, when you're done rinsing those brushes I want you to come talk to me."

My shoulders drooped.

Why did I keep getting in trouble while Theresa got away with being the crazy bully?

"Thanks for that," Paige said when we were inside the dressing room. "I really wish I could be more like you."

"You're welcome," I mumbled. "But being like me isn't great. Now I'm in trouble with Mr. Lowry. He wasn't happy with me last week, either. Because of her."

"Nat, he has to know Theresa's the real problem around here. Not you."

"Maybe."

A few minutes later I found him off stage. He, going through some papers, stood near the center, front row seats. Then an auditorium door opened and Shane wandered in, yawning, wearing jeans, a sweatshirt, and a backward baseball hat.

Had he just woken up?

"Mr. Easton," Mr. Lowry called out, "it's nice of you to finally join us."

He headed down the aisle. "Sorry. I slept in."

"Apparently." To me, Mr. Lowry said, "I appreciate your hard work, Natalie. But for the sake of keeping peace around here, I need you to find a way to get along with Theresa."

I crossed my arms, because this was so not fair. "Mr. Lowry, it's not me. She—"

"I'll be talking to her, too." He lifted his eyes. "Shane, come here for a minute."

He changed direction and stood next to me. And he looked terrible. His eyes were bleary and puffy from exhaustion.

What could've possibly happened between yesterday and this morning?

"I'm putting Natalie and Paige with you and Liam on the scoreboard until it's finished."

Liam. Shane's friend. I'd make sure to remember his name. And I would've felt enormous relief with Mr. Lowry's decision, even giddy. But he made me feel like a troublemaking little kid who had to be babysat by the more mature teenager.

"Okay," Shane said. "She's a good painter. Paige works hard, too."

He looked at me for the first time since walking into the auditorium, and I saw humor flash through his tired eyes.

"Great. Then get to it."

We fell into step beside one another and walked toward the stage. In silence. And I had absolutely no idea what to say, considering we'd gotten close through our texting this week.

"So you're still here," he murmured. "Must mean you haven't knocked Theresa out. Yet."

I smiled. "It was getting kinda ugly just now, before Mr. Lowry walked up to us."

"What happened?"

"It's not important." I eyed him. "Are *you* okay?"

"I didn't get much sleep last night," he muttered. "I almost didn't come today, but I really wanted to—be here." He stopped when we reached the stage stairs. And gave me that smile. "It's probably a good thing Mr. Lowry paired us up, Sunshine. I'd hate to see you get expelled." He paused before adding, "You'd be missed around here."

He turned and jogged up the steps. But I'd glimpsed his

face turning pink, the same way it had at the shop when he'd complimented me.

I bit my lower lip, but it didn't stop my smile. Still, I wondered if Maddie had been the reason he didn't sleep well because they'd been on the outs all week.

My smile disappeared.

I absolutely needed to talk to him about her.

* * *

I waited for him in the auditorium for as long as I could while he helped other kids clean, but gave up. And continuing to wait for him seemed too obvious.

Grams texted they were running late, and the moment I stepped outside into the hazy sunlight I dropped to a stair step. Hopefully he'd be out soon.

He started to look better while the four of us worked on the scoreboard, but still distant. A little distracted, too. But I had found out Liam was actually Shane's best friend, also active in theater. He'd played Tybalt in *Romeo and Juliet* and got Doody, another T-Bird, in *Grease*. He seemed really nice, too. And funny. Just like his best friend.

I rested my chin on my knees and tried to gather what I would say to Shane.

Because we were friends, I could use that approach. He and Maddie had been fighting all week. Maybe being on the outs with her had caught up with him last night?

Jealousy burned inside me. The fact I had no right to feel this way made it worse. No matter my impossible crush on him, we were *just* friends. Who flirted with each other too much. But I loved the Natalie who came out while we texted and when we were together.

My phone buzzed and dinged with a text message.

Are you still here?

My insides turned mushy from Shane's simple question.

I so needed to get a grip.

Yeah. Waiting for my grandparents.

The school's doors burst open behind me. Two boys came out, followed by Shane. His eyes lit up when he saw me, followed by a smile I returned.

The three said quick goodbyes, and the two boys walked by me down the stairs. It looked like they were trying not to stare at me. But it didn't stop me from staring at them.

They headed left. Once they were gone, Shane sat beside me on the step. Close enough his right knee touched my left knee. And my heart beat a tad faster.

I asked what then came to mind. "Where's your bike?"

He smiled, and I hoped he was thinking about this time last Saturday, too.

"Still has a flat tire. No time this week to get it fixed."

Silence fell.

Why couldn't I talk to him all of a sudden?

He seemed to be searching for something to say, which told me he felt the same way. Or maybe he had to give me bad news. Like tell me we had to stop the texting because of Maddie.

We needed to talk about her and better to beat him to the topic. I took a deep breath, released the air and asked, "What are you and Maddie up to over the break?" Not exactly to the point, but at least it got the conversation started.

He, not surprisingly, became tense, but I couldn't let this go. So I waited. And waited.

"Nothing," he finally said. "We broke up Monday night."

Wait...*what* did he say?

My mouth opened. I glanced sharply at him, but he wouldn't look at me. In fact, he looked pretty guilty as he stared down at the step.

Okay. So that's why they hadn't been sitting together at

lunch. This also explained his carefree attitude about our texting and his "I promise we're not doing anything wrong" message.

Though a big part of me wanted to release a sigh of relief and excitement that we could keep texting each other, another part of me ached for him since he looked so guilty. And break-ups never stayed a secret at Pacifica Academy. Especially a week. So I asked, "But...how?" This earned me a confused frown from him, and I shook my head. "Break-ups are usually all over school within a day. You know that."

"Because a lot of kids around here post it on social media as soon as it happens." His frown deepened. "I don't do that and neither do my friends. That's messed up shit. Maddie and I were friends before we started going out, and she's not like that, either."

I gave him a soft smile as my insides became hot *and* mushy.

I guess there were some boys who genuinely respected girls.

He looked back down at the step. "Maddie's great, but we didn't work as a couple. And it's not like *that* was a big secret," he added under his breath.

I watched him while I wrapped my brain around the fact those two hadn't been a couple for most of the week. Wow. I guess if any of our classmates had noticed them being apart, they must've—like me—figured they were fighting. Or maybe kids had been too caught up in spring break fever this week. And it seemed pretty obvious why they broke up, but I sensed he'd been the one who'd done the breaking. Still, their break-up Monday couldn't be the reason he looked guilty and hadn't slept well last night. Especially when I remembered his flirty texts from yesterday morning. But I didn't feel right asking him about that, either.

As I continued to watch him, though, my surprise and

curiosity changed into a strong desire to lean closer, put my arms around him, and squeeze. Hug his breath out of him. But I kept my arms tightly at my side and said, "I know what happened is none of my business, but...do you feel like talking about it?"

It took him several seconds to raise his head, and our eyes met. "Not really. But thanks for asking." I nodded, his answer fair enough, and he added, "I know I probably should've told you, but I didn't want you to think—"

"It's fine. We're just friends." But even I didn't quite believe me as our eyes stayed locked and something like... surprise?...flashed through his eyes.

"Right," he agreed. "Just friends." He dragged his eyes from mine to reach out and playfully tug my ponytail. "I like your hair like this. It's casual. And fits you."

"Thanks," I murmured, so grateful for his subject changing.

"I would've texted you pics of your Camaro yesterday, but it's still a chassis. For now." He tried smiling. "So what are you up to next week?"

"Um...not much. Rehearsing the routine with the club." Which reminded me of us wanting to keep it a secret. "You can't say a word about us being in the competition. Okay?"

He seemed confused, but then held out his right hand and extended his pinky.

I hooked my left pinky with his.

"Sealed with a pinky swear. But why do you want to keep it a secret from everyone?"

Our fingers stayed hooked a few seconds longer than necessary before I unhooked mine. "There are two people who can't know right now."

"Ella and Quinn?"

I nodded. "They don't understand me being in the club. Especially Ella. I'm putting off that conversation for as long as

I can. Especially since I was supposed to be in a routine with them for Ella's campaign." And I cringed at sounding like the worst friend on this planet.

He didn't look at me with judgment, though. It looked like he understood.

"I think it's cool you're doing the competition with your club."

I returned his warm smile and the warmth reached all the way into my core.

"I'm not sure what me and the guys are doing yet." His smile turned mischievous. "But we're meeting up later to figure it all out. I'm also working a few days next week." He leaned against me, and the warmth inside my core turned into white heat.

Just. Friends.

"I'm looking forward to seeing the *real* Natalie Carlisle up on stage in a few weeks."

Now my cheeks were hot. He was so good at making me feel good about the *real* me.

I turned my head. Our faces were close. If either one of us moved a few inches, we'd be able to—I blinked and looked down.

Just...Oh, wow.

"Your grandparents are here," he quietly said. "I'd recognize his Chevy anywhere."

I jumped up and scurried down the remaining steps.

Where had that heat come from? The fact he no longer belonged to another girl?

"Hi, sweetheart," Grams said as Gramps pulled into the pick-up zone. "Sorry we're late. Our golf game took longer than we thought." Her eyes landed on Shane, strolling up to us.

"Hey there, Shane." Gramps leaned over the steering

wheel to see him. "Honey, this is Shane Easton, Gabe's youngest."

She smiled. "It's nice to meet you. We love your family, the shop, and everyone in it."

"Thanks." I heard the pride in his voice. "Nice to meet you, too. Hi, Mr. Carlisle."

I started to face him and force myself to say goodbye when Grams asked, "Are you waiting for someone to pick you up or do you need a ride?"

My eyes widened, because I hadn't expected her to offer him a ride home.

"I was going to walk—"

"Get in," Gramps commanded.

Shane responded by opening the passenger-side's rear door for me.

I smiled my thanks while avoiding his eyes.

My mind became muddled. From he and Maddie breaking up. From my grandparents giving him a ride home. From our almost kiss—I slid across the bright white, leather bench seat, and Shane followed me.

He gave them directions and, after looking around the car's perfect interior, said, "I love this car, Mr. Carlisle. It would've been awesome to work on it."

Gramps laughed. "They did a great job. But I heard your dad has a 70 AMX?"

I released a mental groan. Now Shane knew I'd been talking about him with my family.

I bit my lower lip and peeked at him. Of course he gave me that smile. But after seeing him feeling so bad all morning, the smile seemed like a good sign.

"I would love to see it sometime."

To Gramps he said, "I'm sure I can make that happen."

The car became silent, and I became aware of how close our hands were on the seat. Our pinkies were almost touching.

I remembered our pinky swear and wondered what it would feel like to place my hand over his and feel *all* of our fingers linked. I had a feeling our hands joined tightly together would feel very right. Safe. Then we were at his three-story building.

"Thanks for the ride."

"Of course. Anytime," Grams answered.

Shane opened the door, but paused to catch my eyes. "I'll see you later, Sunshine."

We continued our long stare until he, reluctantly, slid out of the car. He shut the door and headed for his building.

"*Sunshine?*" Grams asked as Gramps drove us away.

I shook my head to clear the haze he created without trying. "It's a nickname."

"He's darling, sweetheart. I approve. Much better choice than the last boy you dated. Who was also too old for you."

"Grams, we're just friends." *Just friends who almost kissed.*

"Then you need to change that."

She'd said it teasingly, but I couldn't find a smile. Because I knew if we did get together so soon after his break-up with Maddie, the harsh judgment at school—especially from Ella and Quinn—would be too much to bear. The unfair part of high school I hated.

I'd miss seeing him this next week, but we apparently needed the physical distance.

Things were getting way too fiery.

Chapter Sixteen

exi blew her whistle and said, "Guys, come on. We can go through it one more time."

She, Warren, and Kassidy were the only ones standing. The rest of us had dropped to the shiny, hardwood dance floor in her aunt's studio. Mirrors lined the left wall. Metal folding chairs lined the right wall where we'd thrown our stuff.

Warren brought a bluetooth speaker to play our Panic! At the Disco song, "High Hopes." He'd chosen the song as a not-so subtle message to our haters. As much as I liked the song and knew it fit us, the power anthem would be stuck in my head forever after hearing it over and over for the last hour. And it was more of an anthem than dancing song. Lexi's choreography included more bouncing in place, strutting, and fist pumping the air than actual dancing.

"This is *soooo* hard," Erin whined while sprawled on the floor.

Paige hugged her knees to her chest and started rocking. "I don't think I can do this. Erin's right. We're supposed to lip sync our lines *and* move around that fast? Without bumping into each other? I'm not that coordinated."

I swallowed my laughter remembering all of us trying to "dance," while holding our papers with the lyrics, as we did crash into each other. I had definitely reached delirious. But it seemed obvious getting ready for this competition would be harder than we thought.

Lexi put her hands on her hips. "Giving up is not an option. We can do this."

And what the hell had gotten into Lexi? With her gym shorts, tank top, Nikes, and whistle, she looked and sounded like a PE teacher with a military background.

She blew her whistle again. "All of you get up. We're going through it again."

Warren took her whistle away. "Enough, Sergeant Lexi."

"I think we're moving around too much," Meg said from right next to me. "No offense."

"Yeah, Meg's got a point," Alisha added. "Keep it *simple*. There's gonna be nine of us up there."

Lexi's face crumbled, and Kassidy put her arm around her and squeezed.

Her sad face weighed me down. She had worked hard to come up with the moves.

I said, "Lexi, you're really talented, okay? But not everyone in here was born to do this."

Everyone stared at me. Probably shocked since I'd never said anything that nice to her. The thought pushed my shoulders down more since we were supposed to support each other.

"Thanks, Natalie." She gave me a soft smile, which I returned.

"I agree." Jade squared her shoulders. "And because this is only our first rehearsal, maybe we need to focus on learning the lyrics before Thursday. Then add the moves?"

Kassidy's face brightened. "That's a great idea." She squeezed Lexi again and stepped forward. "Does everyone have time to work on learning the lyrics between now and Thursday?"

The first part of our rehearsal had been divvying the lyrics and deciding what we'd lip sync together.

Everyone looked at each other and nodded.

"And I'll work on taking out some of the movement," Lexi said.

Warren handed over her whistle. "Ease up a tad on the whistling next time?"

"Sorry about that," she mumbled.

"Okay. We got enough done so let's call it a day." Warren exchanged a sly smile with Kassidy. "But we have one more thing we need to do before everyone leaves."

Everyone but me started smiling like Warren and Kassidy. Then those two and Lexi practically skipped out of the studio, and I stood.

"What's going on?" I asked Meg.

"You'll see," she answered with mischief in her voice.

I shrugged and headed for my bag.

I'd been doing my absolute best since Saturday to stop myself from checking my phone every thirty or so minutes to see if he texted. Which he hadn't. But it's not like I'd texted him, either. Maybe, between his break-up and our almost kiss, he'd been a little freaked out, too? Then again, he had said he'd be busy meeting up with J.R. and Owen, and working.

Even though our connection could never go beyond friendship, I really hoped we hadn't lost anything. I'd probably only have a bunch of chats from Ella and Quinn, but it didn't stop me from wanting to check. Because at some point checking my phone to see if he'd texted had, right or wrong, turned into a full-blown addiction.

I dug through my bag until I found my phone. I took a

deep breath, released the air, then, with one eye open—another addictive, silly ritual I'd started after not hearing from him—I hit the home button.

I opened my eye and smiled.

An addictive, silly ritual which worked this time, and I sagged with relief.

Among the chats from Ella and Quinn, I saw his two texts. The first one included a pic, and I went right into text messaging.

Early birthday present. Parts are coming in for your Camaro, Sunshine.

I tapped the photo to make it bigger. He'd taken a pic of several shiny, brand-new metal parts lined up neatly on a work bench. I couldn't tell what parts they were, but seeing them was another enormous step toward my ultimate goal of freedom.

My smile doubled in size and I read his second message.

Got any big plans tomorrow?

I thought about his question for a second, then typed, *Sleeping. Dinner with my grandparents. My parents are supposed to FaceTime with me, too. Thanks for the pic.*

I sent my message as Meg bounced up beside me. I hit the side button to make the screen go black.

"Who are *you* texting?" Meg asked as she dug through her bag.

"Nobody." I'd said the simple word too quickly based on how she looked at me.

"Uh-huh." She withdrew her phone. "Who's the guy?"

I rolled my eyes.

"Seriously, who is it? I saw you smiling when I walked up. And I *know* that kind of smile." She gave me a playful shove. "It's how I looked when Owen and I started dating."

Shit.

I couldn't really be so obvious, could I?

"Meg, there's no guy."

My phone buzzed and dinged with his response.

Meg stepped closer and angled her head to see my phone I clutched to my chest.

"Natalie, it's okay if you're dating someone. It's not an Anti-Love Club anymore."

"I'm just...texting a good friend. It's not what you think." Not entirely a lie.

She shook her head and focused on her phone.

I pressed my home button.

You're welcome. And sleeping doesn't count. I'll pick you up at 10.

Wait...what?

He so couldn't be serious, and I quickly texted, *What are you talking about? And you don't even know where I live.*

A strange combination of exhilaration, shock, and confusion made me tremble.

What the hell was he up to?

Warren, Kassidy, and Lexi walked back into the studio. All thoughts of Shane disappeared when my brain registered Kassidy carrying a plate of cupcakes with white frosting. The one on top held a single lit candle. Everyone surrounded me and sang "Happy Birthday."

I couldn't move. Frozen solid from being stunned they had done this for me. For my birthday. Ella and Quinn were my best friends and had never done anything like this for me.

"Sorry it took so long." Lexi interrupted that unexpected realization once they finished singing. "We had to find matches."

"We also had to stop Warren from stealing a cupcake." Kassidy glared at him.

"Chocolate cupcakes are my weakness," he stated without a trace of apology.

Tears filled my eyes—another strange reaction for me—

but I blinked a few times and laughed. "How did you guys know about my birthday?"

"I have my ways." Warren pointed at the candle. "Make a wish and blow out the candle before your cupcake gets covered in wax."

I thought of one wish. A wish I'd be wasting because I couldn't have what I wanted. So I made a wish for the club—for us—to be successful and blew out the little blue candle. A thin line of smoke I could smell spiraled off the candle's tip, and I pictured it as my wish going into the air between us.

"I can't believe you guys did this for me." My voice cracked on the words.

Kassidy set the plate down on a nearby chair, and everyone came closer to hug me.

I hugged them back as tightly as I could for it being a group hug. But I held onto Warren and Kassidy a few seconds longer as everyone else withdrew. I didn't know how else to thank them since saying the words would never be enough. Then my phone dinged, and we separated.

As Kassidy removed the candle from my cupcake, I checked his message.

I know where to find you.

Chapter Seventeen

I followed Chloe up the stairs to the main level and paused. My body shook from the anticipation also making my stomach flutter. The fluttering started yesterday with his text, lasted through the night, and I hadn't slept well. But makeup covered the lack of sleep under my eyes.

It took me forever to decide what to wear since I had no idea what we'd be doing. I'd finally chosen my favorite pair of skinny jeans, my *only* pink shirt, and Converse. I'd grabbed a black zip-up hoodie because of the typical, morning marine thickness that might burn off by the afternoon. I'd decided to wear my hair down, with the sides pulled back into a fancy braid.

Grams walked into the foyer and stopped. She looked me over, but not in a judgmental way like my mother would have, then smiled. "I thought you two were 'just friends?'"

I dropped my black cross-body bag and shrugged into my hoodie. "Grams, don't start."

I was already struggling with we-shouldn't-be-doing-this

emotions. I didn't need her teasing me about my *friendship* with Shane. I probably should've backed out of this day.

But I couldn't stay away from him.

She approached me and her smile grew. "What are you guys doing today?"

I picked up my bag and settled it across my body. "I don't know." And relief hit at telling the truth for once. "Where's Gramps?"

"He's been on the golf course since eight."

The doorbell rang, and Chloe yodeled, the normal bark for a Basenji.

I walked the two steps to the front door and Chloe, wagging her butt, met me there. I wondered again how he found my address in Sausalito.

I took a deep breath to steady my pulse and opened the door. And there he stood. Smiling.

Chloe continued to yodel her greeting, and when he turned and bent just enough to pet her, I checked him out. Because he looked *hot*. I scanned his dark jeans, and not the worn out kind he wore to community service, that hugged his lower body the right amount.

He straightened, and my eyes landed on his bluish-gray shirt not quite clinging to his...lean chest. He'd also pushed the sleeves to his elbows, which showed off his defined forearms.

I lifted my eyes to his smiling face and noticed his shirt made his blue eyes stand out.

"You just met Chloe," was all I could think to say as I tried not to stare into his eyes.

"She's cute. Like her owner. I mean—" His face turned cherry red. "Not that you look like your dog or anything. You actually look amazing. But not that—" He sighed.

I giggled, and Grams walked up. Probably to save him from his awkward compliment.

"Hi, Shane."

"Hi, Mrs. Carlisle." His face began to slowly go back to its normal color. "Is Mr. Carlisle here? I have a surprise for you guys. Come on."

He took my hand and led me outside, and Grams and Chloe followed us.

We turned the corner, and I stopped. Then I blinked several times, not believing what I saw parked in the driveway.

Grams said, "Oh, your grandpa is going to be really mad he missed this."

"He's not here?" Shane asked her.

"No. He's golfing."

I walked toward the beautiful car. Also known as his dad's AMX. For some reason, it looked way more ferocious out in the world where it belonged. But how had he managed to get this car, what had to be his dad's prized possession, out of the shop?

I whirled toward him. "How did you talk your dad into this?"

He laughed. "I'll be honest, he said no. About a hundred times. Then I really begged."

At that moment, Chloe headed for the car. Disaster involving her claws flashed through my mind. But Shane, also sensing disaster, scooped her up with a second to spare.

"Sorry," he said to her and she licked his chin. "You're cute. But no dogs allowed in the AMX." He handed her over to Grams and looked at me. "Are you ready?"

"Fu—hell yes."

I caught Grams's disapproving stare before I followed him to the passenger side.

"Have fun," she said. "*Please* be careful."

I waved absently at her and slid into the black, leather bucket seat. And I laughed at sitting in such a fucking hot car.

He sat in the driver's seat, and when he started the

powerful 401 engine, I felt its rumbling in my core. Shane Easton also looked super hot behind the wheel.

"I can't believe your dad let you borrow this," I said while I examined the car.

Everything inside gleamed and smelled of being custom, new, and rarely driven.

He moved the shifter into reverse and carefully backed out of the driveway. "Well, he did say if it came back with a scratch, no one would ever see me again."

I laughed and enthusiastically waved goodbye to Grams as we pulled away. "How did you find out where I live?"

"We have this address on file at the shop and Darlene, the office manager, loves me."

Of course. Why hadn't I thought of that?

"I'm going to try to behave while getting us out of here. It doesn't take much to get this car going." He tapped the gas pedal, and the car roared and lunged forward.

We laughed together, and I briefly caught his eyes. Warm tingles filled me up. Especially as it struck me he'd gone to all this trouble for me. For my birthday.

I had to ask, "Why did you do all this for me? You barely know me."

"That's not true. And I wanted to." He shifted uncomfortably in his seat. "I don't want to sound like a jerk," he began as he stayed focused on the road, "and I know you said staying here was your choice. But it kind've...pissed me off your parents left you for your birthday." He glanced at me and smiled. "Happy birthday, by the way."

I hadn't expected him to say all that and smiled since it sounded like he honestly cared about me. But true friends did care about each other, and I remembered my birthday surprise from yesterday. Something Ella and Quinn had never—no. I so didn't want to think about them.

"Thanks," I murmured. "For all this." I hesitated before

adding, "Being here for spring break hasn't been terrible. I'm really glad I didn't go with my parents."

We drove up to a stoplight, and he rolled his head in my direction. "Me, too."

I bit my lower lip, then asked, "What are we doing today?"

His smile grew. "It's a surprise. So sit back, relax and...be you."

After the stress of the last couple weeks, last week in particular, everything he said sounded like bliss. I just wanted to be here, with him, free and clear from reality.

"And now that we're out of your neighborhood," he continued in a lowered voice, "are you ready to have some fun?"

I glanced at him, his wicked smile infectious as I said, "Drive like you stole it."

"Whatever the birthday girl says." He looked all around, probably for a cop, and his eyes settled on my seat belt.

He gave me a quick wink, and we waited.

The light turned green, and when Shane hit the gas pedal, the AMX flew forward and my head jerked back. But he smoothly shifted the gears.

Laughter bubbled out of me as he actually sped up and zipped around a car going much slower. We also just missed the next light.

I eyed him. "Where'd you learn to drive like this?" Because this bad boy side of him, combined with his confidence driving a 70 AMX, was so Incredibly. Hot.

To the degree I had to catch my breath.

"My brother," he answered while we missed yet another light.

Of course.

I ripped my eyes off of him to roll down my window. I needed air. And my hair started to blow around my head as I took a deep inhale and exhale.

"I'm thinking," he said above the wind barreling into the car, "we should time how fast we can make it across the Golden Gate."

I laughed again while shaking my head. "Whatever *you* say, Kenickie."

I then relaxed into my seat and smiled at my sudden feeling of naughtiness.

* * *

We walked to where the ocean's surf met dry sand, and I breathed in the salty air.

He'd taken us the scenic way down Highway 1 to the Half Moon Bay area and pulled off at one of the beaches.

Up until now, I'd completely let go of all the school drama. The weight had lifted the further we got away from the city. From reality. But with the scenic drive, and ending up on a beach with only us and some people here and there walking along the shore, I couldn't stop one thought—this was so feeling like a first date.

A huge wave thundered, then broke apart on the water's surface. The surf rumbled toward our bare feet, but gradually drifted backward to get lost in another approaching wave.

I stared at the open water and wanted to swim toward the hazy horizon. Battling the frigid water and hypothermia seemed much better than reminding him—us—we were *just friends*.

I opened my mouth, but fear grabbed a hold of me and I blurted out, "You look really good today."

He released a quick laugh. "Thanks. Do I normally look really bad?"

I guess I had sounded a little surprised, and I, in total frustration with myself, started walking north. He fell into step beside me.

"No. Never." I mentally groaned and glanced over to find him looking at me with raised eyebrows. While trying not to smile. "It's just...you didn't look like yourself on Saturday. Because of what happened with you and Maddie?" And now we were out together, not even a week later, on what could be called a date. But he'd agreed we were just friends.

His face darkened for several seconds before he shrugged and said, "It was a long week. I was tired and not in the mood to work on the set."

I responded with silence since what he'd said made sense. But why the dark look? And he really hadn't answered my Maddie question.

"But it's cool you think I *never* look bad," he added.

I looked right and found him smiling again. *That* smile.

"Okay," he said in a serious-but-playful-way voice, "I now know you have a dog named Chloe. You become a bit of a devil when you're in a badass muscle car. Which is very cool."

I laughed. At his teasing. And compliment. And him, once again, changing the subject.

"You hate old music."

We'd gotten into a brief thing about music when he'd tried to keep the radio on some station his dad had programmed that played old rock. But being the birthday girl I'd won, and he'd changed the station to an alternative rock channel.

"You have a house on Oahu because you go every Christmas to see your mom's family."

Something I'd told him during our chat about our families. I'd found out his brother, newly engaged, lived in Burlingame. His sister, Aubrey, was a sophomore and journalism major at NYU. But he'd explained it as his sister "escaping California to do her own thing." The tone of his voice had told me he admired her for leaving. He also admitted if he *were* ever to steal a classic muscle car, it would be his brother's Chevelle, which made me smile.

"What do you want to do after college? I can't see you in the family business."

I huffed. "No. I'd rather jump into the ocean and swim to Hawaii than be stuck in that office all day, everyday." But saying that out loud made me sound ungrateful. I added, "I appreciate how hard my gramps worked and now my dad. But it's not for me."

"I get it. Believe me. So what do you want to do? Something with old cars?" he teased.

I smiled since I did like the idea of turning an old car into something fast and beautiful. "I think working in a shop like your family's would be fun."

"Wow." He laughed. "I was kidding. But I can also see it. The—" He cleared his throat. "The hot girl who knows how to restore old cars. Like on some of those car shows?"

I giggled. "It could be fun." My smile faded, though, when I thought about how my mother would react to that as a career choice. "I don't know what I want to do yet. But I do know I'm going to load up my Camaro next summer and go to college far away from here." I, remembering how he'd answered my question to him being in charge of the shop someday, asked, "What about you? It doesn't seem like you want to be in the family business, either."

"I don't. I want to study Marine Biology."

I stopped walking, then he stopped, and I turned toward him. "Are you being serious?" He didn't seem like the scientist type. Not that scientists couldn't be hot with blue eyes to match.

He nodded. "I want to study sharks."

My mouth dropped open. "You mean, you want to be one of those crazy guys who willingly dives into shark-infested water? Without the cage?"

He laughed. "That's part of what I'll do, but, yeah. Sharks are really misunderstood."

And he couldn't figure *me* out?

"How'd you get into Marine Biology?"

"I love the ocean. Not an original answer. But I love it more than restoring old cars."

I narrowed my eyes. "Do your parents know this about you?"

His smile fell. "I've told them. They'll be paying my college tuition. And my mom sort've gets it. But my dad..." His eyes wandered away from mine. "He wants me to go to college for business. He has this dream of me and my brother running the shop. Which is weird. The shop doesn't need me. My brother can handle it and wants to."

The confusion and frustration I heard in his voice caused me to clasp his left hand and give it a quick squeeze, which made him look down.

I never would've guessed Shane would be up against what he wants versus what his dad wants. The Eastons didn't seem like that kind of family. And we apparently had way more in common than classic muscle cars.

We wanted to break free from our families. Our last names.

He lifted his gaze from our hands, and our eyes snapped together. Like magnets.

He gently pulled me toward him and warning sirens went off in my head. He pulled me so close he could slip his arms around me. And the huge part of me who wanted to shove *just friends* aside began trembling at his closeness, and the fact he, as usual, smelled as good as he looked. But I found the strength to place my shaky hands on his chest.

He lowered his head, and I said, "Shane, we need to talk."

He blinked and raised his head. "Did you call me by my name?"

I groaned, stepped backward, and my feet sunk into wet sand. "You're so not changing the subject this time."

"Sorry. You saying my name surprised me. What do you want to talk about?"

His smile turned wicked, and he looked so adorable I wanted to throw myself into his arms and finish the kiss we started. Twice.

I dropped my eyes to watch the cold surf cover my feet, then rush backward.

I had to tell him the truth. As much as I hated it. Telling him the truth might also bring this awesome day, my birthday, to a swift end. But staying friends would be best. For both of us.

I looked up at him and forced myself to say, "Shane, we have to stay just friends."

Confusion filled his eyes and face. Until he grinned. "Okay." His eyes now gleamed with a hint of challenge. "I'll give you three chances to give me one, really convincing reason why you think that. If you do, we'll stay 'just friends.'"

I squinted at him as another wave pummeled my feet and ankles.

This was so not the reaction I'd been expecting. Challenging me, sure. But not like this. There were many reasons why we had to stay friends.

I crossed my arms and leaned forward. "Reason one. We'll be socially destroyed."

He also leaned forward. "Nope. Not convincing. Because the Natalie I know is in you doesn't care what the kids at school think."

I wanted to be the Natalie he believed in, but said, "I do care. I'm already the bitch nobody at school wants to mess with. If we get together, I'll be the bitch who broke you two up."

His humor vanished. "Stop calling yourself that. Because that isn't who you are. And you won't be alone in the gossip. But my friends and your *real* friends won't care."

His words were incredibly sweet, but what the hell had he meant by my *real* friends wouldn't care?

"Natalie, I like you. A lot." He found my eyes. "I wasn't expecting this." He gestured at me and himself. "I didn't expect you to be who you really are."

He liked the *real* me. I'd never heard that from a boy. Or friend.

My breathing slowed.

"I want to be more than friends and...I know you do, too."

I remained silent. It's not like I could argue with him.

"So, here's a new deal," he continued in a businesslike voice. "If I can't change your mind by the end of today, we'll stay 'just friends.' Okay?" He held out his hand.

This determined side of him, because he did want to be with me, caused me to stare at his hand. At the same time, it made me smile. Because I liked it. A lot.

I hesitated as I ran through everything he'd just said to me, then squelched my apprehension and grasped his hand. A little thrill shot through me as we shared a firm handshake.

And at not knowing what else he had planned for the day.

Chapter Eighteen

I stared at the white roller skates hugging my feet. "I don't know how I let you talk me into this. I haven't roller skated since I was thirteen." I gave him a pretend glare. "I blame you taking me to lunch." Which had turned this awesome day *into* a first date.

His mouth opened in pretend outrage. "Stopping for food is what happens when a girl tells a guy she's hungry. Especially when it's her birthday." He faced the rink. "And skating's like riding a bike. You never forget how to do it."

We stood where we could enter the dimly lit, nearly empty rink. Several multi-colored lights hit the floor in various spots and the floor looked a little on the slick side. There were some moms with their kids, us, and two guys who worked here. It was a Wednesday afternoon and the quiet meant less chance of hurting anyone with our rusty skating skills. But the Top 40 pop song playing right now sucked.

I looked at Shane while remembering the deal we made at the beach. "I'll give you points for originality, Kenickie. But this music is going to drive me nuts."

He carefully stepped onto the rink's floor. "It's skating

music. Stop trying not to have fun and let's go." He skated away from me.

And I decided to check out his super cute butt. His super cute everything.

How had I never *really* noticed him at school the last few years? Because he was one of the hottest boys at Pacifica Academy. Easily top five. Had I been so self-absorbed and against high school boys? The answer came fast, and I frowned. I couldn't even remember why I refused to look at high school boys. I'd never even given one a chance. Just adopted Ella and Quinn's attitude about—my frown deepened.

What else had I missed being Ella and Quinn's Natalie?

He skated back to me. "Hey. Why do you look serious all of a sudden?" His hypnotic blue eyes filled with concern.

I didn't like seeing him looking at me that way, so I smiled and said, "Just psyching myself up for this." Another lie, but a necessary one.

He took my left hand and helped me out onto the rink.

As we got comfortable skating, a group of girls, who looked about thirteen, skated by us. They giggled together and were being so obvious *they* thought Shane was cute.

I glanced at him to find him glancing at me, and I knew my glowing insides showed on the outside as my smile inched into a bigger one.

I teasingly said, "Those girls who just passed us think you're cute."

He gave them a pained expression. "Great. Little girls think I'm cute."

"They have to be around thirteen. And I'd be looking at you—" I stopped myself, and he smiled. That smile.

"The truth finally comes out." He took my left hand and laced our fingers together.

Holding his hand did feel right. Safe. And I sighed. But not out loud.

"So, Kenickie," I said, pulling a Shane-worthy subject change, "is it terrifying performing for the *entire* school?" I wanted his honest opinion since being in the competition would be the polar opposite of my comfort zone.

"It's pretty fucking awesome. Once the nervousness goes away." He squeezed my hand. "Stage fright doesn't kill you. It's easier to be on stage with other people, too."

Hopefully.

One of the guys who worked at the rink whizzed by us, skating backward.

"That's so cool. He makes it look easy."

"It is easy."

Shane looked at me. "You know how to skate backward?"

I released his hand and skated ahead of him. I felt ten times more comfortable and confident after going around with him. I then, and a bit wobbly, turned backward and skated in time with the newest song playing, "Paris" by The Chainsmokers. A song and band I liked.

He smiled. "Where'd you learn to do that?"

I glanced over my shoulder to make sure I wasn't about to slam into anything. Or anyone. "Figure-skating lessons. My mother's second try at making me more like her. A girlie-girl."

"What else did she have you do?"

I faced him. "Beauty pageants, big shocker there, and ballet lessons."

I rolled to a stop, which caused him to stop.

"But you're really a tomboy."

"Yep." I shrugged. "That's what the beauty queen got."

His smile faded. "It sounds like she's really hard on you."

I nodded. "She wants me to be someone I'm not."

"I get that," he mumbled.

Something about the way he said that, and his frustrated expression I totally understood, made me want to skate closer and slip my arms around his waist. Hug him like I wanted to hug him on Saturday. But then he took my hand again.

"Teach me to skate backward."

I stared at him.

Shane Easton. Master at changing the subject.

"Right now?" I asked.

"No. At the beach, Sunshine." We skated closer to the wall to be out of the few other skaters' way, and he gave me a blinding smile. "Okay. Now what."

I had to smile at his pretty cute enthusiasm. "Just...watch and copy me."

"I can definitely handle watching you."

"Would you be serious?"

He exaggerated a scowl and mock saluted me.

I rolled my eyes, skated forward, and glided backward. He tried copying me, but couldn't turn. Or keep his momentum. Then he started basically scooting backward on skates.

I skated right back, rolled in front of him, and stopped. I grasped his—really firm upper arms—and faintly said, "I'm going to skate and push you."

He definitely worked hard to keep himself in shape.

I slowly skated, pushing him backward. My eyes went to watching behind him and back to him. This went on for a bit, and I tried to ignore his goofy smile.

"I could seriously get used to this," he said in a low voice that gave me goosebumps beneath my snug sweatshirt.

He was clearly committed to our deal, and I felt the little thrill shoot through me again, to the point I shivered. But I still gave him my exaggerated scowl and said, "Stop flirting and pay attention, because I'm going to let you go. But move your feet so you don't slow down. Ready?"

He nodded, and I released him. He rolled backward, but watched his feet, as if that would help him actually skate.

"Don't forget to look behind you," I called out.

His head shot up and he looked over his shoulder—and his feet flew out from underneath him. He hit the rink's floor. Right on his cute butt.

I choked on my laugh and skated toward him. But I couldn't stop my laughter while I watched him fall back on the floor and lie there, almost spread eagle.

Across the rink, I heard laughter and saw those same girls, and their moms, watching us.

"Wow, Kenickie. That. Was. Spectacular."

He groaned. "And I'm sure everyone in here saw it."

"Your little fans definitely saw it. And their moms. Anything broken?"

"Just my ass."

I laughed until I could say, "Let me see."

He, now smiling, rolled slightly onto his right side.

"You're good. Everything still looks perfect."

He rolled onto his back. "I guess hearing you say that about my ass makes this worth it." He sat up and shook his head. "I think I'm okay not knowing how to skate backward."

He got into a kneeling position and from there he, very carefully, stood. When he started rubbing his butt, I burst into more laughter.

I couldn't remember the last time I'd laughed so hard my sides *and* cheeks ached.

"This isn't funny," he said around his own laughter. "I'm in serious-ass pain here."

"You're right," I said, then giggled some more. "Maybe we need a break."

We skated to an area right off the rink that had high tables with matching chairs.

He, flinching, sat on a chair, and I sat beside him.

He grinned. "I really like seeing you like this. You're kind've glowing right now."

Yeah. Because of him. Maybe Shane Easton would change my mind after all.

* * *

"That was so much fun," I said after he eased into the driver's seat and closed the door.

He grasped my left hand and placed two fingers on my wrist.

"What are you doing?" I asked.

"Checking to make sure you admitting that didn't kill you."

I pulled my wrist free while laughing. Again. Nobody could make me laugh like he did.

"What's next?" I so didn't want this day to be over. Every trip for my past birthdays didn't compare to this one birthday with him. "Maybe we can find someone to drag race?"

He smiled and turned onto his right side to fully face me. "There's something I actually need to tell you. I probably should've told you when we were still at the beach. But it's—" His face became crimson. "It's kind've embarrassing."

I turned onto my left side to fully face him and couldn't stop myself from saying, "It can't be more embarrassing than what happened in the rink."

He cracked a smile. "This is a way different kind've embarrassing." His face stayed crimson while he seemed to be searching for the right words.

What he wanted to say must be serious. He rarely had trouble speaking his mind.

"I've had a crush on you. For a while."

Wait...*what* did he just say to me?

The smile I'd been wearing all afternoon left as I stared at him while blinking rapidly. Then I decided he was screwing with me. "Right. Since when? That day I kidnapped you?"

"A little longer than that."

He looked at me, and his serious expression made me frown. Which didn't feel right after so much smiling and laughter.

"Shane, what are you talking about? You didn't even know me before a few weeks ago."

"That doesn't mean I haven't noticed you." He cleared his throat, that I now knew he did when he was really embarrassed. "I've had a crush on you since freshman orientation."

It took a few seconds for his confession to penetrate my brain. But as soon as it did, I slowly angled forward and sat up.

Freshman orientation? I barely remembered that day. I then eyed him over my shoulder and, if possible, his face had turned redder.

"How? You *really* didn't know me back then."

He hesitated before saying, "You walked into the auditorium, and I...thought you were the hottest girl I'd ever seen."

Now I felt my face turning the same color as his. But his compliment did make me smile.

I sat sideways, bent my left leg, and tucked it underneath me. "Thanks. I'm really flattered." I smiled softly, which seemed to help his embarrassment. "But why didn't you talk to me? There were a lot of us who didn't know each other. I only knew Ella and Quinn."

"I tried thinking of some reason to talk to you after orientation. But I know I would've looked and sounded like a dumbass." Our eyes caught. "Then I started hoping we'd have a class together. Which we never have. Kind've weird, right?"

I nodded, then frowned again. "Why couldn't you talk to me? I was a newbie like you."

He paused, then said, "Don't take this the wrong way, but you're...a little intimidating. And with your image around school..." His voice faded into nothing.

I sucked in a breath.

I'd never given a boy at our school a chance because they'd never given *me* a chance. Until now. So it had been easy for me to copy Ella and Quinn's high-school-boys-suck attitude.

He reached across the console to take my hand. "I didn't hurt your feelings, did I?"

"No." I gave him a half smile. "What you said explains a lot."

And I hadn't thought of myself as a bitch back then, but I guess I had been.

"I know I was an ass to you that first day in the office and at community service." He glanced down at our joined hands. "I mean, there *you* were, sitting in the office, looking so angry. It was the closest I'd ever been to you. I wanted to" —he shrugged— "finally talk to you. Maybe cheer you up. But when it was obvious you had no idea who I was, it pissed me off."

I really felt like a bitch. This also explained why he'd been upset I didn't know his name.

"I recognized you," I quietly admitted. "But I didn't know your name."

"I know." He smiled. "But you've said it a few times today. That's progress."

I cringed, but said, "I like calling you Kenickie." A thought occurred to me and I added, "And you kind've started that, *Giles Corey*."

We shared a quick laugh, and I lifted myself up, stretched my leg out, and scooted to where we were eye level. Thinking about where my mind went before we started skating, I said, "I'm really sorry I didn't know your name. Know you." And I meant every word.

"I'm sorry I didn't have the guts to talk to you when we were freshmen."

"Me, too," I said without thinking.

Those two little words caught his attention, and our eyes connected.

The electricity between us surged through me, and I knew who I wanted. How could I not after *everything* he'd told me today? After everything we'd done? After all the texting when he had—not counting Monday—been single?

I, giving him my wicked smile for a change, released his hand and grabbed a fistful of his shirt. I pulled him toward me and met him at the console. I bit my lower lip and waited to see if he would stop me. Us. This. But seeing the beginnings of his wicked smile made me pull him the couple inches closer. And we finally started our two almost kisses.

His lips were soft. Warm. Gentle. At first. Then he cupped my face and angled my head slightly back to deepen our kiss. And every part of me warmed and buzzed. The car and every-thing around us became misty. A sigh escaped me during a pause for air, and our mouths fused again. Until we needed more than just a pause for air.

He pressed his forehead to mind while we caught our breath. "So was that your way of saying you changed your mind?"

I slowly opened my eyes, which locked with his that looked a little hazy. Like mine felt. And I, feeling a bit naughty from our *wow* kiss, murmured, "The day isn't over yet."

He, smiling, lifted his head. "I'm not sure whatever we do next could beat *that*—" He released me and sat up. "What time is it?" He grabbed his phone from the center console where he'd left it before we went inside. He then frowned, pressed the button to make the screen go black, and put it back in the console. "We have to go. My dad told me to have the car home by six. He's taking it back to the shop and riding home with my mom." He looked torn. "I have to take you home. Natalie, I'm sorry."

I smiled, a bit on the dreamy side, too. "Don't be. This day has been perfect."

He returned my smile. "Yeah. That's why I don't want to take you home." He tore his eyes from mine and sat forward. He was about to start the engine when he sat back. "Traffic's going to suck, too. I should probably go to the bathroom. Do...you need to go?"

I shook my still misty head, because...*wow*.

He climbed out of the car and moaned. "I think there's going to be a bruise."

I giggled as I watched him almost limp toward the rink's entrance. Then I heard his phone buzz and the screen lit up. And I saw a bunch of green. Missed text messages.

The mistiness and my smile faded as I stared at his phone. Those were a lot of texts.

It couldn't be—I glanced at the rink's entrance, then at his phone. What I wanted to do was so wrong. Especially after our kiss. But I had to know. He'd just been on it and had been a little weird when I brought her up at the beach.

I, keeping my eyes on the still clear entrance, picked up his phone.

I couldn't believe what I was about to do, but I took a quick breath and pressed the home button. And my heart nearly stopped as I scrolled through the messages. All of them were from Maddie. The newest one said, *Please call me. I really need to talk to you.*

Chapter Nineteen

My stomach knotted from what I'd done and seen. Darkness devoured all my light. And reality slammed into me, destroying my trip to Fantasyland.

He'd told me they'd broken up last Monday, and I believed him. I had no reason not to believe him. But why the hell would she be texting him so much—asking him to call her—if they'd broken up? Unless...he had broken up with her and she still wanted him. Another reason their break-up never made it to the school's gossip mill? Because Maddie wouldn't let go?

I pictured us at school on Monday, and acting like we had today.

My stomach knots turned into nausea so strong I swallowed several times to keep from scrambling out of the AMX to empty my stomach.

I'd be branded the real reason he and Maddie broke up. Most of the school would say he'd cheated on her with me. They wouldn't care about the truth. That he'd been crushing on me forever and we had a connection most of them would never understand. I couldn't even be sure Ella and Quinn would have my back on anything. Especially since Quinn and Maddie were friends. And Shane was so well-liked and popular with almost everyone. He deserved better than being labeled a cheating asshole.

He'd absolutely changed my mind, but we really *did* have to stay friends.

My lunch went further up my throat and made my vision blurry. I kept swallowing.

His door opened, and I jolted in my seat. I then realized I still had his phone. And it occurred to me admitting what I'd done might cause him to not even want to be friends.

He carefully slid into the driver's seat and shut his door. "Okay. I feel better and ready to sit in traffic—what's wrong?"

How could he simply look at me and know something was wrong? Then again, I was faced forward, sitting stiff as a tree trunk, and probably looked pale. So not looking the way he left me, smiling and gazing at him like I'd been hit in the heart with all of Cupid's arrows.

"And why are you holding my phone?" He sounded a little panicked.

I swallowed once more and gave him his phone. "Maddie really needs you."

A tense, horribly thick silence filled the small space between us. I sensed his body become as stiff as mine. I could also feel the hurt and anger from his eyes.

"You went into my phone and read my messages? Why would you do that?"

I cringed at his questions and clear outrage. "I—" I had no excuse for what I'd done. Only the truth. I hated irony. "Your phone went off. While you were gone. I saw a bunch of green. And I—" I sounded pathetic defending myself. Pathetic being a quality I couldn't stand. Especially in girls. "I only read the one that just came in. But scrolled through the others."

How could he not flee in the other direction after this?

"Well, that's good to know. You only *kind've* invaded my privacy."

His sarcasm made my defensive side surround me, and I looked at him. Then instantly wished I hadn't, because of the darkness I saw in his eyes. It hurt my heart to see him glaring at me, and after what happened between us minutes earlier. But it didn't stop me from saying, "Shane, what the hell is going on with you two? And have you been avoiding her texts *all* day?"

I didn't know how he could've managed avoiding her texts without me noticing, being so focused on me and us. But maybe he'd left his phone on vibrate and in the car because of her?

"Not *all* day. And this isn't what you think." He lifted himself up enough to shove his phone into his left, front pocket.

Point taken. Loud and clear.

He stayed silent for several seconds, then said, "Maddie and I *did* break up last Monday."

"And I believe you," I firmly said. "But you're obviously not telling me everything."

Did it even matter at this point since we clearly couldn't be more than friends? Something I'd known all along, too. But I'd been so caught up in him and us that I'd, for the first time, followed my heart. A decision I regretted. Because of the tightness in my chest from my heart's first crack.

"All I can tell you is that Maddie has a lot going on right now. And I've been trying to help her. As a *friend*." He released a frustrated sigh. "But now she wants to get back together, and I want us to go back to being" —he shook his head— "just friends."

Outside of Maddie going through something personal, nothing he'd said surprised me. But the tightness in my chest made it a little hard to breath at knowing he was being so awesome, helping his ex through a crisis. It could be why he hadn't slept well last Friday night, too.

"I didn't tell you because I didn't want all this to affect us." His eyes found mine for the first time since he began explaining everything. "But it has. Hasn't it."

"Shane," I shakily said, and in response to the defeat I saw, and heard in his voice, "the timing is just wrong. Especially since you're trying to help her. Which is amazing." I lifted my shoulders. "But this isn't right. We can't walk into school, gazing and smiling at each other after spring break. You have to know how that'll make you—us—look."

"Great," he mumbled. "We're back to that." He buckled his seatbelt and started the engine. But this time I couldn't enjoy the engine's power. "Natalie, kids at school break up and get together with someone else all the time. Why are *we* different?"

I couldn't argue with him. But everyone at school seemed to like Maddie. Where just about everyone avoided me. The bitch. The reputation I'd built and hid behind for almost three years. The only two people who seemed to like that Natalie were Ella and Quinn. Especially Ella.

The Natalie I hardly recognized after this perfect day with Shane. But I still said, "We can only be friends. And that was the deal *you* came up with."

"*Only* if I couldn't change your mind. Which I did. Before you went into my phone," he muttered under his breath.

Okay. I deserved that. It didn't stop me from reaching for my seatbelt and roughly buckling myself in. "We need to go. You're already going to be late getting the car back."

He didn't say a word or move for so long I had to glance at him. And my stomach twisted at his flat expression after seeing him wear his wicked smile most of the day.

"Fine. Friends it is." He then pulled out of the parking space.

I swiftly rolled down my window. I took a deep breath as my hair flew around my head. I'd loved the feeling at the beginning of our day, but now it and this beautiful car represented feeling trapped. Because now we seemed to be lightyears away from friendship.

* * *

When I saw my grandparents' house finally come into view, I somehow stopped myself from releasing the huge sigh of relief wanting to burst free.

Our drive home had been so painfully long and quiet my already uneasy stomach started to ache while we sat in horrible stop-and-go traffic on Highway 101. The only time he'd spoken was when he called his dad to tell him he'd be late. Based on Shane's side of the call, I could tell he'd gotten an earful of crap from his dad.

He pulled into the driveway, stopped, but didn't turn off the engine.

Had I really expected him to walk me to the door?

I froze since I didn't know what to say. Because saying "Thanks for the best birthday of my life until I went into your phone" seemed ridiculous and insane.

I forced myself to look at him, and braced for the anger and hurt. His eyes cut to mine. But instead of anger and hurt I saw confusion and sadness.

Crack. Chest pain.

"Natalie, what are you afraid of?"

His question blindsided me, and I blinked several times like a total idiot.

"What your two *friends* might think?"

This was the second time he'd referred to Ella and Quinn so harshly, and I frowned.

What had they ever done to him?

"Don't you think it's weird you're hiding, from your so-called best friends, the fact you're doing the competition with your club?" His voice now held an edge to it. "I'm friends with most of those kids. They're really cool and nice. And seem to love the *real* you."

His words stung parts of me I never knew existed.

"And why don't you want anybody in school to know the real you?" he continued. "A tomboy who loves and knows about old cars. A girl who has a great smile and laugh and sense of humor." He paused, then said, "I'll bet if we'd run into anyone from school today, they wouldn't have recognized you. You're so different when you're *not* with Ella and Quinn."

"Just stop!" I said, since I didn't want to hear any of this. "You don't know them. We've been friends forever. And everybody has different sides to their personalities." I narrowed my eyes. "You're a drama boy who knows how to drive and work on old muscle cars, but want to be a marine biologist who studies sharks? That's three totally different sides to *your* personality."

He narrowed his eyes, too. "None of that's a secret from my friends, Sunshine. And I don't care who in school knows all that about me."

His words stung my eyes to the point they watered, followed by a long *crack*. The tightness in my chest made it hard to breathe again. I had to get away from him—his judgment I never expected—and I opened my door. "Thanks for everything." I flung the words at him over my shoulder, not sounding at all grateful, and guilt made my stomach clench.

I scrambled from the car, took a huge gulp of air, and somehow stopped myself from slamming the car door behind me. It wasn't the AMX's fault this day ended as an epic failure. I then marched to the front door without a backward glance.

But even in my fury of emotions I noticed he didn't leave until I closed the door behind me.

I blinked the tears from my eyes and caught my breath.

If I didn't get myself under control, I'd never get through FaceTiming with my parents. Or my birthday dinner with my grandparents. I couldn't—wouldn't—break down into a mess.

So much for being *just friends*.

Chapter Twenty

"**Y**ou look like something that would come out of your little dog," Warren said.

I replied with a nasty glare.

"What's its name?"

"Chloe." I grabbed her before she could dart out of the house, then straightened.

He walked into the foyer and closed the door. "What happened to you, Madam Veep?"

I set Chloe down and shrugged. "Rough night." That included more tossing and turning than I had ever done in my life.

Warren and I decided on Tuesday to work on the presentation for Mr. Yates. Grams planned to take us to rehearsal later. Something I wished I could skip.

It had taken every ounce of my strength to drag myself from bed and pull on a pair of yoga pants, a sweatshirt, and pull my hair up into a messy knot.

If my mother saw me right now, she'd faint from repulsion.

"Are your grandparents here?"

"No." I headed down the stairs to my bedroom. Warren and Chloe followed me. "They're running errands." I knew this because they'd left me a note in the kitchen.

As far as they and my parents knew, I'd had an extraordinary birthday. But I'd left out Shane driving the car like he had stolen it. And the amazing kiss. And *everything* that happened after our amazing kiss. But thinking about him caused my lower lip to tremble.

"This is a nice house," Warren said as I led him to my room.

"Thanks," I murmured before biting my lip to stop the trembling.

I then realized he was the only other person from school, besides Ella and Quinn, who'd been in this house. I couldn't count Shane—I stopped that thought and collapsed onto my messy bed. Chloe jumped up beside me, and I rubbed her sweet face.

"I fully plan to be the nosy friend who looks at everything in your room." He set down his backpack and sat in my desk chair.

What really made my heart and soul throb was I had no one to blame but myself. Because he'd been right about me being scared. Yeah, I was the bitch almost everyone avoided. But it'd kept me from being the topic of any gossip for three years. How could I go from that to what would happen if we got together? What would happen with my friends? He obviously didn't like Ella and Quinn. No, they—Ella—weren't perfect, but we'd been friends for a long time. I couldn't throw away our friendship over a boy. Not even a boy like Shane.

But then, why should I have to choose them over my heart?

"*Hello*? What's up with you?" Warren waved his hand in my face.

I lifted my eyes from Chloe and focused on him.

"Did you get your party on for your birthday last night and not invite me?"

The other Natalie, if Ella and Quinn had been here, probably would've been somewhere she didn't belong and partying with a bunch of strangers. I now seemed eons away from that girl. And it didn't feel like a bad thing—my eyes widened.

Ella and Quinn never texted or sent me Snapchats yesterday. On my birthday.

I sighed. "No. I just didn't sleep well. And my *friends* are gone, remember?" I muttered. "They also still don't know I'm not grounded."

I'd never, no matter what, forgotten their birthdays. And the guilt from not being honest with them about my grounding lifted off my conscience. I felt ten pounds lighter.

He sat back in the chair. "Natalie, I think of you as one of my best friends."

We had become close because of the club, and his comment patched a portion of my cracked heart.

"I know something's going on with you. You've been way too nice lately. And smiling and laughing." Warren tilted his head. "It's not like you."

I remembered Shane's brutal honesty from yesterday.

I'll bet if we'd run into anyone from school today, they wouldn't have recognized you.

I frowned since, maybe, what he'd said wasn't too much of an exaggeration.

"I'm not the only member who's noticed," Warren continued. "And you're telling us stuff you're not telling your besties. Are you three on the outs right now?"

I watched Chloe settle into a spot on one of my pillows, not sure how much to say.

"And Meg's convinced you've got it capital B-A-D, bad for a guy you won't tell us about." He smiled. "Which could explain your out-of-character good mood."

Damn Meg and her big mouth. But as much as I trusted Warren, and my other club members, I couldn't tell them—or anyone else—I had it capital B-A-D, bad for Shane Easton. And Kassidy, being active in theater, was good friends with Shane *and* Maddie.

So I responded the only way I could—rolled my eyes and lied. "There's no guy."

"I'm just repeating what Meg told me."

"Well, she's wrong. And we're trying to save the club. We can't do that if we're divided."

Totally the truth and, feeling a bit more weight lift off my soul for being honest, I quietly added, "Ella and Quinn don't know I'm doing the competition with all of you. They wanted me to be in their routine for Ella's campaign." I sighed as more weight lifted.

Warren's expression and eyes softened with sympathy. "Nat, you're gonna have to tell them. They can't be mad at you forever over something like this. And I know we're trying to keep being in the competition on the down low." He shook his head. "But too many boyfriends know about it. And Shane knows. I'm not saying they'd blab. But talk happens."

Everything he'd said mirrored what I'd been thinking.

"Is this really all that's bothering you?"

"Yes." I stood and walked toward my desk where I kept my laptop. We—I— needed to focus on something entirely different. "Let's get this done."

About an hour into creating our presentation, using as many of the positive comments as we could, I realized one idea kept showing up. Being able to talk to other students about stuff they didn't feel comfortable talking about with their parents, or even their friends. But not serious enough to involve a teacher or our school counselor. And a lightbulb came on. As if what I'd read flipped a switch.

Smiling for the first time since watching Shane limp back

into the skating rink, I lifted my eyes from all the papers I held. "Warren, I think I figured out what our new name should be."

Chapter Twenty-One

My heart picked up its pace as I headed for the stage.

There were about the same number of kids working this morning as there had been a week ago, and I easily found him. He was with Paige and Liam, crouched on all fours with his back facing the auditorium, and working on the scoreboard I knew we'd finish today.

His position gave me a great view of his butt.

I remembered his Wednesday wipeout and wondered if he felt better.

Mr. Lowry, talking to a couple kids near the front row seats, looked up when I tried to sneak by him.

"Another late sleeper, I see." He sounded more amused than irritated.

I so hadn't wanted to come today. But making up a half hour would be much easier than making up four hours.

"Sorry. Not feeling well today," I said, not lying, before heading for the stairs closest to where my three partners were working.

I slowly walked up the stairs. My heart now wanted to explode from my chest.

Paige looked up from painting the word HOME. I guess that meant I'd paint the word VISITORS. Liam paused from his painting long enough to give me a friendly smile. He and Shane were painting the bottom portion of the scoreboard.

Shane, dressed almost exactly like he'd been a week ago, including the backward baseball hat, had his earbuds in with the cord tucked behind his sweatshirt. He'd never worked and listened to music before, which meant he didn't want to talk to anyone. Namely me.

He looked up and our eyes met. For two seconds. Then he went back to painting.

I dropped to my knees.

If this was how it would be for the remaining weeks of community service, it might be worth finishing my hours at one of my mother's charities. On the plus side, I didn't see or hear Theresa. Maybe she'd taken my advice from a week ago and flown back to her evil monkeys.

"You don't look any better than you did Thursday," Paige said.

Our rehearsal had been another rough one with the "dancing" while lip syncing. But I'd brought my laptop with me and everyone perked up when we showed them the presentation. Everyone also loved the new name. I'd gotten another group hug, which I'd needed and loved.

"Are you getting sick?" Paige leaned backward, as if I were suddenly contagious with something that could kill her. "I catch everything. So keep your distance if you're getting sick."

I did feel sick, but my sickness wasn't contagious and a hundred times worse than the flu.

I eyed Shane, still focused on his painting, and said, "Paige, I'm not sick. I just haven't been sleeping well."

"Well, it must be going around." She pointed at Shane and made a sour face. "He's in a *really* bad mood."

Just what I needed. More guilt.

"Paige, I can hear you." Shane lifted his head and yanked his right earbud out. "My music isn't that loud."

I stared at the scoreboard.

Had he heard what I said? But maybe he needed to hear he wasn't the only one hurting.

"Sorry," Paige mumbled and focused on her painting.

"Paige, don't listen to him." Liam gave his best friend a hard stare. "You're not pissed at her, so don't be a dick."

Wait...*what* did that mean? Had he told Liam about us? But if he had, Liam probably wouldn't have given me a friendly smile when I got here. So had he been referring to Maddie?

Shane's expression became flat. Just like it did before we left the rink's parking lot.

He twisted his earbud back into place and continued painting.

Liam glanced at me and mouthed "O-kay."

Guilt lowered my shoulders, and I picked up the extra paintbrush.

He'd told me Maddie had a lot of personal stuff going on and was trying to be *just friends* with her again, but based on what Liam said, I had a feeling that wasn't going well. And I'd all but ripped the car floor out from underneath him three days ago.

I couldn't really blame him for being in a rotten mood.

We worked silently as we finished the scoreboard. Totally fine with me, too, because I, like Shane, didn't feel like listening or sharing.

Mr. Lowry walked over when we finally finished. "Looks great. Shane, can you and Liam lean it up against the back wall? Then I need to talk to you and Natalie. Paige, you and

Liam can help with the backdrop. We need to get it done today."

I halted.

Why did he need to talk to us? Had the tension between us—in our group—been that obvious?

I peeked at Shane. He'd taken out his earbuds when we started cleaning and they were hooked over the collar of his sweatshirt.

With that flat expression, he said, "Sure. I'll be right back."

He and Liam carefully picked up the scoreboard and carried it to the back of the stage.

Paige sent me a what's-that-all-about frown, then walked away.

I bit my lower lip.

My heartbeat went back into overdrive as I searched my brain for a reason Mr. Lowry wanted to talk to us. Outside of our tension, we hadn't done a thing to warrant his attention.

Shane walked up to me and Mr. Lowry, and stood at least a foot away from me.

Apparently, we now had The Great Wall of China between us.

My heart would've cracked further. If it hadn't been beating so hard.

"You're Kenickie and know what Mrs. Chaplin wants for the 'Greased Lightning' number." Mr. Lowry's eyes went to me. "You said you wanted to work on the car."

My breath slowed.

Oh, shit.

"You two also seem to work well together. So, I'm putting you guys on the car. Starting now. You'll have three Saturdays to get it done. And that's all you'll be doing."

A week ago this would've been a gift from the car gods. But now? No. This could so not be happening. And I didn't dare look at Shane to see his reaction.

"Before you leave today, you'll need to sit down and figure out what supplies you'll need to build the car. I can have the supplies for you here next Saturday. Okay?"

I shook my head, stepped forward and pushed some hair behind my right ear. "Mr. Lowry, I don't know anything about building a car. Not like Shane does. It would be better if he and Liam—"

"I need Liam on the backdrop and other things. You two will do great. I know it."

Mr. Lowry walked away, leaving us and our sickening tension behind. And there went my desperate thought about working with my mother.

His continued silence caused me to sigh and say, "Shane, I'm really—"

"It's fine." His eyes connected with mine for the second time. "We are *just* friends."

I clenched my teeth at the way he said that. And at his mouth curving into a smirk.

He took a step back. "I'm going to go find some paper and a pen so we can get this done. I'll meet you out in the house."

I gave him my back and marched toward the stairs.

Okay. I'd made a pretty bad choice picking up his phone and hurt him on Wednesday. But we were somehow going to have to make peace.

He walked up with a pad of paper and pencil, and flopped down in the aisle seat, two seats away from me. I guess that meant his butt felt better.

I quietly said, "Shane, we're going to *have* to be friends— or at least be friendly—to get the car done. We were friends before Wednesday." My voice hitched on the word, but I added, "There's no reason we can't go back—"

"And pretend like everything between us never fucking happened?" He faced me.

The hurt and sadness and confusion in his dim eyes squeezed my soul. But I couldn't look away from him.

"What do you want from me, Sunshine? Besides *friendship*," he muttered.

I ignored that, took a shaky breath, and whispered, "I want you to understand I'm doing you and us a favor."

"No," he whispered back. "You're not doing me any favors. That's about you."

Oh, what was it about his honesty that made me feel like I'd suddenly been stung a million times? And I *was* protecting him. He deserved better than being judged and the topic of horrible school gossip. Why couldn't he see it that way?

He leaned forward. "I opened up to you on Wednesday because I'm crazy about you. You opened up to me for the same reason." He shrugged. "But you care more about what everyone at school will think of you, and us being together, than being the awesome girl from Wednesday." He stood. "I can't do this with you right now. I'll work on the list this weekend and give it to Mr. Lowry on Monday."

He headed for the auditorium doors.

I wanted to follow him and scream what did *he* want from me?

But it's not like I didn't know the heart-clenching answer.

Chapter Twenty-Two

I dragged myself into school Monday and wanted to turn around and drag myself out.

The school buzzed with back-to-school-after-a-break commotion. The office looked busy with parents and students. The hallways were filled with loud, excited chattering and laughter. Kids talking to their friends about their trips or how they'd spent their break.

A headache started on the right side of my head.

I made my way upstairs and hoped I wouldn't see him. I never did, but after everything that happened between us, I half expected to run into him. That would be my luck.

I turned the corner and my steps failed at who I saw standing at my locker.

Ella and Quinn were waiting for me. They looked the same and at the same time different. Like they were strangers. I couldn't remember the last time the three of us hung out together when we weren't at school. It must've been right before I got grounded. But I couldn't remember what we'd done together. I couldn't remember that Natalie.

I headed for them.

Quinn looked up from her phone first and waved. Ella lifted her eyes, barely smiled, and went back to her phone. I knew right then she was still pissed at me for backing out of her campaign routine for the competition. For supposedly still being grounded.

I also had the terrible feeling she'd never forgive me for doing the competition with my club. And I remembered what Shane said to me on my birthday before I walked away from him.

Don't you think it's weird you're hiding, from your so-called best friends, the fact you're doing the competition with your club?

I knew at the time what he meant. If they're really your friends, why would you have to hide that from them? He'd also indirectly asked if they're really your friends, why would they not understand and accept us being together?

I pushed those thoughts aside and plastered a smile on my face.

"Hey," Quinn said when I reached my locker. "What happened to you over the break? You were, like, never on Snapchat."

Not entirely true. I'd gone in a few times to see their posts. But only out of boredom. Quinn and her parents had gone to Seattle to visit her brother. He went to college up there. I'd never been to Seattle, but I'd spent a week in New York City with my parents and grandparents the summer before our freshman year. Ella's pics and posts were nothing I hadn't seen and done before. And after they'd forgotten my birthday, I hadn't cared about what they were doing.

"Did your grandparents take away your phone, too?" Ella asked.

I opened my locker and stared at everything inside like I'd never seen any of it before.

"No. I was busy." I wanted to add something bitchy about them forgetting my birthday.

But I focused on what I needed to get through my morning classes.

"Does that mean you're not grounded anymore?" Quinn sounded excited. "Because Chad and his roommates are having a big party this Saturday night."

I held onto my groan and lied. Again. "I don't know, Q. I won't know until I'm back with my parents tonight." Another reality I didn't want to face.

"Well, how was your break?" she asked. "Mine was okay. But I hate the weather in Seattle. I don't know why my brother likes it there so much."

I unloaded and loaded my backpack, and began counting the hours until dismissal. At least Quinn talking about her trip saved me from lying about my break.

Quinn came closer to me. "Okay, so it's only the first day back after break, but there's already serious drama." She paused, then said, "I guess Shane and Maddie dumped each other that week before spring break."

I froze as I was about to shut my locker door.

How the hell had that gotten out?

"Not a huge surprise since they fought all the time," Quinn continued, in full gossip mode. "I can't *believe* no one found out, but—"

"Quinn, maybe no one around here gave a shit about those two," Ella interjected.

I gripped my locker door at her words and nasty tone.

Quinn shrugged. "But the real drama is that Maddie wants to get back together with him and he *doesn't*." She shook her head. "I feel kind've sorry for her. She looks terrible today."

But I knew that could also be due to whatever else was going on in her personal life.

At that thought, my patience snapped, and I looked at Quinn. "Where did you hear all this?" Because Shane had made it crystal clear he and Maddie would never post it all over—

"It's all over Snapchat." She frowned. "Like I said, you're *never* on there anymore."

Which meant one of their friends must've blabbed.

My insides ached for them, but mostly for Shane.

"Well, I think she's pathetic for acting like that," Ella stated. "Over some drama loser?"

That made my temper snap.

I slammed my locker door shut and faced them. "You don't even know him, Ella." I glanced at Quinn. "And there could be more going on here than just their break-up."

I probably shouldn't have said that, and maybe I'd been a little too obvious. But I sure as fuck couldn't let them talk about Shane *or* Maddie like that.

They gaped at me, and I shrugged into my backpack's straps.

"What, like *you're* good friends with him?" Ella snidely asked.

"Jeez, Nat," Quinn grumbled. "It's school drama. You usually like hearing this stuff."

Their Natalie liked hearing this stuff. This Natalie—the real one—wanted no part of this ugly conversation. My stomach somersaulted just thinking about what Ella had said.

"I'm not in the mood for it today. I'll see you in Yates's class."

I spun from them and marched toward the classroom.

The anger at them and myself and even Shane burned inside me. Though he hadn't done anything wrong. Accept have the guts to be himself. Unlike me. Which he had absolutely no trouble pointing out on Wednesday and Saturday.

Maybe that's why my anger burned so strongly inside me.

I dropped my backpack and sat down in my seat behind Warren.

He, like he always did, turned to talk to me. "You look awful. And grouchy. Still not sleeping well?"

"No," I answered without looking at him.

"You'll feel better once you talk to Ella and Quinn. Oh, and I talked to Mr. Yates. I had to sorta beg, which I didn't like, but he agreed to give us fifteen minutes at our meeting on Friday."

I managed a small smile. "Good. Thanks for doing that."

He nodded. "So did you hear about Shane and Maddie breaking up *before* spring break?"

Oh, my God.

Was this day ever going to end?

* * *

The noise level in the cafeteria drilled into my aching head. I needed to eat and take some aspirin, or I wouldn't make it through my afternoon classes.

I dragged my sluggish legs toward where I sat with Ella and Quinn. I didn't know what to expect when I walked up. Quinn had been a little distant during American Government and Ella had ignored me in English.

Most of my club members sat with J.R., Owen, Nate, and other jocks. The pull toward them almost overwhelmed me when Kassidy, Meg, Jade, Lexi, and Warren smiled and waved.

I waved back, then slid my gaze across the cafeteria. Because I did want to see how he looked. To make sure he was okay. But he sat with his back facing the cafeteria. And him sitting that way seemed like another way of ignoring me. Like he had most of Saturday.

A thick sadness joined my already heavy load as I finished my walk. But when I saw Ella, Quinn, and *Maddie* sitting together, my heart dropped into my stomach, landing with the impact of a boulder.

"Hey," I murmured, and I placed my lunch bag on the table.

Maddie looked pale, and her big brown eyes were bleak and red.

I so wasn't in the mood for this, and debated turning and sprinting from the cafeteria.

"I invited Maddie to sit with us since she can't sit over there. With him," Quinn said. "Way too awkward. And..." She leaned forward. "She found out Sloane told Brandy *everything* going on with her and Shane, and Brandy took it from there." She straightened. "So she certainly can't sit with those two anymore."

A growl inched its way up my throat, but I swallowed it and tried to give Maddie an encouraging smile as I lowered myself to a chair. But I also didn't understand why she would be friends with someone like Sloane, the she-devil—my eyes went to Ella, focused on her phone.

"And she's going to be our third person in the routine," Quinn cautiously added. "She's obviously great at stuff like that and needs the distraction."

Of course.

Could this day get anymore screwed up? And weird?

Ella raised her head and smiled at me, but there was something truly she-devil about it. I'd never been on the receiving end of her evil smile and a bit of fear settled around me.

Something huge had shifted in our friendship. There's no way she could've found out about me being in the competition with the club. Not in less than four hours of our first day back. I could only assume she didn't like me challenging her so much and all of a sudden. I'm sure she also didn't like the fact I'd stopped blindly following her. Like Quinn and *that* Natalie did.

"We're going to be talking a lot about the routine. You'll

probably be bored," she said, and in a way that made me feel very unwelcome.

I met her cold, steady gaze, but didn't have a chance to reply.

"Thanks for letting me sit here." Maddie stared at her lunch and tears filled her eyes. "I just can't believe Sloane did that to me." She looked at Quinn, then me. "I was the *only* person in the *Romeo and Juliet* cast who would hang out with her. No one in the *Grease* cast likes her, either." She pushed her food up, folded her arms on the table and rested her forehead on her hands. "Now Shane's barely talking to me," she said into the table. "But I trusted Sloane."

Quinn shot me a what-the-hell-was-she-thinking look as she patted Maddie's back.

"I know Shane only wants to be friends again, but I was still hoping..." She sighed. "We didn't *always* argue. And he can't already like someone else."

Shit.

My discomfort with this entire situation became another noose around my neck.

"Maddie, seriously, he's so not worth it," Ella said while still on her phone.

I gritted my teeth and leaned forward to defend him again when Maddie lifted her head.

"You don't know him. He's not just cute. He's one of the nicest boys in this school." She released a miserable laugh. "And he's funny. He could make me laugh until I couldn't breathe."

Jealousy replaced my anger with Ella, filled my bloodstream, and went straight to my head. My vision blurred.

I needed to leave, or she needed to stop. Or my aching head would explode.

"I was angry the day we broke up, but..." Her voice wavered. "I miss him."

The bitchiness of Natalie past had definitely come back to bite me in the ass.

"Let's talk about the routine." Quinn's eyes darted to me. "Nat, you won't care, right?"

I shook my head since Quinn basically read my mind.

And I was officially in hell.

Chapter Twenty-Three

My dad waving his hand in my face made me jump and pull off my Beats. I had the volume cranked while focusing hard on the lyrics. I'd hoped the high volume would drown my thoughts. It had worked. But only a little.

He grinned. "Dinner's going to be ready soon."

I paused the competition song I downloaded to my phone. "You're home early tonight."

The words came out sounding like an accusation, and I instantly regretted it. I liked it when he came home early. He eased the tension between my mother and me. He also made real food for dinner. When the beauty queen and I were alone, we usually ate fish. And salads.

"I haven't seen you in over a week. FaceTiming doesn't count." He sat on my bed's edge. "What's the loud music all about? That competition you're going to be in?"

I nodded.

I'd told them about it during our FaceTime call on my birthday and only because I had to. I needed to get to and from our rehearsals the next couple weeks. And they'd been surprisingly supportive. Though my mother added it better not affect my schoolwork.

"I think it's good you're doing that with your friends."

I pulled my legs up to my chest and hugged my knees. "Thanks."

"But you never mentioned Ella and Quinn. Aren't they doing it, too?"

I so didn't want to get into all the drama. I still had to get used to the fact Maddie, of all people, would be the third person in their routine. And be sitting with us at lunch. Indefinitely.

Bitchy Natalie wanted to walk up to Sloane and Brandy tomorrow and slap them.

"They're doing their own routine with another girl."

He frowned. "Is everything okay with you three?"

No. Things weren't okay. At least not between Ella and me. "Yeah."

"Are you sure? You haven't been talking about them lately."

We were closer than my mother and me, but his attention hit my defensive button and my armor surrounded me. "I've only seen them at school lately," I mumbled. "I was grounded? And they were gone over break."

"So it has nothing to do with you liking and dating Shane?"

No. Absolutely not. This conversation was not happening. But I started to ache all over. Like I did have the flu. Influenza H. For heartbreak.

I stopped myself from groaning and said, "I'm not dating Shane. We're just—" Even I was so over saying those two stupid words. And it was a bigger lie now since we weren't even friends. But I couldn't escape the fact we would be dating. If I had the courage to be with him.

"That's not how it sounded when you were telling us how

you spent your birthday." He smiled. "I have to admit I felt a little jealous hearing you talk about that AMX."

I could only sort've smile.

"It sounded like a date to me. And your mom. Your grandparents seem to like him. It sounded like he went out of his way to make your birthday special."

His smile grew, and I noticed how handsome he was when he relaxed long enough to be himself. Richard Carlisle. Dad, husband, son, and classic car lover.

Maybe struggling with being two very different people ran in the Carlisle genes.

"Shane's like that. A really nice guy. So not a big deal." But the heavy, thick words almost stuck to my tongue as I said them.

Because I missed *him*. Missed the texting. Missed the anticipation of getting a text from him. Missed talking to him and his smartass comments. I really missed the laughter from those comments. Missed his wicked smile. Missed the "awesome girl from Wednesday" he brought out of me. But none of that changed the fact I'd done the right thing by walking away.

I still couldn't believe I'd picked up his phone and done such a rotten thing to him. To us. But what if I hadn't? His break-up with Maddie would've been a million times worse today if we'd walked into school together, being a boy and girl who were crazy about each other.

Thinking all those things, and knowing what I had to deal with at school until the competition ended, caused me to snap, "Dad, I don't want to talk about this, okay?"

He held up his hands. "I'm done." He stood. "I need to finish dinner."

He looked as frustrated as I felt, and I said, "I'm sorry. It was just a bad day today."

His face softened a bit and he nodded.

I suddenly realized what I wanted and needed. Besides Shane. I wanted my dog. Snuggling her always made me feel better. And I couldn't stand her not being here with me.

"Can you talk to Mom again about letting me have Chloe here? Please?"

His look transitioned into full *hell* no.

"I know having a dog in here is a lot of work. But she's not a puppy anymore, and I promise I'll walk her. She doesn't shed *that* much. And if Mom doesn't want her running around when nobody's here, I can always put her in her crate."

She'd hate being in her crate, but I'd rather have her here than in Sausalito without me. And my heart needed all the support it could get.

He stayed silent for so long I figured he was searching for a nice way to say *hell* no.

"I'll try," he finally said. "But I'm making no promises."

I smiled. My first real smile in...I didn't know how long anymore. "Thanks."

He returned my smile and left.

He'd have to get her on a great mood day, but I knew he'd do his best convincing her to let me have Chloe here. And I allowed the hope he'd be successful fill another portion of my cracked heart.

Chapter Twenty-Four

Warren faced the classroom after getting Ms. Simmons's laptop hooked up to the Smart Board and bringing up the presentation we'd created in Google Slides.

Mr. Yates sat right up front and Ms. Simmons sat beside him. The eight of us were behind them and staying silent from the pressure. I knew all of us were feeling the weight, the importance, of this presentation going well. Especially since Mr. Yates didn't look happy to be here. One of the reasons we'd decided Warren, our president, should do all the talking. He had way more patience with Mr. Yates than I did.

Warren's eyes found mine, and I gave him an encouraging smile and nod.

After this rotten week, I so needed this to go as we all hoped it would.

Warren took a quick breath and said, "Mr. Yates, the reason we asked you to be at our meeting today was to explain and show you what this club is really about. And that Pacifica Academy needs a club like this. For social *and* academic reasons."

Mr. Yates didn't make a sound.

I glanced at Kassidy, sitting beside me. She sent me a confident smile, and I relaxed. But only a fraction.

"We created a poll and gave it to past and current members," Warren continued.

Mr. Yates released a laugh that also sounded like a grunt.

"We went over all the answers we got and created this presentation. And because of the answers, the first thing we were able to do was come up with a new name."

He used Ms. Simmons's mouse to click on the first slide. And there was our new name in bold, black print. A name I'd come up with.

A tingle of pride shimmied through me when I remembered how everyone responded to the new name.

"Our new name is Students Supporting Other Students. Or S.S.O.S. And we would be a student group, not a club."

"That's wonderful, Warren. Really," Ms. Simmons said, and I heard the kindness and encouragement in her voice.

Mr. Yates, on the other hand, didn't say a word.

I looked around at my other club members and saw wide eyes. Fear of the unknown. Fear of not knowing how to interpret Mr. Yates's silence. But Warren had six slides to go.

"Thank you, Ms. Simmons."

He clicked to the next slide, a summary of how everyone responded to our first question. Not our strongest point since we'd lost several kids after Mr. Yates went to that meeting almost a month ago. Though we all blamed him for losing so many kids.

"We've lost kids in the last month," Warren said while doing a great job not looking at Mr. Yates. "But before a month ago there were twelve of us in here." He went to slide three, a summary of question two. "And, yes, kids showed up because of personal relationship reasons."

Our nice way of saying we'd been dumped or rejected, and were mad as hell about it.

Warren chose slide four. "A few original members still come to the meetings. Their main reasons for coming to the meetings are for the close friendships they've found here and support." He smiled. "Some kids wrote they also liked being in here because nobody judged them."

I'd written that, but so had a couple of other kids.

"Reasons for kids leaving" —he chose slide five— "varied."

Which really meant we didn't include the answers, "Because of Mr. Yates."

"Many kids left *only* because they were ready to move on from whatever brought them in here to begin with." He looked right at Mr. Yates. "And they wrote we helped them with their confidence by being supportive. And listening. These kids also consider most of us in here to be their good friends."

Definitely one of our strongest points, as was the next slide.

"Our last poll question was kids needed to list two things they love about the club." He went to the slide. "The two things that came up the most again were the friendships and support. But our group activities also came up. Like other school clubs or groups or the sports teams, we've done things to build each other up." He extended his thumb to get ready to list our group activities. "We've gone to two school dances together, and not because we didn't have dates. And some of us plan on going to prom together."

Mr. Yates released another laugh-grunt.

I'd refused to go to Snowflake Formal with them in December. I'd gone to some party with Ella, Quinn, and her boyfriend. A stubborn, not-supportive decision made by *that* Natalie.

"We've done movie nights," Warren went on. "We got together in December to study for finals and want to do the same thing in May. We're also going to be in the lip sync competition." He lifted his shoulders. "So the only difference between this club and the other clubs and groups in this school is what we talk about."

Warren chose the final slide—our final argument. "No, we don't talk about fundraisers or themes for dances—no offense, Jade."

I glanced at Jade, sitting behind Kassidy, and she laughed.

"We don't talk about how to win the next game or computers or chess maneuvers." He took a step forward. "Mr. Yates, we talk about way more personal stuff. And this got back to you as us hating on other kids in this school. But it's not like that. We're just venting." He stayed focused on Mr. Yates. "We're teenagers. Aren't we supposed to vent? Not hold it all inside so we don't explode?" He gestured toward the classroom. "And most of the stuff we talk about in here isn't serious enough to go to a teacher or the counselor. We just want to talk to each other. Because we understand what it's like to be a kid in this school."

Mr. Yates stayed silent and continued sitting there with his arms folded across his chest.

"In conclusion," Warren said, straightening, "we feel to be successful in our classes and with our schoolwork, we have to feel good about ourselves. And that's what this club—this group—is *really* about."

I smiled. Because Warren had nailed it. But the room remained silent.

"I'm done," he added, his eyes skittering over us.

Ms. Simmons sat up. "Excellent work."

She turned in her seat to face all of us, and I wished her proud smile meant everything would be okay. But we were trying to convince Mr. Yates.

"Do you have any questions for Warren?" she asked Mr. Yates.

He shook his head and stood. "No. But I do need to talk to all of you before I leave."

Oh...That so didn't sound good, and I tried to control the dread building inside me.

Ms. Simmons raised her eyebrows, and I shared a fleeting glance with Kassidy.

"Warren," Mr. Yates quietly began, "you and everyone else did a good job on this. And if it were for a grade, you'd all get an A. You made some good points."

No. We'd made nothing but fantastic points.

I gripped the edges of my chair to stop myself from jumping up and speaking my mind.

"And I appreciate you putting all this together for me."

No one spoke as we waited for the *but*, and my dread doubled in strength.

"But if students in this school are struggling that much, socially speaking, they *should* be talking to an adult," Mr. Yates said. "Be it a teacher, the counselor, their parents, older siblings, or other family members." He eyed each one of us. "Like Warren said, you're teenagers. Meaning you're children. And have no business *counseling* each other."

I started to shake as anger joined my dread at the way he emphasized "counseling."

"What you say and do off school campus is obviously your business." He shook his head. "But this isn't the place for venting. That's not what school-sponsored clubs and groups are for."

Kassidy did jump up. "Then why were we allowed to start it at the beginning of the year? JF—Josh told me what we had to do to start it and that's what we did. And Warren explained what this group really does for kids in this school."

I wanted to hug Kassidy for being able to say what I wanted without losing my temper.

"You weren't given all the proper information," Mr. Yates stated. "And that isn't your fault. But this club started before I authorized it, and I took it to Mr. Hathaway."

We looked at each other with wide eyes since Mr. Hathaway was our principal. And everyone seemed as lost as me.

"Ms. Simmons and I met with him in September," he continued. "After listening to her, and her positive feedback, Mr. Hathaway decided to let the club stand."

Even back then, Ms. Simmons had been fighting for us. For the club.

I wanted to jump up and hug her, too.

"But, and I'm sure Ms. Simmons remembers this, it came with a warning."

I swung my eyes her way to find her face had become stony.

"If it started causing problems, which it has," he added, "I could shut it down."

I held onto a frustrated sigh.

She'd never told us that. But I'm sure she, like us, never expected—

"And because of the negative comments I'm still getting about the club, this will have to be your last meeting."

Wait...*what* did he just say?

My mouth fell open as I turned toward my club members. Their eyes were also wide with *their* mouths hanging open.

No. He couldn't have said that. Not after the poll and how hard we'd—Warren and I— worked on putting together the presentation, and Warren's awesome—

"Ms. Simmons, I'm sorry I didn't have a chance today to meet with you about this."

She was silent for several seconds, then said, "Yes. That *would've* been nice."

If I hadn't been stuck in shock, I *would've* smiled at her icy tone.

"But Mr. Yates—"

He gave Kassidy a sharp look and said, "I'm sorry. But that's my final word on this." He nodded at Ms. Simmons and walked out.

The silence in the room made the *tick, tick, tick* coming from her wall clock the loudest sound I'd ever heard. And with each tick, my anger began to pulse inside me.

"Why did he make us go through the presentation if he knew he was shutting us down?" Kassidy muttered to one in particular.

Because he's a twisted, miserable old man who needed a power trip.

Warren dropped into the seat on my right as Ms. Simmons faced us. Her expression had relaxed a bit, but her eyes held a mixture of irritation and sadness.

"All of you did such a good job on everything. I'm so sorry about this."

"It's not your fault," Lexi said. "I can't believe that's it. And what about the competition? We've been rehearsing so hard and it sounds like we never even had a chance with Mr. Yates."

Nobody spoke.

The longer I sat there, the stronger my anger became. With Mr. Yates. And this horrible week. Trying to deal with my cracked heart while listening to Maddie talk to her new bestie, Quinn, about *Shane* this and *Shane* that. He, of course, had been sitting across the cafeteria with his buddies and not caring his ex was sitting at *my* table. I also listened to Ella and Quinn talk about their rehearsals and girl power routine. Which sounded like *it* could be unbeatable.

I should've spent the week hiding in the library with my lunch and schoolwork. But Ella's she-devil look on Monday had also felt like a challenge, and I hadn't wanted her to think she'd won that battle. I still didn't know what had caused the war between us.

I'd lost the boy I wanted and had to work on that *stupid* fucking car with him for the next three Saturdays. I'd lost Ella. I'd lost my club. All in one week.

"I think we should still do the competition," Warren said. "It'll be good for us."

"No," I snapped. "I'm so done."

I felt everyone's eyes as I stood and picked up my backpack.

"Natalie, we're all upset," Kassidy said. "But Warren and Lexi are right. We've been working hard on the routine and—"

"I don't care, Kassidy. Not anymore. I'm out."

I flung my backpack over my shoulder and fled the classroom.

I was sick of being two different Natalies. I needed to choose one. Since I couldn't have the boy I wanted and my club, that made the choice easy. Hopefully I hadn't lost Quinn.

I stepped outside and pulled my phone from my sweater pocket. My mother wouldn't be here for a few minutes. Plenty of time to text Quinn about the party tomorrow night.

I could finally tell them I wasn't grounded, with the competition being a week from today and being out of it altogether. And so much weight came off of me I thought I might start to float.

Totally forgot to tell you I'm not grounded anymore and can go to the party.

I took deep breaths of the dreary, salty air while I waited for her reply. With each breath, the guilt of leaving my club members—former club members—the way I did left me.

I felt more control over myself. My emotions.

Yay! You and Ella will stay the night with me. Like always. We'll get ready here and Chad will pick us up. So excited.

I read her message a second time and smiled, already feeling like the old Natalie.

Chapter Twenty-Five

"You look nice today," my mother said as she drove me to community service.

I'd taken the time to put on makeup and pull my hair up into a fancy ponytail. I'd also chosen a snug pair of jeans and my favorite, snug, Linkin Park black tank top I'd bought at one of their concerts. But I had to put on a light zip-up hoodie because of the chill in the air.

I woke up this morning so done with people telling me I looked like shit.

"Thanks."

"But couldn't you have chosen a nicer shirt than that tank top?"

I rolled my eyes.

Why did most of her compliments come with a *but* attached to them?

"I'm going to community service." I ground the words out. "Not a beauty pageant."

She didn't respond to my bitchy jab, and I continued staring out my window.

I so didn't want to deal with her. Or community service.

Or him and the car we had to start building today. The only thing keeping me going right now was the party tonight.

"I've been meaning to tell you your dad and I talked about Chloe."

I looked at her, but based on her frown and firm tone I knew the answer.

"*We* decided she belongs with your grandparents. In a house. And the subject is closed."

My cracked heart shattered and turned into cold rubble in my chest.

"No, *you* decided that," I snapped. "Dad doesn't care."

We came up on the school, and I wanted to get as far away from her as possible. I also didn't know when I'd ever speak to her again.

"Natalie, a dog belongs in a house. And I don't appreciate the way you're talking to me. If it continues, you'll be grounded again and for much longer. Do you understand me?"

She pulled up in front of the school.

I unbuckled my seatbelt, got out of her Beemer, and slammed the door behind me.

She wasted no time driving off.

I approached the doors on shaky legs, and with equally shaky hands I pulled out my I.D. and let myself into the school. I had to calm down before I walked into the auditorium. Before I had to face him. I couldn't let him see me weak. Not after the last rotten ten days.

I started breathing deeply. By the time I reached the auditorium doors, my shaking had almost stopped. I took a bigger deep breath and opened the door.

I immediately saw him on stage with Paige and Liam. They were standing around a pile of materials I assumed he and I would turn into Kenickie's stupid Greased Lightning.

I, with my chin angled up, headed right for the stage. And

I sensed his eyes were on me, but I made it a point to ignore him since two could play that game.

I stopped next to Paige and said, "Hi." I then smiled at Liam.

"Hey," she answered. "You look like you're feeling better. Are you?"

I knew what she was asking, but I smiled and said, "I'm fine."

She frowned, but out of concern. "Are you sure? You were really upset when you left yesterday. Warren and Kassidy were going to chase after you, but Ms. Simmons talked them out of it. She said to give you some space."

A burst of warmth tried to piece my heart together at hearing Warren and Kassidy had cared enough to want to come after me. But I'd left that Natalie in Ms. Simmons's classroom. And damn, Paige, and *her* big mouth. I wanted to muzzle her. I didn't need her saying anything else about yesterday in front of Kenickie.

Before I could tell her nicely to shut up, Theresa and her minion walked by us.

It looked and sounded like *everyone* was back today. The noise level being higher with activity and excited talking.

They stopped, and Theresa's eyes fell to the Greased Lightning materials.

She smirked at me. "I didn't know princesses knew anything about building cars." Her gaze shifted to Kenickie, standing across from me. "I feel *really* sorry for you."

Oh, this bitch did not just say that and call me princess. For the second time.

A dark silence surrounded us. Everyone seemed frozen in place.

Until Kenickie said, "Theresa, you need to—"

"No." I looked at him. "I've got this." And I, feeling the full power from this Natalie, unleashed the she-devil stare I'd learned from Ella. "Look everyone," I enunciated, "isn't it *awesome* Theresa made it back from visiting her evil monkeys?" I leaned forward. "Without getting water dumped on her head and melting."

Paige and Liam, standing behind me, released muffled laughter. I even saw, from the corners of my eyes, Kenickie's shoulders shaking with quiet laughter as he looked down.

Theresa and her minion returned my glare, but theirs wasn't nearly as powerful as mine.

"You and your little minion can go now," I added.

"What's going on over there?" Mr. Lowry yelled from across the stage.

Theresa and I continued staring each other down. Until Mr. Lowry appeared between us.

"Girls, I've talked to you about this. What's the problem?"

I gave him a sweet smile. "We were getting ready to start working on the car when Theresa walked up. She was trying to give us suggestions, but we really don't need her help. Do we, Shane?" I glanced sharply at him and, with my eyes, dared him not to go along with my lie.

He smiled. That smile. "Nope. We're all good."

I tore my eyes from him and looked back at Mr. Lowry, now frowning at Theresa.

"You two have your own assignments today. So get to it. And I better not see you two over here again. I don't have time for this nonsense." He faced us. "Paige, Liam, you need to get to work, too. That backdrop has to be done today so we can get it up and out of the way."

Everyone scattered at Mr. Lowry's borderline barked orders.

Guilt tried surrounding me, but I pushed it away and dropped to my knees.

Kenickie silently knelt down across from me. "Feel better?"

I heard the humor in his voice and lifted my eyes from the hot mess of materials between us. Our eyes did that dumb magnetic thing, but I broke it before his eyes affected me.

I also tried *not* noticing he looked better than good. Wearing tight jeans, a tight, faded-red Vans T-shirt and no baseball hat. I sensed him checking me out, too, and squashed the tingles.

"Yes," I replied. "I do. She deserved all of that."

He started laughing again. Which pissed me off. Especially after everything I'd been through this last week, including the recent moment with my mother.

I glared at him. "Don't you dare sit there laughing like we're friends. Because we're not. We're nothing!"

He stopped and stared at me. As if he couldn't believe what I'd said to him. And I immediately regretted it since I'd sounded beyond bitchy. Almost cruel. Like Ella.

"Ouch," he murmured. "Right for the jugular again, Sunshine."

The hurt in his voice matched the hurt I saw.

He'd said something like that to me in the office when I'd made it clear I didn't know his name. I'd hurt his feelings then, only he'd done a better job of masking his hurt.

This round of guilt I couldn't ignore.

"I'm sorry," I mumbled and went back to staring at the mess. "I shouldn't have said that."

He was silent until, "Yeah, well, maybe I deserved it. Between last Saturday and Maddie...I've seen her sitting with you guys at lunch. I never thought she'd do that. And I don't know what the hell she was thinking, telling *Sloane* about..." He sighed.

Nothing he'd said about Maddie surprised me, but all of that didn't help my mood.

"I really wanted to send you a text," he quietly continued. "To apologize. For that and last Saturday. But thought it would mean more in person." He paused, then said, "Natalie, would you look at me?"

I so didn't want to look at him, but gradually brought my eyes to his. They were full of the apology I heard in his voice. And way too much sadness.

I hadn't been expecting the real Shane today and didn't want this Shane. I wanted hurt and pissed off at me Shane, and my defensive armor went up.

"It's fine," I flatly responded. "It's been *super* fun being around your ex this week."

He frowned. "It isn't fine. None of this is fine. And I'm trying to apologize to you."

I shrugged. "Okay. Apology accepted. Are we done? Can we focus on this now?" I threw my hand out and toward the Greased Lighting materials.

"What's with you today? It's like you're about to explode or something."

That's exactly how I felt, but I didn't like him noticing or his sudden snarky tone. I snapped, "I'm fine. Thanks for asking."

"Stop saying that," he snapped back. "And why didn't you sit with Kassidy, Warren, and your other club members at lunch?"

"What club?" I muttered without thinking. Then mentally slapped myself.

Now he would start asking questions I didn't want to answer.

"What does that mean?" he asked in a nicer tone.

I started sifting through the materials—wood, metal, nails —like I knew what I was doing.

All around us other kids were talking, laughing, working. Having a great time. At least they weren't paying any attention to us. Our heated tension and words.

"Natalie, what happened? And is that what Paige was talking about when you got here?"

Of course he'd heard. But it's not like she'd spoken quietly.

I couldn't get out of this, and stopped my sifting and sat back on my heels.

"There's no more club." I crossed my arms. "We couldn't save it. And Mr. Yates, because he's supposedly still getting complaints, told us yesterday was our last meeting."

His face became dark. The darkest I'd ever seen it in our lightning brief time together. But why? A question so strong I had to ask.

"Why are you mad? You have nothing to do with the club."

Hurt again flashed across his face, but his reaction didn't make sense.

"You're right." He sighed. "But I know how much the club meant to *you*."

I didn't need or want his kindness and understanding. Not now. Not ever again.

Shane Easton and that Natalie Carlisle were done.

He took a deep breath and leaned forward. "Natalie, there's something—"

"I. Don't. Want. To. Talk. Any. More."

He slowly sat back and kept his eyes locked with mine. Until he looked away. He then picked up papers stapled together and tossed it onto the Greased Lightning mess.

"That's what we're building," he said without emotion. "We need to start."

I silently released the air inside my lungs.

Finally we were on the same page.

As he started going through the materials, I started the countdown to the party. To officially letting go.

Chapter Twenty-Six

I swallowed my third tequila shot with Daniel, Chad's friend, new roommate, and my blind date, and coughed. At all the other parties I'd been to with Ella and Quinn, I'd never drank this much. Maybe a shot, then sipped a beer the rest of the night. Though I hated the taste of beer.

But with each tequila shot I'd taken, the alcohol burned up one emotion after another. Guilt...anger...more anger. But not sorrow.

The horrible hip-hop music and partying around us in the small kitchen, and that I heard coming from the first floor of the boys' townhouse, started to become hazy. Almost dreamlike.

I stood at the square island counter with Daniel. The sticky countertop held bottles of alcohol. Different types of juices. Cans of Coke. And big red cups and empty shot glasses. The only other counter in the kitchen looked the same.

Daniel had made a little space between us on the messy top for our shot drinking.

"Again?" he asked.

"Definitely."

He smiled at me before he started to pour two more shots.

Not a terrible looking boy. But I didn't like his hair. Too dark and shaggy. Not short, soft and...sandy-blond. I didn't really like his eyes, the same color as his hair, either. They weren't...San Francisco Bay blue. At least he was tall. But not as tall as—no.

He handed over my glass, and I tried to return his smile before we drank.

This time the tequila burning my throat didn't make me cough, but the haziness in my head doubled. As Daniel looked me up and down. Again.

I had the same shoe size as my mother and *borrowed* her black, Jimmy Choo sandals. She owed me for keeping my dog away from me. And the sandals went with my black, sleeveless ruffled dress. That landed mid-thigh and had a *low* neckline. I'd also flat-ironed my long hair. The only other thing I had on was my black crossbody phone case.

I knew I looked like the...beauty queen my mother wanted me to be based on the way Daniel, and other boys at this party, kept staring at me.

Daniel leaned down and placed his lips near my ear. "How are you feeling?"

I shuddered. At his breath on my skin. And the thought of being someone I'm not.

His heavy cologne mixed with tequila filled my nose and foggy head. But I gave him a plastic smile and said, "I'm great."

"Want another?"

I should've said no. But I had to get rid of sorrow. "Sure."

While he poured us another shot, I swung my head left, right, but...didn't see Quinn and Ella. The last time I'd seen them was during shot one. A group shot with them. Then Quinn and Chad left. And Ella left me with Daniel in the kitchen...in search of her own guy. Far from me.

Daniel handed me my glass while giving me a lazy grin that made my flesh rise. He then tapped his shot glass to mine.

I took a breath, drank, but this shot made me almost gag. And the *ooonly* thing I felt was...my fuzzy head spinning. "I think I should...shtop." I shook my head.

He laughed and pulled the glass from my hand. "So how long have you and Quinn been friends?"

"Shince...we were twelve." Soooo *needed to stop drinking*.

"She said you're really into college guys."

He moved closer to me and...slowly checked me out.

Ickiness slid up my spine as I swallowed. To keep the tequila down.

"But I can't believe you don't have a boyfriend," he said... softly...in my ear. "The girls I went to high school with didn't look anything like you."

I shuddered again at him and...his words...and leaned back.

"Are you cold?"

"No."

The hip-hop music sounded louder. I felt its deep... pulsing in my stomach's pit. The voices and laughter all around us sounded like I was...surrounded by flocks of geese.

"I need to...sit," I carefully said. "I'm not...used to drinking like...this."

He put his arm around me, hugged me to him and we started walking. Into the music. Then there were stairs. A hall- way. Voices. A dark room that became bright. The music sounded muffled. And we were suddenly on a bed and his hot, tequila-tasting mouth was on mine.

Panic gripped my voice and stopped the spinning.

But my stomach heaved as he ended up on top of me.

Oh, shit.

How did I let this happen?

"You're the hottest piece I've ever been with," he mumbled against my mouth.

I turned my head and did think of Shane. What he'd said to me on my birthday. In the car.

His words from that day—his feelings for me—filled me with the power to grab Daniel's hand and stop it from sliding up my bare thigh.

"Get off me," I said with surprising strength and clarity.

Then my fight response fully kicked in. I tried to squirm out from underneath him, but he had almost all of his weight on me.

"Relax, baby. I promise we'll have fun." He smashed his mouth against mine.

I wiggled my hands between us, onto his chest and, with all my strength, pushed him up.

"I said get off me!" I yelled and followed it up by kneeing him.

Right where it would hurt the most.

He yelped and rolled off me.

I scrambled off the bed and, just to make myself crystal clear, kicked him as hard as I could in his leg. With my mother's eight-hundred-dollar Jimmy Choo sandal.

He moaned. "What the *fuck's* wrong with you?"

"You're the biggest piece of shit I've ever been with." I headed for the closed door while straightening my dress. And phone case.

Once I was on the other side of his closed door, I paused long enough to take several deep breaths. To keep my tequila-filled head clear.

I needed to get out of here. Now. Because I didn't know what Chad's *friend* might do to me if I didn't leave. But first I had to find Quinn and Ella.

I tried not to stumble, and ignored two girls waiting for

the bathroom as I walked toward the stairs. I went down them as fast as I could in my unsteady, high-heeled feet.

I scanned the crowded living and dining rooms for Quinn and Chad. Nowhere in sight. With my luck, they were in Chad's room doing what Daniel had hoped to do with me.

I wanted to empty my stomach at that thought. I'd have to brush my teeth until my gums bled to get the taste of him off my mouth. I'd have to burn this dress, too.

What was I going to—that's when I spotted Ella. In a sudden opening made by partiers heading toward the kitchen. She was on the couch and plastered against some guy with obnoxious biceps. I didn't want to rely on her, but I had no choice. And maybe she knew where I could find Quinn and Chad. Though all of them would be pissed at me for us needing to leave.

I wobbled toward her. I'd been so dumb to drink like that.

But heartbreak and anger had made me stupid.

"Hey," I said to her. "I need to talk to you. Now."

She glared at me. "A little busy right now. What happened to that Daniel guy?"

I looked over my shoulder to make sure he hadn't followed me. No sign of him. Yet.

"That's what I need to talk to you about."

She made a big show of rolling her eyes before looking at her guy. "Save this spot for me?" she flirtatiously asked. "I swear this won't take long."

He smiled and winked at her as she slowly pulled herself away from him.

I took Ella's hand and practically dragged her out the front door, into the night, and through a smaller group of college kids drinking outside. Still no sign of Quinn and Chad.

She jerked her hand free from mine and stopped about a foot away from the door.

Not nearly far enough for me.

"What's wrong with you *now*?"

I ignored that and said, "Where's Quinn and Chad? We have to go. Like now. Daniel's a complete dick. He took me upstairs to his room and—"

She laughed, and the sound chilled me to my core.

"Can you blame him? Look at how you're dressed." She gestured at my dress and shoes. "And you started drinking the minute we walked into this place. What did you *think* he would want with you?"

I stared at her, blinking, not sure I'd heard her right.

"Ever since you got grounded, you've changed. And that stupid club's changed you, too." Her hazel eyes flashed with disgust. "You used to be like me. Kids at school would get out of your way when you walked down the hall. Now you're one of them. A nobody. And I hate it."

I, mouth open, stood in front of her as my mind went blank from her visible hatred.

She took a step toward me. "I also know you're doing the competition with the losers in that club. You've been lying for weeks."

Oh…This is why she'd turned hateful bitch on me. But how did she find out? It couldn't have been anyone in the club. Had she heard one of the boyfriends talking about it?

A massive tequila headache started to form.

"How…did you find out?" I asked, sounding weak and beaten.

"Nothing at that school stays a secret." She leaned forward. "How could you do that to me? You *were* my best friend."

Shane's words to me from earlier drifted through my muddled brain.

Ouch. Right for the jugular.

"And now I'm stuck with Maddie Harrington." She all

but spit the words at me. "A drama loser who won't stop whining about that asshole she wants back."

I squared my shoulders, but forced myself not to do something really awful and dramatic.

Like slap the crap out of her.

"But you won't win the competition."

The hatred burning in her eyes stole the air in my lungs.

"And I don't know where Quinn and Chad are. Even if I did, I wouldn't tell you." She subjected me to the she-devil stare. "We're. Staying. Here. You can do whatever the fuck you want." She walked away. Right through the college kids who'd probably heard and watched us.

I continued standing there. Staring at...nothing.

I'd been friends with Ella Walker since sixth grade. Back then she'd just been snotty. Her nastiness didn't really start until her dad decided to run for mayor over a year ago. I'd seen this side of her too many times to count and now knew what it felt like to be on Ella's shit list. The guilt of standing by—glad she wasn't lashing into me—and allowing her to treat kids at school like this covered me. Like I had put a heavy blanket on my shoulders.

If not for the club, being grounded, and Shane, I might've ended up like her.

I turned from the townhouse and wobbled toward the parking lot. I had no other choice.

I slowly picked up my pace—I had to get as far away from there as possible. But then the cool darkness made me shiver. The music and loud talking and laughter from the party and others in the complex sounded like I was in a tunnel. That's when the reality of my situation—and every shitty day I'd had since walking away from Shane—burned my eyes.

I blinked, and the tears fell and slid down my cheeks.

I crossed my arms tight around my shaking body. Out of protection and to block the night's cold wet air. I hadn't...

brought a sweater. I hadn't planned…on being outside…longer than going from a car to…inside a house. Between my tears and exposed skin, I felt like prey…out in the wild. Alone.

My heart began thumping inside my chest.

How was I going to get out of this?

I had one credit card for emergencies…but I'd left it in my purse. At Quinn's place. I never carried cash—my shoulders shook as the tears fell faster and harder.

I was…one of the richest kids at school and had…no cash for a cab. But I did have my almost fully charged phone. I'd had the sense to charge it up while we were…getting ready. For our first night out together…as best friends—I sniffed and swiped my nose with two fingers.

I couldn't think about Ella's…cruelty right now. I needed to stop…crying…and focus on getting myself out of here.

I, through blurry eyes, took out my phone. And I stumbled. My right ankle went sideways. I put my phone between my teeth and yanked the Jimmy Choos off my feet. Once I was steady, I tucked the shoes under my left arm, continued walking, and went into my phone.

I couldn't call my parents. I'd be grounded until I graduated if they found out about any of this. They were also at some fancy party at a hotel downtown.

Who at school had a license and access to a car? And would drop whatever they were doing on a…late Saturday night…to come all the way down to this part of the city to get me.

His face flashed through my mind. I knew he'd come get me, too. Even after how badly I treated him at community service and after. When I'd…left him and the start of Greased Lightning the minute my phone said noon. Without a goodbye or…backward glance.

But I'd rather *die* out here by Lake Merced than have him see me…like this.

I wiped the tears from my cheeks with the back of my hand.

I scrolled through my contacts until I reached the K's and my bleary eyes widened.

Kassidy.

She had her license—my shoulders dipped. Her dad was an ER doctor and they only had one car. But maybe she and J.R. were together? Yes. She *had* to be with him. And I knew he had his license *and* access to a car. He didn't like me...not that I'd ever given him a reason to...but I had a feeling Kassidy could talk him into anything. Including driving all the way down here to get me. I only hoped she wasn't mad at me for how I...acted yesterday.

I stopped walking, chose her name, then begged the black sky she would answer. And she did. After several of the longest rings I'd ever waited through.

"Hey, you," she said, sounding friendly. Warm. And concerned.

Good signs. But her warmth and friendliness refueled my tears. Because of how my *ex*-best friend had spoken to me. I also didn't feel I...deserved Kassidy's kindness.

"I meant to call you to see if you're okay. But I had a busy day today. I'm sorry."

I lost my voice as tears again streamed down my face.

"Natalie?"

I sniffed and said, "Hey, Kass. Are you and J.R. busy?"

I heard a burst of laughter in the background. Which meant yes.

"We're at Bree O'Neil's birthday party with a bunch of kids from school. Why?"

Right. Bree's eighteenth birthday party. Something I hadn't thought twice about all week since we weren't friends. I'd never even spoken to her.

"Natalie, what's wrong?"

"I'm…" I sniffed a couple more times and tried to stop crying long enough to beg for help. "In trouble." My voice cracked on the words. "Can you guys come get me? Please?"

Another pause, then, "Yes. Absolutely. Hold on a sec."

I smiled at the sky and closed my eyes, which pushed out more tears.

It sounded like she'd pulled the phone away from her mouth, but I could just hear my name and "trouble" and "we need to go."

Panic stopped my tears. I didn't need the entire school knowing about this total humiliation. I would have enough drama to deal with Monday morning.

"Kassidy, *please* don't tell anybody about this."

"I won't. I promise. Where are you?"

Her question caught me, and stupidly, off guard. I looked around me. I walked quite a distance from the townhouse, but was still surrounded by off-campus student housing.

"I'm…down by the San Francisco State campus," I said as I searched for street signs.

She gasped, and I cringed.

Hopefully they wouldn't change their minds about coming to get me.

"Okay. We're leaving now. But it's going to take us a while to get down there. Bree lives a few blocks from school. Can you give me any street names?"

That's when I noticed what looked like a bus stop. Several feet in front of me and located in the middle of all the housing.

I awkwardly grabbed the shoes from underneath my arm and speed walked toward the stop. "I'm heading for a bus stop. It should have a stop name or address."

"Text it to me so I can get the directions. Will you be okay until we get there?"

I released a soft huff. "I think so. It's not a...bad area. Just student housing."

"Well, I'll keep checking in with you. But call me if you need me."

The tears picked up right where they left off seconds earlier. "Thanks, Kass."

"Natalie, don't thank me. We're friends. You'd do the same for me."

Yes. I would. Because *that* was the real Natalie.

Chapter Twenty-Seven

Yet another cool breeze hit my skin, covered in goosebumps that hadn't gone away since I sat down on the bus stop bench...forever ago. I rubbed my arms with my shaky, clammy hands, and could no longer feel the lower half of my body, especially my butt. So when I saw the approaching headlights of a slowly moving car that looked like a smaller SUV, my shoulders—my entire, trembling body—sagged with relief.

I put my phone in its case. It was *finally* them. Kassidy had also texted they were close.

My phone and bitchy side had been my only weapons against unwanted attention from other college boys, staggering by me on their way to the next party. Some had even staggered off the bus that stopped once. But my strength had weakened. From the cool air. And emotional and physical exhaustion. My head was full and heavy. My latest tears were stuck to my cold cheeks.

The SUV got closer. I could just see Kassidy and J.R. in the front. Her face brightened in relief when she saw me and she waved. Even J.R. looked relieved to see me.

Definitely a good sign he wasn't pissed at driving all this way to come get me.

I picked up my shoes, pried myself off the bench, and stood on my numb feet. And I noticed they weren't alone. There were two people in the backseat.

My pulse fluttered.

Who the hell could be with them? She'd promised not to tell anyone about this.

I squinted into the headlights, and noticed my eyes were gritty and puffy.

J.R. steered the black SUV toward me and, as they pulled up, I saw Meg and—my heart stopped when my eyes connected with his.

Oh, my God.

I turned, and now shook from being cold and *complete* mortification.

But of course he'd been at Bree's party.

Car doors opened and closed. Then Kassidy and Meg were beside me. They pulled me into their arms for a hug. Though the hug and warmth felt awesome, I started crying. Again.

"You're freezing," Kassidy said and pulled away. "We need to get you in the—"

I groaned and said, "Kass, what is he *doing* here? You promised not to tell anyone."

The tears I didn't know I had left fell fast.

"I *promise* no one knows but the four of us. And Owen. He wanted to come, too, but there wouldn't have been enough room for all of us in the car." She came in for another hug. "Shane was sitting with us when you called. He and Justin and Owen were talking about their rehearsal today. He heard what I said to Justin. About you being in trouble and needing to come get you." She squeezed me. "He wouldn't stay, and I wanted him to come with us."

My tears stopped, and I stared at her as she leaned back.

"I had a feeling something was going on with you two. Before tonight."

I, speechless, blinked the wetness from my eyes.

"You did?" Meg asked. "Because I sure as hell wasn't expecting him to jump up like he did and want to come with us. That came out of nowhere."

Kassidy gave me a tiny smile. "I saw the way you were looking at each other. The day they came to tell us about the competition? Like you two had a big...secret."

And I'd thought we'd been sneaky. Until he'd told me the answer to my one trivia question the way he did.

One thing that caught my hazy, exhausted mind was Kassidy and Meg weren't looking at me with judgment. Even though no one had seemed to know about him and Maddie breaking up.

"He was ready to come out here before we pulled up, but I stopped him." Kassidy grasped my left hand and squeezed. "I figured you needed the girls first."

I tried smiling at her.

Meg's eyes became round. "You were texting Shane that day. At rehearsal?"

I bit my lower lip and nodded-shrugged. Then my eyes watered up. Thinking about him sitting steps from me right now. What would I say?

"I can't face him," I whispered. "Look at me. I'm a fucking mess."

"What happened tonight?" Kassidy quietly asked.

"My stupidity." I placed my frigid hands on my face and wiped my wet cheeks.

"Nat, he won't care." Meg hugged me. "He's worried. And was scared. All of us were."

I squared my shoulders and took a quick breath. I had to get this humiliation over with. I also couldn't stop trembling from being out in the cool damp air forever.

"Does my face look as awful as it feels right now? Tell me the truth."

Kassidy lifted her shoulders. "It's obvious you've been crying. But that's it."

Thank God for waterproof mascara.

"There's a box of tissues somewhere in the car. I'll find it for you."

Kassidy went back to the SUV, and Meg gave me an encouraging smile.

I paused as another wave of tears hit, but I frantically cleared my eyes and turned.

I followed Meg toward the passenger-side's rear door as it opened. She went around the back of the SUV, and Shane got out. He took a step away from the opened door.

I forced myself to look up, and our eyes met. My barely held together dam almost broke for the hundredth time. At seeing his concern. Relief. And no anger. No judgment.

I stopped when we were in touching distance. "Hi." Totally lame. But I didn't know what else to say. Could a person die from humiliation?

He took my shoes from me. With his free hand, he took my right hand and gently pulled me toward him. The second he wrapped his solid warm arms around me my tense insides melted. The goosebumps slowly disappeared as my skin absorbed his heat. I relaxed against him and breathed in the safety of his arms. His warmth. His gentleness. And being right where I belonged.

I also breathed in his familiar scent I'd missed. Terribly.

"You're shivering," he said, hugging me tighter. "I need to get you in the car."

I nodded and reluctantly pulled away from him. I kept my face down, hidden behind my hair, and slid into the backseat beside Meg. He slid in after me and closed the door. I became sandwiched between them, but allowed myself to lean into him.

He wriggled his arm behind my lower back and hugged me to his side. And a tiny sigh escaped from my chest as Kassidy handed me the box of tissues.

J.R. turned in his seat, his expression like everyone else's. Relief mixed with concern.

Kassidy was right about him. He, like Shane, wasn't like most of the boys at our school. Most boys on this planet.

The guilt from how harshly I'd treated J.R. back in the fall filled my eyes.

How could I have any tears left?

"Thanks for coming to get me," I murmured before grabbing a tissue.

His face relaxed. "I'm glad you're okay." His eyes flicked to Shane and back to me. "So where are we going?"

I started to give him my parents' address, but stopped and released a quiet moan. I didn't have my keys. Those were also in my purse, sitting on the floor in Quinn's bedroom. My parents probably weren't even home yet from their party. A good thing. If I had my keys.

"Shit." I wiped my wet eyes. "I don't have my keys to get in and my parents aren't..." My voice failed me. I didn't know how much more rotten I could take.

"You can drop us off at my place," Shane said.

I sniffed and peeked at him.

He couldn't be serious. And what would his parents think when I walked into their place looking like I'd spent the night in a cold version of hell? Which I had.

He hugged me tighter to him. "It'll be fine. Don't worry about it."

I relaxed since I didn't have the strength to worry. And I trusted him. Completely.

"Okay." J.R. faced forward. "Do you need the heat turned up higher?"

I shook my head, even though I couldn't stop trembling. The only warmth I wanted and needed happened to be right against me.

After a few minutes of silence, the kind of silence that wasn't uncomfortable but not comfortable either, Kassidy angled herself to see the backseat. To see me.

"Do you want to tell us what happened?" she quietly asked again.

No. I sure as hell didn't. Especially while snuggled against Shane. But because they'd left their party and driven all this way to come get me, I knew I had to tell them something. The highlights. But that word made my stomach tighten. Nothing about what happened the second I stepped into the townhouse had been a high. Though I'd convinced myself acting like a careless high school dummy would make me feel high. Help put my heart back together.

Everyone waited for me to say something. Anything.

Hopefully none of them—Shane—would hate me after all this.

"Well, let's see," I said with a bit of sarcasm to hide my embarrassment, "I had a really horrible week and—" Shane became tense. Because he felt somewhat responsible for my horrible week. But I forced myself to continue. "I thought it would be a super idea to go out with Ella and Quinn and forget...everything. So I drank...way too much." I stared at my lap as I twisted the tissue back and forth. "I...was hanging out with this...guy." I couldn't say his name. Didn't want to. I also couldn't look at any of them. *Him*. Not during this next part. "And he...wanted more than to just hang out. But I—" My voice broke and sickness crept up my throat.

The car became so quiet all I heard were the moving tires beneath us.

I wanted the backseat to swallow me whole while I waited for the judgment. For someone to blame me for what happened. Like Ella did. My dress and the shoes were pretty flimsy. And I had drunk way too much. Maybe careless and dumb Natalie had been asking for it.

"Did he hurt you?"

I ripped the tissue at Shane's softly spoken question. A question I'm sure all of them had.

"No." I laughed, but it sounded close to hysterical. "I kneed him hard, you know where, and kicked the shit out of him."

Meg growled. "You should've *ripped* it off, too. No offense to the boys in here."

Her comment made me smile and eased some of the tension in the car. Her comment also eased my embarrassment since there'd been no judgment. By anyone. If anything, it seemed they agreed with Meg. But Shane became rigid. No longer warm.

Did he hate me now? For this newest mess I'd caused him? Us?

"You obviously got away from him and out of there, which is great," Kassidy said. "Is that when you called me? What happened to Ella and Quinn?"

The tears I'd been doing a good job fighting came back with a vengeance.

"I couldn't...find Quinn. But I found Ella. And when I tried...to tell her...what happened she—" I let the tears fall as I recalled her hate.

Shane relaxed, and his arm tightened around me.

Meg took away the ripped tissue, pulled out a new one for me, and handed it over.

Shaking from my emotion, I wiped my cheeks and mumbled, "She's not my friend."

None of them needed to know the awful things she'd said

to me and about them. My real friends. The people I...loved. Especially him. And I cried harder when I remembered how I'd treated him that morning. I so didn't deserve to be curled against him like this.

"I left," I said during a break in my tears. "When I was far enough away, I called you."

Kassidy reached out and clasped my free hand. "Natalie, can I tell you something?"

I sniffed twice, swiped my nose with the tissue, and shrugged. Too exhausted to respond any other way. But I tried to prepare myself for a truth I probably didn't want to hear.

"Quinn seems okay. I guess." She paused, then added, "But I don't know why you were friends with Ella. She's evil. Nothing like you."

My eyes caught hers. And I saw compassion. After how Ella treated me, I so needed to hear we *were* nothing alike.

I squeezed her hand, and she nodded and smiled.

"Yeah," Meg agreed. "I'm not voting for Ella Walker. I don't care who her dad is."

"Me, either. She's nuts," J.R. said. "Shane sits between Ella and me in math. Sometimes I can hear her talking to Quinn who sits on her other side. All she does is bitch about everything. And text during class. I can't believe the T-Rex hasn't caught her yet." His eyes shifted to Shane in the rear-view mirror. "I don't know how you can sit next to her."

I never knew Shane sat by Ella in the T-Rex's class.

"I tried getting the empty seat on the other side of you and behind Owen. But he told me no one's allowed to sit back there." Shane smirked. "He's caught too many kids *texting*."

J.R. shook his head.

"You're too good for her, Natalie," Kassidy said before she turned forward in her seat.

A smile tugged at my mouth as she and J.R. laced their fingers together, then rested their arms on the center console.

I snuggled a bit deeper into Shane's arm and side.

I still had a chill that probably wouldn't go away until I took a scalding shower. To burn off Daniel and the rotten night. Which stopped being rotten when my *real* friends rescued me.

Then it hit me—Quinn had yet to text. Because she hadn't noticed I left the party.

Chapter Twenty-Eight

I walked into the third-floor condo. Shane followed me and shut the door.

The living room, barely lit up from a lamp on a table, was straight ahead. The room looked big, but cozy at the same time. Filled with cushy furniture and fat pillows. A big part of me wanted to head straight for the sectional couch and collapse. Put my head on one of those pillows and lose myself—my thoughts—in its warmth and softness. With him beside me.

Then I thought of his parents.

"Your parents are asleep?" I whispered. And what would they think if they woke up and saw me here with their...perfect son? Their perfect son who was way too good for me.

"They're not here." He walked around to stand in front of me. "They took off in the AMX for a few days. I think our trip on your birthday brought out my dad's romantic side."

I heard the smile in his voice, but still couldn't find the courage to really look at him.

Embarrassment had gripped me and refused to let go.

"But my brother and his fiancée have been staying here

while they're gone. They're remodeling their house and needed to get away from the mess and noise." He stepped toward me. "They're not here right now, either. They went out with some friends."

So we were alone. And wouldn't have to stumble through any lies about what I was doing here this late.

A breath of relief came out of me in a soft puff. But knowing we were alone made me feel exposed. I looked at my skimpy dress, bare legs, and feet. The bottoms had to be black.

I crossed my arms and the trembling returned.

Shane dropped the Jimmy Choos on the floor and stood close enough his heat found my cold skin. He hesitated before reaching to cup my face and gently tilt it upward.

"Natalie, look at me."

It took me a few seconds to find the courage to do what he'd sort've asked. When I did, our eyes, of course, did the strange, magnetic snapping together.

My breath left me at what I saw in his eyes. Still relief and lots of concern. And more than a little anger. But not toward me. Or the huge mess I'd gotten myself into tonight.

"Now that we're alone, be honest with me. Did that asshole hurt you?"

His concern and the way he was staring into my eyes sparked several pieces of my heart, and they clicked back into place.

"Shane, I swear he was the only one who got hurt in *that* mess."

He gave me a quick nod and kissed my forehead.

Tears filled my eyes, and I hated I couldn't stop crying. I wasn't even sure how I hadn't fallen into his arms from emotional exhaustion.

"I'm so sorry," I blubbered. "About this morning and tonight and you missing your party and...*everything*. Especially looking at your phone. I wasn't thinking."

"Natalie, don't apologize." He leaned back to catch my eyes. "And you wouldn't have even gone out with *them* if you hadn't been pissed at me. And Mr. Yates," he muttered.

He released my face to run his hands through his hair, which caused it to stick up in several directions, and I smiled. For the first time in forever. I then noticed how incredible he looked. In a black, untucked button-down shirt with the sleeves rolled to his elbows...dark jeans and...black Vans. A casual, but totally hot, birthday-party look.

I stared at my dirty, cold bare feet almost toe-to-toe with the tips of his shoes.

I should've been at Bree's party with him and my real friends. But I'd been too much of a coward to be with him. To be me. And this is where fear had gotten me—standing in front of the boy I now knew I loved and looking like Frankenstein's daughter after getting drunk, assaulted, and having Ella dump me as her best friend on a sidewalk in front of strangers. Then walk away and abandon me like I didn't exist. Had never existed.

Oh, I so needed this night to be over. But I couldn't stand the thought of leaving him.

"Shane, I was pissed at Mr. Yates. Not you. But I wasn't expecting to deal with Maddie. All week." I sighed. "I also didn't know she and Quinn had become such good friends."

"I really am sorry about that. And for being such an ass last Saturday."

I slipped my arms around his waist and nestled my head on his shoulder. A much better way to accept his second apology while fixing the way I'd accepted his first one.

He hugged me tight, then said, "You're still shivering." He released me and clasped my hand. "If my sister was still at home, you could wear something of hers. But what she left was boxed up when we moved and put in a closet somewhere around here." He tried smiling as he led me left and down the hallway. "I'll have to give you something of mine. But they won't fit."

The thought of wearing his clothes gave me tingles I didn't squash.

He stopped us at the end of the hallway where there were only two rooms and a closet.

His part of the condo?

He flipped on his bedroom light. To the right of me and across his bedroom was a bathroom, and I realized I needed a bathroom. But not to use the mirror.

I had *zero* interest in seeing my face.

He led me into his bedroom, but my steps stalled as a wave of shyness tackled me.

I bit my lower lip.

He walked to his dresser on my left, and my eyes drifted across his...neat room. For a high school boy. He had a big desk that fit in and took up the far left corner of his room. The top held a bunch of books, some school books, notebooks, papers, and his laptop. To the right edge of his desk was a big window with closed blinds.

My face warmed at his messy queen-sized bed sitting against the right wall. The blankets were falling off and his three pillows were bunched together at the head of the bed. He also had a couple of nightstands with lamps and—I smiled. He had an alarm clock on each table.

"What's with the two alarm clocks? You phone's alarm isn't enough?"

"No. Because I'm *not* an early-morning person," he said as he dug through a drawer.

My smile grew as I continued inspecting his room. He didn't have much on the walls. A bulletin board over his dresser that held a bunch of pictures. Over his bed's headboard, he'd hung a poster-sized picture of a 70 Chevelle. It looked almost exactly like his brother's car.

And it struck me—we had pictures of our dream cars over our beds.

Wow. So weird. But in a happy chance sort of way.

I stepped further into his room. "No posters of sharks?" I teased him.

He pulled out what looked like a pair of comfy and warm pajama bottoms.

My tummy did a somersault. The awesome kind of somersault.

"That would be weird. Going to sleep every night with sharks watching me?"

I giggled. A Shane only giggle.

He pulled out a gray T-shirt and opened another drawer. "But I have a lot of books on sharks over on my desk. I also take over the T.V. during Discovery Channel's *Shark Week*."

My phone buzzed and dinged, and I jumped. I'd forgotten all about my phone after putting it away the moment they'd shown up.

Shane looked up and over at me.

It could only be one person, and I pulled my phone out. "It's Quinn."

"She's just *now* texting you?" he asked with clear anger in his voice. "Blow her off."

"I can't. I was supposed to stay at her place tonight." I frowned at my phone. "If I don't text her back, she'll freak out, her parents will freak, and they'll call my parents." I still didn't know how I would handle them.

Where the hell are you? You attack Daniel and take off without telling anyone?

My jaw tightened.

Of course Daniel the dickhead would play the victim, and Ella would play dumb about what happened between us.

Shane walked up. "What'd she say?"

"You don't want to know," I mumbled. "It'll just make you angrier. Give me a sec to text her back."

I paused, thinking about what to text since I didn't need her parents flipping out.

Once I had what to say, I typed, *My friends picked me up. I'm fine, by the way. Just bring my stuff on Monday. And Daniel is a lying dick.*

I put my phone back in the case. "That should give me time to figure out what's next."

"I'll take you home when you can get in. My parents left the keys to their other cars."

But I didn't want to go to that home, and I couldn't stay here with him. The next best thing was my Chloe.

Had it really been this morning my mother told me she had to stay with my grandparents?

I fought the tears. These were angry tears, though. And I was about to ask the world of him, but I hated the thought of going back to my parents' place. Especially after this night. And, hopefully, my grandparents would understand after I gave them only bits of the truth.

"I know this is a lot to ask, but...can you take me to my grandparents' house?"

His eyes widened. "Natalie, it's after midnight. Won't that cause you more trouble?"

The tears won, again, and slid from my tired eyes.

He pulled me toward him with his free hand. "Sorry. I don't think that came out right."

"No. It's not you. I hate...my parents' place. And I want... my dog." I sniffed. "My mom...told me...this morning...I couldn't have Chloe...here in the city."

I cried on his shoulder, again, and he hugged me tight.

"You really have had a shit week," he murmured into my hair. "Okay. Whatever you need. I'll text my brother and tell him I'm taking a friend home, so he doesn't worry."

Friend.

I now hated the sound of that word coming from him and cried harder.

After several moments of letting me sob into his shoulder, he gave me a quick squeeze and said, "You should get changed." He slowly leaned back. "And call your grandparents?"

I sniffed a couple times, swiped my nose, and nodded. Which made the world spin for a few seconds, and I gripped the sides of his shirt.

"Sorry," I said around a shaky breath. "My head's still... spinning a little."

"It's okay," he murmured, letting me hold onto him.

When my head became a bit clearer, I let go of his shirt, and he handed me his clothing.

"Pajama bottoms with a drawstring, a T-shirt, a sweatshirt, and socks. All of it should warm you up. Need anything else?"

My still aching head made me say, "Aspirin and some water."

"I'm on it." He started to lower his head, but stopped.

He lifted his eyes. That were filled with affection, but also wariness as he searched my face for something. Then he opened his mouth, hesitated, sighed, and stepped back.

Maybe I needed to rethink checking my reflection in his bathroom mirror.

He'd wanted to kiss me. I thought. And tell me something. But I'm sure my hideous face had been a glaring reminder of what I'd been through. Specifically with Daniel, who I needed to scrub off of me. Off my mouth. So I didn't really mind Shane had stopped himself.

But I shuddered at remembering Daniel's tequila-tasting mouth smashed against mine.

I would definitely have to figure out how to purge that memory from my brain.

"I'll be back in a few minutes," Shane softly said.

He walked around me and closed his bedroom door behind him.

* * *

I shifted onto my left side in the passenger seat.

Shane was focused on the road and the only sound in the car was the rhythmic *da-dun, da-dun* as we started across the bridge toward Sausalito.

Between being covered from head to toe in his baggy, but snuggly clothes, the heat blowing from the car's vents, the steady *da-dun,* and feeling beyond safe, my eyelids kept drooping. But I so didn't want to miss a second of this time with him. That would soon end.

So I said, "Thank you for doing this." But what I really meant was *I love you even more for driving me all the way to Sausalito so I can be with my grandparents and dog.*

"You don't have to thank me," he replied. "But I hope you don't get in huge trouble."

He turned his head enough to flash that smile. Which made me smile. And tingle all over.

"It would really suck if you got grounded right now," he added.

I giggled. "I think it'll be okay." Maybe...not. I still said, "My grandma mostly sounded worried." After I'd blubbered through a *less*-truthful and brief version of what happened. Which I'd told Shane, so our stories were straight. But I couldn't think about what my parents' reaction would be to all this.

No. I didn't even want to go there. Not now, when my life felt pretty close to perfect.

I nestled deeper into the seat. "Say something funny.

You're the only one who can make me laugh when I need it." I also needed to stay awake.

"Okay." He paused before saying, "A horse walks into a bar and the bartender asks, 'Why the long face?'"

I rolled my eyes, but the silly joke did make me giggle.

"My dad used to tell us that joke all the time when we were having bad days." He frowned. "But that's all the funny I have. So how about a few easy quiz questions?"

I wanted to tell *him* to stop looking serious. Remind him that I was fine. And that Daniel hadn't hurt me. But I didn't want to bring it all up again and said, "Sure."

He laid his head back. "Question one. Pontiac GTO. Convertible or hardtop?"

I grinned. "Hardtop. Definitely."

He nodded. "Question two. Sixty-nine Charger or 69 'Cuda?"

I yawned and said, "The 'Cuda. No contest."

He smiled. "Final question. Plymouth Road Runner or Road Runner Superbird?"

"The Road Runner," I stated. "The Superbird is too weird looking."

He laughed. "And it's official." He tore his eyes from the road and they caught mine. "You're the perfect girl...for me."

That made my sleepy eyes widen. He refocused on the road. But I could see, from the bridge lights illuminating the car, his flushed face.

An enormous burst of warmth from love pieced more of my heart back together.

I also wanted to throw myself across the console and into his arms. But we so didn't need to add a car accident to the night's list of unfortunate events. And then all my bad choices from the night—the last several days—filled my mind.

I cringed. Because I didn't deserve such an amazing compliment.

"Thank you for saying that," I mumbled. "But perfect girl? Especially after *this* night? I don't think so."

"Natalie," he said, shaking his head, "you made a couple of bad choices tonight and some *dick* college guy" —he gripped the steering wheel— "tried to take advantage of you." His hands relaxed a fraction. "But you got yourself out of it." He glanced my way. "You're incredible. And I wish more kids at school knew this about you."

He gave me a quick smile before looking forward.

My smile was huge and goofy. I never wanted this new perfect moment with him to end. And more pieces of my heart fell into place.

Maybe it was time the kids at school did know the real me.

"Natalie Carlisle," he declared. "You know how to take care of yourself."

I, still smiling, snuggled my seat while imagining it was him. "Sometimes."

"And that's why you need someone like me around."

"Then I guess," I said around a full-body yawn, "I'll have to keep you around."

And I closed my dry, heavy eyes.

Chapter Twenty-Nine

My eyes fluttered open and landed on Chloe, panting and sitting on an empty pillow by my head—my eyes fully opened.

What the hell?

I rolled over to see sunlight trying to break through my closed blinds. That's when I realized I was sweating under my covers since I still had on all the clothing Shane had given me last night. A nightmare which turned into a dream with a happy ending.

My head was still tight, and my dry mouth told me I needed a gallon of water, but I smiled, stretched and rolled back toward Chloe. But how had I gotten from the car to my bed?

I searched my fuzzy mind and found hazy, snapshot memories. Of Shane waking me up. Then helping—maybe more like carrying me?—into the house. My grandparents waiting at the door and talking with him and...nothing else.

I did, however, clearly remember all the *incredible* things he'd said to me in the car.

My smile tripled in size and I wanted—needed—to text him.

I rubbed Chloe's face, then tossed my blankets aside and sat up. I also pulled off his heavy sweatshirt, and not because I wanted to take it off. It was just way too warm. The complete opposite of how cold I'd been—what time was it?

I looked at my one clock. Almost 1:00. Wow.

I crawled to the foot of my bed and scanned my room for the bag Shane had given me for my dress, shoes and phone after I changed. He must've given it to Gramps or Grams before leaving, but where...that's when I spotted the bag. On my desk.

Seconds later I had my phone and *six* text messages?

I smiled at seeing two were from him. My smile faded, though, when I saw two messages from Quinn. I also had a text from Kassidy and Meg.

I read Quinn's messages first that came in late last night. Or early this morning.

I'm not mad anymore. Glad you're okay. But what happened?

Then, *Daniel said you two were having a good time, he took you upstairs because that's what you wanted, then you went crazy. Ella has no clue what's going on.*

"Asshole," I muttered. "And lying bitch."

I didn't know how she'd gotten away with her lie, either. It's not as if other partiers hadn't seen our confrontation. I still couldn't believe the things she'd said. The hate I saw in her eyes. And of course I'd have to tell Quinn the whole truth tomorrow. If she'd listen to me.

I went to Kassidy's text, *Did Shane get you home? Let me know how you're doing.*

Yeah. Feeling much better. Thanks again for coming to get me.

I then responded to Meg's, *How are you feeling this morning?*

Much better. Thanks for being there last night.

Now for his messages, which came in around eleven this morning.

Hey, Sunshine. I'm rehearsing with the guys today, but I'll call you when I get home. You're pretty cute when you're sleeping. And snoring.

I rolled my eyes while also fighting a smile.

His second message said, *Just kidding about the snoring. Hope you're feeling better.*

So much better. Because of you. And everyone else who rescued me last night.

I almost added one of those cutesy emojis, like the blowing kiss face or the hugger or pink hearts. But I wasn't certain we were at cutesy emoji stage just yet, so I hit send.

Now I needed a shower. The hottest one I could stand. But I also needed to check in with my grandparents first. So they knew I hadn't died after getting me into bed.

I left my phone on my bed and, with a ridiculous spring in my step, headed upstairs with Chloe right at my heels. I turned left and stopped. Then my blissful bubble burst seeing my parents in the living room and talking with my grandparents. That is, until everyone saw me.

Oh, shit.

Grams must've called my parents after hanging up with me. Still, I wasn't at all ready for this to happen now. Not at— I guess it was 1:00 in the afternoon. But I hadn't formed my full story. And what about the bazillion questions they'd ask?

My dad stood, his face set in unhappiness. "Good. You're up. Can you come in here?"

Okay. I could tell them about everything but the drinking. And the horrible things Ella said to me. Maybe I'd even get sympathy points because of what Daniel tried to do to me.

"Sit down," my dad said.

I sat on the couch's edge near Grams and Chloe jumped in my lap.

I held her close. As if she were a shield.

My dad sat down beside my mother on the loveseat across from me. Gramps sat on the other side of Grams. And I suddenly felt like I was trapped in one of those intervention shows.

My mother looked me up and down. Her face paled, and I straightened, ready for battle.

"Whose clothes are you wearing?" she asked with an edge in her voice.

"They're Shane's," I answered. More like snapped.

Her face paled even more, and my dad sighed.

"You need to explain yourself," he said. "You scared a lot of people last night, including Quinn and her parents who also called us. But after your grandparents." His frown deepened. "The point is, they were *extremely* worried because they didn't know where you were."

I couldn't really blame Quinn for the confusion she'd passed on to her parents. My text last night had been vague. But I didn't feel very generous or forgiving when it came to her.

"Sweetheart, what really happened last night?" Grams asked.

I shrugged. "I told you what happened when I called—"

"Natalie," Gramps interjected, "you've never done anything like this before. And we're all finding it hard to believe a fight with your friends led to Shane bringing you here, and in the condition you were in, at such a late hour."

My face burned at his words. "*Please* don't blame him. He didn't do anything wrong."

"We're not blaming Shane," my dad stressed. "But what happened?"

I took a slow, deep breath, to give myself time to find the right words.

And hopefully I *wouldn't* be grounded for the rest of my high school life after this.

"Okay. We...went to a party at Chad's place. He's Quinn's boyfriend." My confession caught everyone's attention. "And his roommate got...aggressive with me." Definitely the truth.

My dad sat up, and his eyes and face hardened. Which I took as a sign in *my* favor.

My mother's eyes tripled in size, and my grandparents became uncomfortably silent.

"What did he do? Did you get some help?" my dad asked.

"Nothing," I swiftly answered, because of how angry he sounded. "I...pushed him away from me and left the party."

Their faces and postures relaxed at hearing me say that. And everything I told them next—minus Ella's cruelty—was the truth.

Until my mother asked, "What kind of party was this? Was there drinking?"

I had to lie on this one. But I also knew Ella and Quinn would never admit to drinking.

"No. Just a party with Chad and some of his friends."

She raised her eyebrows, clearly not convinced. Just like my dad and grandparents.

"Do Quinn's parents know what kind of friends their daughter's boyfriend has?"

I sensed the bad direction this was headed in and said, "Mom, I don't know. And I don't need you talking to them about what happened. It'll embarrass me and get Quinn in trouble." Which really meant more trouble for me, and I so didn't need more trouble.

The corners of her mouth tightened, but I didn't give a crap.

"Honey," my dad began, sounding exhausted. I guess I had

worried them. "It's good you got yourself out of there, and your friends and Shane picked you up. But why didn't you come home? How did you end up in Shane's clothes and here at your grandparents' house?"

More honesty poured out of me and led to, "Shane gave me all this to change into." I gestured at the baggy bottoms, gray T-shirt, and white socks. "He was being awesome."

My mother's face slowly relaxed and went back to its normal color.

"That explains the clothes," my dad continued. "But why didn't you call us about what happened and have Shane bring you home? We were home from our party before midnight. And you coming home would've been easier on everyone."

Maybe it was all the time I'd spent explaining—reliving—last night that made my defenses snap at his words, and I blurted out, "I didn't want to go to *that* home."

I shocked everyone into silence. I even saw hurt flash through my dad's eyes. And my mother was now focused on her hands tightly folded on her lap. But all I cared about at this moment was continuing my honesty streak.

"*This* is my real home. With Chloe. Where I can just be me. And not judged because I'm nothing like her." I stared at my mother. Now she actually looked hurt. But I kept going. "I hate leaving this house. Chloe. My room. Where I can have a picture of my dream car over my bed."

"Natalie," Gramps said in a low voice, "we understand you had a terrible night. But that's no excuse for your tone or talking like that."

I gripped Chloe and stood. "I'm sorry. But it's the truth." I hugged her as tight as I could without making her squirm. "I'm not leaving this house again without my dog."

I turned from them and headed back to my room.

I hadn't meant to hurt their feelings. Even my mother's.

And I flinched remembering my dad's hurt. But speaking nothing but honesty made me feel a little more weightless.

I stepped into my room, shut the door, then locked it.

I had no idea where my rebellion would leave me with my parents after today. And it's not like my grandparents would kick me out.

But maybe...just maybe...they *and* my dad would be able to convince my mother to let me have Chloe when I stayed in the city.

Chapter Thirty

I headed for Quinn, waiting outside school with my overnight bag and purse, as Gramps drove off. She was frowning. Probably because she hadn't expected him to be dropping me off.

I had absolutely no idea what to say to her. Except the truth. But would she listen?

"You're back at your grandparents' house?" she asked.

I shrugged. "My parents are traveling this week." Grams had told me that yesterday. After my parents left without another word to me. And that's all Quinn needed to know.

She handed over my bags. "Here's all your stuff."

"Thanks."

I headed up the stairs and she followed me.

When we were inside the building, I looked for Shane. He'd told me before we hung up yesterday he'd find me when he got to school.

"Why didn't you text me back yesterday?" Quinn asked, with a hint of irritation.

I stopped when we reached the stairs. I needed to get this over with. She'd also given me a pretty perfect opening. So I released a quick breath and said, "Because I was pissed at you."

Her eyes narrowed into slits. "*You* were pissed at *me*? For what? My parents freaked when we showed up at my house without you. And Chad's upset with me because of what you did to Daniel. He'll probably never invite us to another party again."

My temper flared inside me and I started quivering. Because she was still taking Daniel the dickhead's side. And had yet to ask for *my* side of that rotten story.

"I don't give a crap," I hissed. "Because Daniel—" I stopped when my brain registered the disdain radiating from her eyes.

Quinn was supposed to be the "nice one." The one who took the time to understand and not jump to assumptions. The opposite of Ella.

Okay. Maybe I had gotten Quinn into a little trouble with her parents. And, yeah, I'm sure Chad wanted nothing more to do with me. Which didn't bother me one bit. But she and I were supposed to be...what *were* we?

"Daniel...?" Quinn crossed her arms. "What did he do, Natalie? Because he's always been really nice to *me*."

I stared at her for several seconds. Then burst into laughter. Because telling her the truth would so not be worth my breath. And it's not like I'd ever be going to another party with them.

Those days were over.

She looked at me as though my laughter had slapped her across the face. "Ella's right. You've gotten so weird since you got grounded."

I guess Ella had shared *those* feelings with Quinn. But hearing her name reminded me I did have to tell Quinn the truth about Ella and me.

I shook my head. "It doesn't matter what Daniel did to

me. Or tried to do," I muttered under my breath. I looked at her. "But Ella lied to you, too, Saturday night."

Her eyes rolled sideways. "What are you talking about? She has no idea why you—"

"No!" I snapped. "I pulled her outside, to tell her what happened with Daniel, but she didn't give a crap." I leaned forward. "She chewed my ass for being in the competition with the club, then left me out there."

She stared at me. "You're doing the competition with your club?"

Really? That's all she'd heard? And I guess Ella hadn't even told her that much.

I truly no longer existed in her world.

"Yes. I am. And I'm excited about it." I just needed to make sure I told them that at lunch.

I planned on sitting with them starting this afternoon.

Quinn's stare turned into a glare.

I pressed my lips together and nodded once.

Of course she would fly to Ella's defense.

"How could you do that, Natalie?" She stepped toward me. "*Ella's* your best friend. Not those kids." Her glare turned into a sneer. "And no wonder she lied and didn't seem to care about what happened to you Saturday night. You lied to her. Us. And betrayed her."

Wow. At least I now knew where I stood with Quinn.

"Well, she made it perfectly clear Saturday night I'm not her best friend anymore." I started to go around her to head upstairs. "Because of what you said, I guess we're done, too."

"Nat...wait." She sighed. "I'm sure she didn't mean it—what do *you* want?"

I was about to run up the steps when I looked over and saw Shane had walked up.

Relief filled every part of me, and I wanted to throw my arms around him. Especially since I'd been practically comatose when he dropped me off at my grandparents' house.

He returned Quinn's glare. "I'm here to talk to her. If that's okay with you?"

Several more kids walked into the building. The hallways were getting louder.

"Why?" Quinn snidely asked.

A muscle in his jaw pulsed before he said, "I think the answer to that question falls under none of your business."

Her face turned so red it looked like her blonde head would burst. "Ella's right. You are another jerk high school boy. Maddie's, like, devastated because of you." She flounced around me and stomped up the stairs.

And I couldn't work up an ounce of anything but more relief.

A swarm of kids came through the doors and were talking at full volume.

Shane came closer to the stairs. "Well that was a fantastic way to start the day," he grumbled. Our eyes connected and his face softened. "Are you okay after dealing with her?"

I nodded. "Yeah. But..." I grinned. "I'm better now that you're here."

He came around to my right side and we walked up the stairs together. "*That's* a fantastic way to start the day." His eyes drifted down and up me. "You look much better than you did the last time I saw you. Natalie Carlisle's back," he added in a lowered voice.

I bit my lower lip. "Stop looking at me like that, Kenickie. No one looks good in these awful uniforms." Except him. He managed to look hot in anything he wore.

"You're not seeing you through my eyes," he quietly said.

We reached the second floor, and my entire body flushed.

We walked to where we'd be out of the way of other kids coming upstairs.

"So are your grandparents still pissed at you about what happened with your parents?"

I nodded-shrugged. "I hate when they're upset with me. But I can't help my feelings."

Also known as the truth.

"At least you didn't get grounded." He smiled. That smile. And I laughed as he asked "Are you ready for today?"

I sighed. "Yeah. But I have Yates first. And Quinn's in there. But so's Warren."

The first two being a double dose of reality I had no interest in dealing with.

"And I'll have to beg Ms. Simmons for a new seat because of Ella being in *there*."

"Natalie, it's Ms. Simmons. You won't have to beg."

True. But I would have to get to her class as fast as I could to avoid Ella altogether.

He stepped closer. "You really do look great. I mean" —his face turned an adorable shade of pink— "you did look pretty cute in my clothes. But the awful uniform fits you."

I giggled at his words. And pink face. "Thanks. But I forgot to bring your clothes."

"Don't worry about it, Sunshine." He leaned down and placed his head beside mine. "I know where to find you if I want them back."

A jolt of electricity shot up my spine and from there exploded and spread everywhere.

My head became a little misty.

He straightened. "I have to go to my locker. Looks like you do, too." He nodded at the two bags I held. He started to turn, then stopped. "But I'll see you at lunch."

Wait...what?

For some reason, I hadn't even thought about us sitting together at lunch.

He winked at me and headed down the hallway.

I went in the opposite direction toward my locker, but paused. To scan the faces of kids walking through the hallway. But nobody was paying any attention to me. No looks of surprise. Or judgment. So if anybody had noticed Shane and I standing so close, smiling blindly at each other while we talked, it hadn't made an impact. A good sign nobody did care, but would that change after lunch today?

I started walking as excitement mingled with fear built inside my stomach.

I'd been really set on sitting with Kassidy, Meg, Warren, and all of them at lunch. But what if he wanted me to sit with him? With his friends? Was I even ready to meet all of his friends? And what if they hated me? Bitchy Natalie. Then Shane's question appeared in my mind. A question that now seemed pretty loaded.

Are you ready for today?

I shoved the fear to the back of my mind and lifted my chin.

Yes. I'd prove to myself *and* him I was ready. For more than just sitting together at lunch.

* * *

Smiling, I entered the cafeteria and went straight for my new table. I also made it a point *not* to look over at the table where I used to sit. But not knowing what Shane had meant by "I'll see you at lunch," I did give his side of the cafeteria a quick glance—my smile dipped.

He wasn't there.

Where could he—I halted when I reached my new table. Because he was on Kassidy's left side, an empty chair between them. J.R. sat to her right.

Everyone stopped talking when they saw me.

A twinge of fear took a hold of me. There was an empty

chair beside Shane, but—everyone gave me warm, friendly smiles. Except Shane. He unleashed that smile.

My brief moment of tension left my body in a quiet breath.

"Hey." Kassidy scooted her chair closer to J.R. "I had a feeling you'd be sitting with us, so we saved you a spot." She casually eyed the space between her and Shane.

I smiled at her and everyone else, and went directly for my seat right next to him.

I sat down, and Shane clasped my left hand under the table.

My tummy did a little *flip*.

"I'm so glad you're sitting with us," Lexi chirped from her seat next to Warren, sitting across from me. "Are you okay? You were so sad on Friday."

As more pieces of my heart came together, I said, "I'm a hundred times better, Lexi."

She gave me a bright smile and popped an orange slice into her mouth.

Shane turned his head away from everyone. "I figured you'd be more comfortable sitting here," he whispered in my ear. "So where's your new seat in Ms. Simmons's class?"

His soft breath on my ear made me shiver. But the kind of shivering that made me want to be All. Alone. With him. Especially since he'd sat over here for me.

I swept those thoughts aside—for now—and whispered, "Thanks. And the opposite side of the room."

I'd slyly watched Ella, handing out buttons to kids before class started. She had exactly what she wanted. All the attention for her campaign. Something she would never give up, meaning she and Quinn wouldn't breathe a word about Saturday night, either.

It would take the attention off of Ella.

I guess it was a good thing for me she-devil Ella Walker wanted to be the first female president of student council.

My eyes then landed on Warren, Lexi, and Jade and Nate, who were sitting on Shane's left side. And a soft smile lifted the corners of my mouth. Because they didn't seem too curious about Shane, or me, sitting with them all of a sudden.

Maybe we really had been super obvious that day during the meeting.

Or maybe nobody *did* care.

"Lexi, Natalie wasn't just sad on Friday. She was pissed. Like all of us," Meg said. She sat between Warren and Owen. "I'd love to know who's been hating on the club."

"Same here," I grumbled.

Shane gave my hand a quick squeeze and released it.

I felt the childish urge to face him and push out my lower lip. But I guess we couldn't eat our lunches with one hand.

"Guys, we'll never know that," Kassidy stated. "We have to let it go."

"But we don't have to let go of the competition." Warren spoke directly to me. "You seem to be in a much better mood today. Though I did notice things were *very* chilly between you and Quinn. And now you're sitting here. What's going on?"

I busied myself with emptying my lunch bag. I had a sandwich and chips today instead of salad and fruit, and I grinned at the really nice change.

Shane, Kassidy, Meg, J.R., and Owen had also become focused on their lunches.

"It's a long story," I finally said. "I'll tell you about it some other time."

Warren's eyes bounced from me to Shane and back. "Okay. We'll absolutely talk later. But what about the competition?"

"Nat, we know Friday was rotten." Jade leaned forward to

see me past Nate and Shane. "But please change your mind. We can still have fun and kick some ass."

I laughed at hearing Jade talk like that and sensed everyone's eyes were on me as I said to her, "I did change my mind. And we're *so* doing the competition."

Silence followed my strong statement. Until my club—my friends—laughed with relief.

"*Yay.*" Lexi quietly clapped her hands. "I'll call my aunt after school and tell her we'll still need her studio this week."

I caught Shane giving me an I-told-you-so smile. Meaning they did love the *real* Natalie.

Something about his smile made me want to grab the folds of his sweater and kiss him. Over and over...

"Our routine's gonna to be so awesome," Owen said before taking a bite of his sandwich.

That earned him a dirty look from Meg, followed by her elbowing his side. Which made him choke a bit on his food.

"Owen." J.R. took one of Kassidy's grapes and threw it at his chest. "Shut the fuck up."

"*Okay,*" he muttered, rubbing his side while retrieving the grape that fell into his lap.

Then I noticed Shane had become weirdly still. But was fighting a smile.

Between that and J.R.'s reaction to Owen's comment, I knew they were up to something.

I looked at Meg, then Kassidy, and their narrowed eyes told me they felt the same way.

"Shane Easton," Kassidy said, a bit loudly, "you swore you weren't going to make you guys look *that* good."

He whipped his head in her direction. "Why are you blaming me?"

"Kass, relax," J.R. said. "You guys will love it. I promise."

She wrinkled her nose at him and went back to eating her grapes.

And the amount of joy and love surrounding this table overwhelmed me. To the point I had to sit back in my chair and find my breath.

This was what I'd been missing. What it felt like to have *real* friends.

"Hey." Shane gently nudged me. "Stop looking so serious."

I opened my mouth, peeked at him—then burst into a wave of giggles at his exaggerated scowl, which reminded me of "teaching" him to skate backward. And I laughed harder when I pictured his *spectacular* wipeout.

He gave me a pretend dirty look. "I don't like the sound of that laugh."

"Um" —Warren cleared his throat— "do we need to leave you two alone?"

Oh. Right. We were surrounded by our friends.

I dragged my eyes from Shane's addictive blue eyes, lit up with humor, and focused on Warren. Giving me a confused, slightly irritated stare. Probably because he'd just figured out I lied to him that day he came over to work on the presentation.

Guilt pricked my conscience as I remembered all the lies I'd told. And for nothing.

I definitely owed him a long, catch-up conversation that would include an apology.

"So," I said, going for a Shane-worthy subject change, "I have to be honest about the competition. It's not these guys I'm worried about." And I didn't feel an ounce of guilt for what I was about to do. "Ella has a really awesome routine planned. To go along with her campaign?"

Warren's face transitioned to interest and he leaned forward. "Spill it, Madam Veep."

I also leaned forward to spill everything I knew.

Chapter Thirty-One

My phone buzzed with a text and I smiled as I shoved my backpack into my locker. There were several kids, talking and laughing loudly, doing the same thing as me since it was lunchtime. And because afternoon classes had been cancelled with it being competition day. We'd also been given a rare free dress day, but nothing "too revealing or inappropriate." So the crazed energy in Pacifica Academy today rivaled the last day of school.

I wanted to sprint to the cafeteria as a way to burn the competition nerves making my tummy flutter. But I also couldn't wait to see him. Another reason for my tummy flutters. Lunch—my new favorite part of the school day—was the only time I'd really seen him this week.

Smiling like the lovesick high school girl I never knew I had in me, I pulled my phone from my back jeans pocket.

So I know I'll see you in a minute, but there's too many of us sitting here to say you've been glowing this week...Sunshine.

I giggled and replied with, *Guess that nickname finally fits me...Kenickie. I'm on my way.*

I closed out of text messaging and shoved my phone back

into my pocket. I then grabbed my lunch, shut my locker door, turned—and found myself looking at Maddie.

My smile disappeared. Like I'd been caught doing something criminal.

Especially since her normally friendly brown eyes were filled with cold fury.

"It's your fault," she said with so much bitterness I drew back.

My heart started thudding against my chest.

"You're the *real* reason he didn't want to get back together with me."

Oh, shit.

Though we were together, nothing had hit the school's gossip mill. Which I'd taken as an awesome sign that nobody *did* care. But it's not like we'd been walking around school and holding hands. Just quick, very friendly morning hellos, and sitting together at lunch. With our friends. And some sneaky texting throughout the school day.

Fear slithered through me.

My eyes darted left, right, but the kids still in the hallway seemed focused on their friends and getting their lunches.

"I can't believe it's you," she said. With clear disgust in her voice.

I stood there, mute, not sure what to say. *It all started with my 68 Camaro and classic muscle car trivia* sounded lame in my head.

"I don't get it." Tears filled her eyes. "Sure. You're really pretty. And rich. But you're...bitchy Natalie Carlisle. Who hangs out and parties with college boys on the weekends."

I straightened. She'd just clawed a very sensitive spot.

Would I *ever* get rid of that image?

"What does he see in you? What does he have in common with you?"

My phone buzzed with his reply.

Of course.

Her tears started flowing from her eyes. "I also can't believe...Shane Easton...of all the boys in this school...chose you over...me." Her voice broke on the last word.

I glanced again at the kids and my stomach lurched.

Now they were watching and listening. She didn't seem to care, either.

My heart felt like it might beat through my chest. And here I'd been loving the fact I'd been so happy. Free of guilt and fear.

"I don't care what...Kassidy says about you. That you're *really* nice. You sat there...all last week...listening to me...pretending to care...and the whole time—you're horrible." She sniffed. "And have been...since we were freshmen. I'm not the only one...who feels that way."

Okay. I had to snap out of it and say something in my defense.

"Maddie, Shane and I...started out as friends and—"

"I know...you'll get bored with him and break...*his* heart. I've seen the way he looks at you...since you've been sitting together at lunch."

I heard the jealousy in her voice. But imagining her watching him—us—made the hair on my arms shoot straight up.

I knew she had serious stuff going on outside of school. Still, this creepy behavior didn't seem like the Maddie Harrington Shane had talked about and tried to help. As a friend.

She leaned forward. "I just hope I'm around so I can see the look on his face when you crush him into a million pieces." She sniffed a couple times, wiped her cheeks, and gave me a she-devil smile. "And Ella's right. I do feel *much* better."

I froze for a few seconds, then gritted my teeth. Because now this all made perfect sense.

Maddie spun from me and bolted down the hallway.

And of course Ella had talked Maddie into confronting me right before the competition.

That crazy bitch.

Had I really called her my *best friend* for five years?

I stared at the floor as my body trembled from rage. I also took the deepest breaths I could to get myself under control. I couldn't walk into the cafeteria looking beaten. Because I knew Ella would be watching for me. I also didn't need Shane or my friends knowing anything was wrong. Not today of all days.

I raised my head, avoiding the stares of kids walking by me who'd caught the rotten confrontation, then turned and headed in the same direction as them and Maddie.

Fear of what just happened hitting the school's gossip mill by the end of lunch tried to replace my anger, but I squashed it with each step closer to the cafeteria.

I couldn't—wouldn't—let this ruin such an important day.

Chapter Thirty-Two

Meg, Paige, and Erin were almost cowering by the stage's back wall in front of the Rydell High backdrop. Greased Lightning had been pushed to the stage's right side, opposite of us, and covered with a blanket so lip syncing competitors wouldn't screw with it.

"I can't do this." Paige sounded like she might start hyperventilating. "I'm gonna be sick. And I didn't even eat lunch today because I was so nervous."

"Totally agree with everything Paige said." This from Meg.

We were up next. After a few sophomore girls on stage finished their routine to some Ariana Grande song.

I eyed Kassidy who looked pale. A little weird, too, since she was used to this.

"I'll take Paige and Erin, and you take Meg?" I asked.

She nodded, and we closed the small gap between us and the three other girls.

Kassidy started her pep talk with Meg.

I said to Paige and Erin, "Look at me." They raised their heads and looked like death was coming for them. "You know what you're doing. Our rehearsal yesterday was awesome. We've *so* got this."

They didn't look convinced, but I felt I deserved an Academy Award for my strong words and equally strong performance from the moment I walked into the cafeteria. But then, everyone had been bursting with lip sync competition excitement. And nerves. Well, except Shane.

I smiled softly, remembering his face bright with more excitement than nerves. But getting up on stage and performing was his thing.

Lexi came up and stood between Kassidy and me, which brought me back to the now. The reality the competition was here and we were up next.

My tummy went back to fluttering. Probably a good thing I, like Paige and Meg, hadn't eaten much of my lunch.

"Everyone's been *soooo* good," Lexi said while she played with the end of her braid.

We—the girls—had voted to wear our hair in two braids, to keep it out of our faces. Warren had decided all of us should wear black jeans, Converse, and "positively white" T-shirts.

"But I have to admit," Lexi continued, "I'm kinda happy Ella's group wasn't as good as we thought they'd be."

That made me smile. Wickedly.

Ella, Quinn and Maddie's lip syncing and dancing throughout their routine to "Salute" had been really...off. The older girl power song fit Ella. And her campaign. But they hadn't rehearsed enough. So none of us could argue with Lexi, and my friends shared relieved smiles.

I held onto my wicked one.

Warren, Jade and Alisha walked up. They'd been watching the sophomore girls.

"They're not bad, but look nervous," Warren said. "We can beat them."

"But what about Drew's group?" Jade whined.

"Drew's routine was perfect," Warren said, and then sighed. "Because *he's* perfect."

I affectionately patted his arm.

Drew's "Happier" routine with Liam, two other boys I vaguely recognized from the plays, and Bree, the only girl in their group, had been pretty cool *and* perfect. Their applause had been loud. As I'd watched them, I'd wondered if Shane would've been in their routine if he hadn't joined up with J.R. and Owen. Those three were going last and, because of that, had been assigned sitting on the other side of the auditorium from us. Which totally sucked.

JFK walked up to us holding a clipboard and pen. He, as the soon outgoing president of student council, had been running the competition with help from Mr. Yates and Mr. Lowry.

"They'll be done in a few seconds," JFK said. "Are you ready?"

Warren nodded for us, and JFK walked away.

The nine of us came in for a silent group hug.

The other music stopped. We heard the applause. The three sophomore girls appeared backstage and burst into relieved laughter.

"Okay," we heard JFK say into his microphone. "Next we have Warren and Friends."

We broke apart and headed for the enormous thick curtain blocking the audience from seeing the backstage. And as I looked at my *incredible* friends shaking from excitement and nerves, courage erupted from my soul.

I said, "Jade was right on Monday. Let's kick some ass."

Jade gave me an enormous smile and giggled. Then we strutted onto the stage.

The opening notes of "High Hopes" exploded from the sound system.

We launched into our club power routine.

And all of us nailed our lip syncing parts and power anthem dance moves.

What seemed like two-and-a-half *seconds* later, we jogged off the stage and collapsed into laughter. From success and relief.

"*OhmyGod*," Paige said around her laughing. "I'm *so* glad that's over."

"Totally agree with what Paige just said," Meg said, trying to catch her breath.

"But did you hear the boys hollering and whistling for us?" Jade asked.

I'd heard it, but thought it was my adrenaline making all the applause and hollering and whistling sound louder. But I giggled, thinking about Shane, J.R. Owen, and Nate, sitting somewhere behind the competitors, reacting to our routine that way.

"Yeah, because we did kick some *serious* ass," Lexi snarled. But in a triumphant way.

I laughed harder at this way different side to super sweet Lexi. And the fact she was right.

"Who *are* you right now?" Warren asked Lexi, his eyes round with awe.

"Sorry," she replied as we headed for the stairs to go back to our seats. "I have a pretty intense...competitive side. From years of dancing competitions."

"'Intense?'" Warren mumbled. "More like scary."

We sat together in the third row on the right side of the auditorium. All the competitors had been assigned seats up front for quick access to the stage.

A gigantic part of me wanted to stretch my neck up to find them—Shane—on the other side of the auditorium. But that would be too obvious. And silly. So I settled into my seat between Kassidy and Warren as a group of boys walked onto the stage...and did a routine to a really annoying hip-hop/rap song. But I stopped myself from rolling my eyes since the boys looked pretty wobbly from nervousness.

Getting up on that stage, in front of peers and teachers, wasn't easy. And I smiled at the fact I'd conquered and done something so fucking insane. Despite Maddie's confrontation, too.

My smile grew as more of my heart came together. To the point it was near whole again.

* * *

JFK walked out, holding a microphone in his right hand, the clipboard and pen in his left. "And, as the last group for our first lip sync competition, we have J.R., Owen, and Shane."

He left, and the boys sauntered out.

My smile became lovesick, goofy at the sight of him.

They'd chosen to wear snug, red T-shirts and jeans.

They stood there, with their heads angled down, and the music started. It had an upbeat, pop song feeling to it. Then J.R., standing a little ahead of Shane and Owen, lifted his head and started lip syncing and moving to—

Kassidy gasped. "Oh. My. God. They chose 'I Like Me Better,'" she cooed while her mouth curved into a sappy smile. "It's why they're wearing *red* shirts."

I glanced at Meg, whose expression matched Kassidy's.

I watched J.R. lip syncing and moving with the music, and focused on the song I didn't recognize since I never listened to music like this. But as I listened to the lyrics, my mouth drifted open. Because they'd chosen a love song.

They lip synced the super sweet chorus together, then broke out some well-rehearsed dance moves during an instrumental break.

I released a quick laugh. And my smile became sappy, and

I pictured me, Kassidy, and Meg looking like cartoon girls with hearts popping out of our eyes.

"Oh, no." Warren sighed. "Almost every girl in this auditorium who didn't compete, and maybe even some guys, are going to vote for them. So much for first place."

I laughed as Owen and J.R. smoothly switched places, and Owen lip synced the second verse. And did as good a job as J.R. He even seemed comfortable with the dancing. But not as comfortable as J.R. Or Shane. Who could dance really well.

My insides crackled and zinged as I watched him.

I shook my head and leaned forward to see Meg, sitting on Kassidy's left side. Her mouth was slightly open and in a half smile. And Kassidy had her hands over her mouth as she giggled.

After the chorus and their dancing, Shane and Owen smoothly switched places, and Shane lip synced the bridge. Which had a high part at the end that he exaggerated. In a cute, drama boy way. And just enough to earn laughter. Then the song stopped, and they stood the way they'd looked at the beginning of their *ridiculously* sweet and adorable routine.

We joined the very loud applause. And hollered. Meg even whistled.

They, smiling like they'd just beaten the devil, sauntered off stage.

JFK came out and told everyone, who hadn't been in the competition, to cast their votes.

All I wanted to do was hunt Shane Easton down, grab the front of his red T-shirt, kiss him, and tell the truth. That their routine *and* him had put the rest of my heart back together.

Chapter Thirty-Three

"Okay. We have our winners," JFK said to the packed auditorium buzzing with anticipation, "for Pacifica Academy's First Lip Sync Competition. Are you ready?"

The auditorium exploded with applause and hollers.

All nine of us glanced at each other, our eyes wide with nervous excitement.

We'd done as good as the other groups, if not better than most of them. We had to have at least placed. I felt that in my trembling body. But, at the same time, did it even matter?

"We have a tie for third place."

Kassidy, Warren, and Lexi, on Warren's right side, straightened.

"Our third-place winners are...Bryan and the Soccer Boys with 'Don't Go Breaking My Heart' and...Ella, Quinn, and Maddie with 'Salute.'"

Bryan, a senior, and two of his friends were sitting in the front row of our section and, as they laughed, ambled onto the stage. They'd exaggerated their lip syncing and dancing to their song, sung by some boy band, and while wearing their soccer uniforms.

I slouched in my seat and applauded, but for Bryan's group. They had been funny.

"Seriously?" I muttered. "Ella, Quinn, and Maddie got third place?"

I looked at my friends, and their expressions were full of surprise and disappointment. At the total unfairness. Them getting third place also meant Ella might actually be elected the first girl president of our student council in a couple weeks. But none of us would be voting for her.

"I hate to say this," Warren said, "but Ella did choose a pretty perfect song. And I knew Bryan Costello and his friends would get something."

Okay. I could give Ella Walker that much credit, too. But still—

"There's two more places that could also have a tie!" Lexi whispered.

I swallowed my giggle at her fierceness as I watched Ella, Quinn, and Maddie, who'd been sitting in the center section, walk onto the stage to get their ribbon. And I again smiled wickedly from the fact Ella *wasn't* smiling about her third place. Or that she'd tied with Bryan's silly routine. She must've really thought she'd get first place, and I rolled my eyes.

Bryan and his friends, still laughing, dramatically bowed after JFK gave them their ribbon. Which made lots of kids applaud louder.

All of them stayed on stage while JFK said, "In second place, no tie, we have...our lover boys, J.R., Owen, and Shane with 'I Like Me Better.'"

Everyone burst into rowdy applause. Including the nine of us. Because they deserved it.

"I can't even be mad at them about this," Kassidy said with a huge grin as she clapped.

"Yeah," Warren agreed around a sigh. "I think I'm in love with them now."

I giggled as I clapped harder. But as they walked slowly onto the stage, I could tell by their deer-caught-in-headlights expressions they were shocked by the win. They didn't want the win, either, since they weren't smiling. In fact, they looked really guilty.

"They feel bad," I said to Kassidy and Warren when their applause died down. And my smile faded a bit at seeing their guilty, confused expressions since they'd *earned* second place.

Kassidy nodded. "You're right. Another reason I can't be mad at them."

Lexi leaned forward. "Guys, there's still first place! Why can't it be us?"

Wow. Warren had been right. This side of Lexi *was* a little scary.

I laughed. Because I so didn't care about winning first place. I'd won way more than some silly trophy or ribbon this week. I just wanted to get the hell out of this auditorium, this school, and be All. Alone. With Shane.

JFK lifted the microphone to his mouth and said, "And finally our first-place winners, who will get the trophy we had made for the competition, are..."

Kassidy and Warren, and I'm sure Lexi, took deep breaths.

"Drew and Crew with 'Happier.'"

* * *

I glanced at Shane as we walked to his place. He'd decided not to go into work today so we could spend some time alone, talking. Hopefully doing other stuff, too. Like finally having our second kiss. And a million more after that. So his flat expression made my stomach twist, because I'd put it there. Again. After telling him what happened with Maddie.

But I'd left out she'd been watching him. Us.

"Hey." I gently nudged him. "Stop looking so serious."

I waited for him to look at me so I could give him my exaggerated scowl. But he didn't.

"I knew something was up with you at lunch," he grumbled.

I frowned. "How? I acted totally normal." Seriously, how did he know me so well?

"Yeah." His eyes cut to mine. "But you weren't glowing."

Oh. I guess when it came to him, award-winning performances would never be possible. But I smiled, since I was beyond okay with that.

"I figured it was because you were nervous about the competition." He cracked a smile. "You guys were freakin' awesome, too. I love that band. And song. You looked incredible up there. And deserved to place. Not—" His flat expression returned. "Natalie, why didn't you tell me Maddie did that to you? It's not like her to act like that, either." He shook his head. "But she's pulled away from her *real* friends the last couple weeks."

The concern in his voice, combined with what he'd said, tugged my heart. Because I now understood that whatever Maddie was going through outside of school meant she needed and deserved to be surrounded by her *real* friends.

"I hate hearing she's doing that." I clasped his left hand and laced our fingers together. "And I didn't tell you because I knew it would upset you." I smiled. "Telling you might've affected *your* incredible performance today, Kenickie." I squeezed his hand. "You guys really deserved first place."

He, not smiling, stared straight ahead. "But we weren't supposed to be incredible enough to place. That wasn't the point."

"Shane..." I practically groaned. Because I needed and wanted the real Shane right now. "Me, Kassidy, Meg, Warren,

Lexi—*all* of us—know that. I promise it's fine." Another truth hit and I said, "At some point, being in the competition became something I had to do. I don't care that we didn't place or win." Sharing that truth with him made me give him a blinding smile.

"I get it, Sunshine," he murmured. Without looking at me.

Okay. We needed to wrap this up and get back on the same page of finally being alone together for the first time since early Sunday morning on the way to my grandparents' house.

"And the whole thing with Maddie—"

"Do you want me to talk to her? I mean, we're obviously not friends anymore. But I'll talk to her on Monday if you want me to."

"*No!*" I said, and too sharply. But we wasn't listening. "I hate hearing you're not friends, but don't blame her. Because she was mostly under the influence of Ella Walker." But saying that made his flat expression become dark.

"Yeah," he muttered. "And when all of us were walking off the stage there at the end, I caught Ella off to the right with Maddie and Quinn." He glanced at me. "I couldn't hear what she was saying to them, but she looked *pissed*."

I cringed, imagining the nasty things she must've said, mostly to Maddie. Ella had probably blamed her for their rough performance and third-place win. Which tugged my heart even more. But Maddie had made her choices. Hopefully she'd find her way back to her *real* friends after seeing the *real* Ella. And Quinn. Who'd probably done nothing to defend her.

I pushed those images from my mind, then stopped walking, which made him stop.

Time to pull a Shane-worthy subject change.

I closed the tiny gap between us, slowly hooked my arms behind his neck, and unleashed *my* wicked smile. "Kenickie, we're about to be all alone, at your place, for at *least* a couple hours." I guided his head down to mine. "Let's try a new topic. Something like—"

"No." He leaned back, his eyes filled with sadness and guilt. "I can't do this anymore."

Silence filled the small space between us. Then sirens started going off in my head as I became very aware of how he was leaning so far back I had to tighten my hands to keep them folded behind his—I removed my arms from around his neck and stepped backward.

What the hell was going on here? With him?

I lifted my chin. "What does *that* mean?"

His shoulders fell with frustration. "That didn't come out right." He cleared his throat. Which so wasn't a good sign. "I've been trying to tell you something for a week. But the timing's been...wrong. And I've hardly seen you. It's another reason I took this afternoon off."

The sirens in my head became louder.

Apparently, he'd planned on more talking than other stuff.

"I don't want to do this now, but I have to because of what Maddie and *Ella* did to you."

It sounded like he'd said those last few words through his teeth.

"I've also—" He looked at me and his eyes softened. "Fallen for you. And I'm sick of secrets."

Okay. He'd fallen for me.

My neck, shoulders and back gradually relaxed as I allowed his confession to sink into my head...my heart...my soul. And I wanted to leap into his arms. Then kiss him. Until we couldn't breathe. But what kind of secret did he have that would upset him this much? And even after saying something so unbeliev-ably amazing? Maybe he needed to hear what I felt for him?

I smiled. "Would it make you feel better if I told you I feel the same way about you?"

He smiled, too, but it didn't reach his eyes. That were more gray than hypnotic blue.

"Yes...and no. Because I'm afraid what I'm going to say might make you mad. At me."

The warning sirens returned as my smile eased back into a frown.

He released a quick sigh. "Ella and Quinn were the ones who got your club shut down."

Chapter Thirty-Four

Wait...*what* did he say?

I stared at him as he concentrated on kicking a raised portion in the sidewalk with the toe of his shoe.

No. He didn't just say what I thought I'd—

"I overheard them in the T-Rex's class," he mumbled, still looking down. "Talking about leaving typed messages about the club in the student council suggestion box...when Mr. Yates wasn't around. So he wouldn't know it was only the two of them."

Oh, my God.

But of course it'd been Ella. Fucking. Walker. She'd always hated me being in the club. Blamed the club for my change into the *real* Natalie, who she also hated. But *Quinn*? She'd always seemed more accepting of the club and my club—my friends. And other kids in school. That's why we'd always called her the "nice one" of our little group. Or former group.

The fact they'd typed the notes, probably to avoid Mr. Yates noticing the notes were coming from the same handwriting, felt like an additional blow. And my breath left me at one thought—they'd gone to a lot of trouble to get my club shut down.

Betrayal and rage then filled my blood and went straight to my eyes.

I now understood the phrase "seeing red."

I blinked Shane into focus and narrowed my eyes. He'd known about this. But for how long? Maybe he'd only known for a week. He'd said something about trying to tell me—

"I knew it," he muttered. "I can tell by the way you're looking at me you're pissed."

"And feeling a little betrayed. Not much." I took two steps backward, which put me almost on the sidewalk's curb. "How long have you known?"

He flinched.

Another really bad sign. But I closed my eyes, willing him to say—

"Do you remember that day I fell off the grid? When I never answered your trivia question for me?"

Oh, *shit*.

I opened my eyes.

His face had turned crimson. He was also kicking the sidewalk again.

How could he have held onto this for over three weeks? And after I'd told him a week ago we'd been shut down—oh. *That's* why he reacted the way he did.

I started walking—more like marching—away from him. "How could you wait so long to tell me this?" I snapped at him. "What the hell were you thinking?"

"Okay," he said, following me. "I fucked up. And I tried to tell you—would you *wait?*" He managed to clasp my right hand and stopped us.

I pulled my hand from his, crossed my arms, but kept my eyes on the ground.

"I tried telling you last week at community service. But you..." He sighed.

Okay. Fine. I hadn't exactly been in a talking mood that horrible day. But him telling me a week ago was still a couple weeks too late.

"I should've told you anyway," he finished. "I should've told you right after I found out. Because if I had, you probably wouldn't have ended up at that *fucking* party with them."

I looked up, and our eyes snapped together.

"Natalie, I'm so sorry."

The guilt radiating from his eyes and face deflated me. My shoulders fell forward, and my arms fell to my sides. And my anger with him evaporated. But confusion held on tight.

"Shane, I understand why you didn't tell me last Saturday." I leaned forward. "And what happened with that *asshole* and my really bad choices weren't your fault. Okay?"

He didn't say a word or move. Until, finally, giving me a slight, curt nod. Though he clearly *didn't* agree with me. But I couldn't focus on that right now.

I shook my head. "What I don't understand is why you didn't tell me right away."

He lifted his shoulders. "I didn't think you'd believe me."

I squinted at him. "Why?"

He frowned. "They were supposed to be your best friends and you were so defensive of them. And didn't know me very well." He went back to kicking the sidewalk. "I also didn't want to piss you off. Right as we were...you know."

Maybe he had a small point about me not believing him. Then again, the week before spring break had been the beginning of the end of my friendship with Ella Walker.

"I might have surprised you," I quietly said. "And if you'd told me *three weeks ago* all of us could've gone to Mr. Yates and—"

"I did go to Mr. Yates. That day."

My eyes widened.

He'd gone to Mr. Yates about this? Really? Like he said, we hadn't known each other very well three weeks ago. Had it only been *three* weeks?

It didn't seem possible so much of me and my life had changed in such a short time.

"I told him the notes he was getting about your club were bullshit. I didn't use that word," he swiftly added, "but he didn't believe me. Or didn't want to. And all of that's why I had such a bad day. And didn't text you back."

I stayed silent as I let his words sink into my overloaded brain.

It *was* nice he'd gone to Mr. Yates. But I couldn't let go of the feeling if he'd told me sooner, the entire club could've gone to the student council advisor and talked to him.

"Thank you for going to Mr. Yates," I said. "But I wish you would've told me sooner."

Because how could Mr. Yates have ignored all of us saying the same thing? About my former, evil best friends. And I still couldn't believe Ella had talked Quinn into helping her with that nasty mission. Or maybe I could believe it. Quinn had always been the true follower.

Though none of this was my fault, the guilty weight returned to my shoulders. For my "so-called best friends" getting the club shut down.

So-called best friends.

How many times had Shane called them that? Because he'd known the truth about them. Which he should've told me three weeks ago. But maybe I should've seen their evilness. And would I have believed him then?

"I feel so stupid right now," I mumbled.

"Natalie, you trusted them," he quietly said. "You're supposed to trust your friends."

I nodded-shrugged. I then remembered Shane showing up

at our Thursday meeting with J.R. and Owen. And he'd fallen off the grid Wednesday.

Had all this been the real reason he'd—I looked over at him. I had to know.

"Is this why you were in the competition with J.R. and Owen? Because of guilt?"

Hurt hit his eyes. "No. I mean, I know it might look that way, but...*no*. I was supposed to be in it with Drew and Liam and those guys. But J.R. and Owen were talking in class that Thursday morning about not being able to be with you guys and—" He straightened. "I did it for the same reasons as J.R. and Owen."

I looked away. Though he had seemed and sounded sincere.

Still, another question appeared in my mind.

How had this perfect week with him—almost perfect day —ended like *this*?

Shit.

My defensive armor came up. I folded my arms tight across my chest. "Since we're done talking, which you said was the reason you took off work, I want to go home."

He'd planned on taking me when his mom or dad got home from work. But this *awesome* and honest talk had definitely killed the excitement of being alone with him.

"Natalie..." He sounded and looked defeated. "I can't take you home until—"

"It's fine." I pulled my phone from my back jeans pocket and faced the direction we'd come from. "I'll call my grandma and wait for her at school."

Had I been almost bouncing alongside him minutes earlier? Trying to cheer him up?

And the whole time he'd known this conversation was coming. Probably another reason why he'd held onto his dark mood so tightly.

My stupidity tripled in size and strength. But I had to give him credit for being a great actor today. Because I hadn't seen any of this coming. Especially after their performance.

"You can't be serious." He stepped toward me. "My place is really close."

"I told you it's fine," I said, going around him.

"Okay. Then I'm coming with you."

"No." I stopped to look at him over my shoulder. "I know you're feeling guilty about what happened last Saturday night. About all of this." I sighed. "But I'm sick of secrets *and* drama. And I just want to be alone right now. To...process."

His expression went back to flat.

"I'll see you later." I turned and headed in the direction of school.

I trembled at the thought of this newest thing coming between us.

Last time it had been the shock from Maddie's texts to Shane I never should've seen. And a combo of Ella and Quinn and fear of school gossip. Fear of harsh judgment.

I'd slowly shaken off the fear of gossip and judgment. Just by being around him. Being around my real friends. And my *everything* was lighter because of letting go of all that crap.

But we couldn't seem to go very long without drama blowing up between us.

Chapter Thirty-Five

"Sweetheart?"

I slid my eyes from my bulletin board to Grams, standing in my bedroom doorway.

"We're about to leave."

I managed a smile. "You look really nice." My smile inched into a strong one. "Gramps is going to have the hottest date tonight."

She laughed and smoothed down the front of her modest, but elegant, black evening gown. "Thank you. But I'm wishing this dinner was another night." Her eyes filled with concern. "It's not right your grandpa and I have plans while you, our beautiful granddaughter, are home alone on a Friday night."

I shrugged. "Grams, I'm fine." But that was such a lie.

Had lying become, at some point, a physical part of me I'd never shed?

"I also wish you'd tell me what happened with Shane."

In truth, I wasn't pissed at him.

I went back to focusing on my bulletin board. Specifically, some polaroids of me with Ella and Quinn, the three of us huddled together and smiling for the camera. Like we were best friends.

"Alright," Grams said. "We'll be home pretty late. I'll see you in the morning."

I nodded while still staring at the photos. "Have fun."

I'd stupidly been a loyal friend to Ella Walker and Quinn Abbott since we were twelve. I'd also stupidly followed Ella's rotten lead, because I thought it made me stronger. The girl no one wanted to cross paths with for fear I'd rip them a new one. Like I'd done to Shane before I allowed myself to really know him. And some kids, like Theresa Flanagan, had deserved my bitchy side. But some of them, like Shane and sweet Lexi and awkward Erin, hadn't. Like so many others. I didn't want to think of the number.

I'd gained a horrible image being that Natalie. The one Maddie threw in my face. And though I blamed Ella and Quinn for most of this, I also blamed myself.

I narrowed my eyes.

I'd seen Ella's nastiness toward others too many times to count. But I hadn't really seen *their* phoniness and lies when it came to me. They'd been my harshest judgers, too. I'd wasted so much time being their friend. Wasted three years of high school. I'd only been to one school dance. I'd never gone to any school games. And the only club I'd joined had originally been about anti-love—I shook my head.

I'd found my real friends who loved the *real* me by joining an Anti-Love Club.

I'd also missed out on having Shane Easton as a boyfriend all this time.

Of all the school shows he'd been in, I'd only paid attention to *Romeo and Juliet* and could barely remember his part. But I couldn't wait to see him on stage as Kenickie, performing his big "Greased Lightning" number on the car we were building together.

Yeah, he'd made a huge mistake not telling me the truth sooner. But it's not like I hadn't made some huge mistakes in the last few weeks. I couldn't lose him twice. Not over this.

Because I did deserve him. Deserved to be happy.

I was so done. With Ella. With Quinn. With that Natalie. With any remaining fear.

I had been stupid. But not anymore. And I knew exactly what I needed to do tonight since I'd have the house to myself for hours. I also needed him to be a part of it, since it would feel that much more real.

I took a deep breath and picked up my phone.

I could only hope I hadn't blown it by pushing him away. For a second time.

But he picked up after only a couple rings.

"Hi," he said, sounding shocked and not just a little relieved.

My heart fluttered at hearing his voice. "Hi. Thank God you answered."

"Thank God you called."

We shared a quick, nervous laugh.

"Because I didn't think I'd...ever hear from you again," he quietly added.

I leaned back in my chair. "Guess that means I did surprise you."

"Yeah. You do that a lot." I heard the smile in his voice. "So this must mean you don't hate me?"

"Never." I picked at the edge of my desk. "Shane, I'm sorry for walking away from you. Again. I was just hurt and confused, and needed time."

"Natalie, no more apologies. Okay?"

I smiled. "Yes. And I agree no more secrets."

"Or drama," he added. "But I wish I was there to make it official with a pinky swear."

I hesitated, then said, "It's funny you should mention that. Are you busy right—"

"No."

I giggled. "Great. Because I need you to be here for something pretty important. And my grandparents," I playfully added, "are out for the night."

There was a pause on his end before, "I'm leaving now. And I'll drive my mom's car as fast as it'll go."

I shook with more giggles as we hung up, then stood.

With the night being comfortable, we could do this on the deck. I just had to find a metal bucket, lighter fluid, and matches. And a fire extinguisher. To be safe. But I'd go easy on the lighter fluid. I didn't need the fire department showing up like they had at Meg's house in September. I then reached out and, one-by-one, plucked *those* photos off my board.

* * *

I opened the front door. And Chloe darted out. But Shane caught her.

"Thanks," I said, gobbling him up with my eyes as he straightened.

It looked like he still had on his clothes from the competition, but had pulled on a black, Vans hoodie sweatshirt. His hair was tousled, too. Like he'd had his window rolled down.

I wanted to pounce on him. But he was holding my dog, enthusiastically licking his chin. And pouncing would have to wait. For now.

"Come on," I said. "We're going to the deck."

He closed the door, carefully put Chloe down, and followed me.

"I'll be honest," he said around a quick laugh. "This wasn't exactly how I saw this moment going the entire way over here."

I laughed. "Just wait, Kenickie."

And then we were on the deck, but I'd closed the sliding-glass door. To keep Chloe inside and the smoke outside.

I peeked at him and bit my lower lip as his eyes swept over the display.

I'd placed all my purging tools as far from the house as possible. I'd also dropped what I'd—we'd—be burning in a pile near the bucket.

He raised his eyebrows. "You've been busy, Sunshine."

I dropped to my knees in front of my pile. "Welcome to The Purging."

It was really Phase One of the Natalie Carlisle purging. But that was between this Natalie—the real one—and the old Natalie.

"The Purging..." he murmured while taking in the dark mistiness surrounding us.

The only significant light we had came from one lit lamp in the living room.

"Why do I suddenly feel like I've walked into a horror movie?"

I rolled my eyes. "Sit down. It'll be fun. And fine. I promise."

He dropped beside me, crossed his legs and eyed me. A bit warily. "And why do I get the feeling you've done this before?"

I ignored that and picked up the stack of photos I'd collected from my board and frames on my bedroom wall. "All the photos of me with *them* I had in my bedroom." I dropped them into the bucket. "And I've already deleted all the photos I had of us on my phone."

He nodded and smiled.

I picked up the worn bracelet. "A *friendship* bracelet Quinn made me in the sixth grade. Actually, she made one for the three of us." I tossed it into the bucket.

His smile grew.

"And you'll especially like this part." I picked up the flimsy dress I'd worn to that *fucking* party almost a week ago.

I held the dress out so he could see it.

His eyes lit up with recognition, but his mouth tightened.

"I wish I could burn that," he muttered. "And the images of you getting away from—"

"Shane, that's what tonight's for. Burning all the bad stuff." I balled the dress up, threw it into the bucket, and roughly wiped my hands on my jeans. "And moving on. Starting over." I caught his eyes. "Without all the ugly emotions. Like fear. And guilt."

He was silent for several moments, then sighed. "Okay. You're right." He closed his eyes for a few seconds, then opened them. "Consider those images in the bucket. But the guilt..." Our eyes locked. "That'll take more time, Sunshine."

My heart and soul hurt at hearing him say that. But, maybe, all this would help him move past the guilt a little faster.

"Okay," I softly said. "I think we're ready for the lighter fluid."

He handed it over. "Be careful with this. It won't take much for that stuff to ignite." He huffed. "And burning down your grandparents' house won't earn me any points with them. Or your parents."

"I know." I squirted a quick round of fluid into the bucket. "Trust me."

He handed me the matches and took the lighter fluid. "We shouldn't be this close, either. I really hate hospitals."

We stood, and I took out a match. But before I swiped it against the side, I mentally said, *Ella and Quinn, you give friendship a bad name.*

I lit the match and...let go.

And I burst into laughter after a somewhat tame flame shot out of the bucket; the crackling from inside the sound of the old Natalie Carlisle becoming nothing but ashes. Maybe I'd even release them into the air. But much, *much* later. To be very safe.

"Feel better?" he asked with a trace of humor.

I turned toward him. "Fuck yeah." Though I still had two more phases to my purging.

But right now I wanted to focus on him. Us. Starting over.

"Thanks for being here for this," I said. "Do *you* feel any better?"

He smiled. "Yeah." His eyes darted to the flame. "Wow." He shook his head. "Setting things on fire wasn't even on my radar when you said you needed me to be here for something."

I reached out, grabbed a fistful of his sweatshirt and tugged him toward me. "So what *was* on your radar, Kenickie?"

He slipped his arms around my waist and smiled. That smile. "I was hoping you'd ask."

He lowered his head, and I tilted mine up.

And that's all it took to finally start our second kiss.

Chapter Thirty-Six

"H i."

I looked left at the sound of my dad's voice. Then he, my mother, and grandparents walked into my room. I hadn't known they were back from their trip.

And all of them being in here couldn't be good.

"Can we talk to you for a bit?" my dad asked.

I nodded, and he and my mother sat on the foot of my bed. My grandparents kept standing. They were giving me warm smiles, but I had Chloe in my lap and hugged her to me.

"What are you doing?" My mother looked at the empty picture frames on my bed.

"I'm redoing my pictures," I stated. "I'm not friends with Ella and Quinn anymore." Also known as Phase Two of my purging.

"Are you not friends anymore because of what happened last weekend?" my dad asked.

I shrugged. "That's part of it. They're just not who I thought they were." I gestured to the photos I'd already printed on thick copy paper. "They're my real friends."

"I'm sorry to hear that about Ella and Quinn. Can I see

those?" My mother pointed at my desk, and I picked up the sheets with my photos and handed them to her.

The pictures I'd been printing were the few I had with me and my real friends. I'd also printed the one picture I had of me with Shane I'd taken on my birthday at the skating rink.

Of us standing really close and posing with exaggerated selfie pouts.

Thinking of him brought back memories of our *incredible* night. Especially all the kissing. Like we'd never be alone again.

My faced burned as hot as the fire in the bucket. That we'd actually doused with water before getting lost in...other stuff. And we'd cleaned everything up and he left. A half hour before my grandparents got home.

I took a tiny breath to settle my flickering insides.

Now so wasn't the time to relive last night.

As my parents looked at the pics, Gramps said, "Natalie, we know how much you love being here with us. And we obviously love having you here. But this isn't where you belong when your mom and dad are in town."

My shoulders dropped.

My parents were here to take me home. Though being in the city put me closer to Shane and my friends—definitely a good thing—I still didn't want to leave my Chloe.

I squeezed her little body.

My parents finished looking at the photos and handed the sheets to Grams.

"Honey," my dad began, "what gave you the impression you can't hang a picture of your Camaro in your room at home? You've always been able to do that."

I glanced at my dad. "There's something about that place. It doesn't feel like home."

Wow. That truth had come out without me blinking. And more weight lifted.

I sat up a little straighter.

"Maybe it would feel more like home to you if you decorated your room like this room," my dad countered.

I stared at the top of Chloe's head.

What he'd said *was* true. Maybe I'd never put effort into making that room my real room.

"You don't feel like you can be yourself there," my mother said.

I sighed. "Mom, I'm not like you. Okay? I'm like Dad and Gramps. And I hate looking *perfect* all the time." A little more weight came off of me. "It's not me. I like looking like this." I pointed at myself, still wearing my community service jeans, snug T-shirt, and Converse. I also had my hair pulled up into a tight ponytail. A hairstyle I'd started loving since Shane seemed to love playfully tugging my ponytail. "Especially on the weekends."

"I know you're not like me," she calmly said. "I've known this for years." She tilted her head to the left. "And I know you think I'm unreasonable. But it would be really nice to see some of me in you every now and then. Because you're my daughter, too."

Her surprising honesty hung between us for several quiet seconds, and I nodded.

Maybe what she wanted from me wasn't *so* unreasonable.

She smiled. Affectionately. "I know there's some of me in you, since my Jimmy Choo sandals are missing."

Oh. I'd forgotten about those shoes. But it's not like I'd been home to put them back.

"I wore them last Saturday," I confessed. "They're here. I just need to clean them up."

Her smile deepened. "You can have the shoes. I've only worn them once."

Honesty, an affectionate smile, and a pair of eight-hundred-dollar Jimmy Choo sandals?

My near tantrum last week had actually caught their—her

—attention. And my body felt almost…light. Like floating was a real possibility.

"Perhaps you having those shoes will remind you that you're also *my* daughter?"

I gave her a tiny smile.

I guess there was hope for me and my mother.

Grams, smiling, handed over the sheets with my pictures. "Did you and Shane work things out today at community service?"

Okay. Sometimes I would have to tell *little* white lies.

"Yeah. We're all good." I laughed. "We had a pretty fantastic day, working on Greased Lightning." Trying to stay focused on the car and not on each other.

I then caught my parents and grandparents staring at me. While smiling.

"Are your dad and I ever going to meet him?" my mom asked.

I smiled. "That would be really nice." Especially since I planned on Shane Easton being around for a *long* time.

My parents stood, and my dad said, "We were going to bring you home. But since you're in the middle of redoing your pictures—that you can *also* hang up in your real room— maybe your grandparents can drop you off tomorrow?"

I flushed at his words. But I would definitely print a second round of pics.

"Of course," Grams said. "After we get back from golfing."

Oh, no. They couldn't leave. Because we still had one more thing to talk about.

I stood, too, hugging Chloe to my chest. "What about her?"

My dad and grandparents focused on my mom, and she straightened.

"I'll give it two weeks."

That, too, hung in the air for numerous seconds. Until I

squealed, then laughed. I also wanted to throw my arms around *her*. But we weren't there.

"If there are any problems whatsoever," she continued, "Chloe comes right back here. Without a fight from you. Do you understand me?"

"Yes! There won't be." I hoped. "She'll do great." I bounced in place, squeezing Chloe.

My dad did come in for a hug, and I put Chloe on the floor. He was a great hugger, too. Like Gramps. And me. Must be a Carlisle thing.

"Alright," he said. "We'll see you tomorrow."

They all left, and I sat down. Back to Phase Two of my purging.

The final phase would come first thing Monday morning.

* * *

I marched past my locker and weaved my way in between students toward Ella. She stood at her locker, where I knew I'd find her. And, of course, Quinn stood right beside her.

I had a lot to say to my ex-best friends before this school day started.

When I reached them, I said in a low voice, "You really are an evil bitch, Ella Walker."

She seemed startled. At first. Then her face oozed boredom.

"Like I give a shit what *you* think of me." She continued loading up her backpack.

Quinn remained silent while she watched both of us.

"I know it was you." I glanced at Quinn. "And you. Who lied to Mr. Yates about the club and got it shut down."

Ella rolled her eyes, but Quinn, surprisingly, turned bright red.

Her embarrassment—and maybe some guilt?—fueled the power burning inside me.

"You two were supposed to be *my* best friends. And you jumped down my ass for not being your best friend and doing the competition with you?"

Ella slammed her locker door shut. "We were trying to stop you from *more* social destruction. And totally wasted our time." She gave me her she-devil smile. "But we did get it shut down."

I wanted to slap that smile off her face as I leaned forward. "And I wasted my time. Being your friend for the last five years. Following you around and acting like you." I smiled. But with victory. "I'm nothing like you and I love that feeling." I eyed Quinn, whose face had paled. "And I stupidly thought you were the nice one. But you're just an Ella Walker wannabe." I shrugged. "You'll probably follow her to whatever college she goes to."

Quinn looked away. From my nasty tone.

I guess I still had some of that Natalie in me.

"Are you finished?" Ella asked. "Because I'm bored and need to get to class."

"No." I shook my head. "Not even close." I knew many eyes were on us. Kids were probably straining their ears to hear us, too. "I have *real* friends now. And I have the best, cutest, funniest boyfriend. Who's *not* a loser. Or an asshole," I added in a lowered voice. Then I smiled. Wickedly. "Those words describe the college guys *you two* date."

Quinn's eyes widened. But Ella released a huge sigh.

I glanced at kids nearby. I even spotted Theresa. All of them not bothering to hide the fact they were watching and listening. Some were smiling. And laughing. Like Theresa. Of course.

"In case anyone was still wondering," I said in a raised voice, "Shane Easton is my boyfriend. And we're crazy about each other." I laughed. "No. That's not even enough." I tilted my head back and said even louder, "I love Shane Easton and he loves me. And I don't care who knows it." I lowered my head and turned to look at Theresa, and a couple kids I recognized, but didn't know their names. "Did you hear that?"

The two kids, with wide eyes, slowly nodded. Theresa's eyes rolled upward and she walked away. But Ella and Quinn's mouths had inched open as they stared at me.

"I also love, for anyone still listening," I loudly continued, "fast, *classic* muscle cars. Like a 70 AMX." I focused on a girl standing nearest to me with red glasses. "Do you know what that is? Or what about a 68 Camaro?"

She, looking fearful, shook her head.

"That's too bad." I gave her a bright smile. "My first car and my dream car is a 68 Camaro. I'm Natalie, by the way. What's your name?"

She hesitated, probably not sure if she should answer the girl acting nuts at school on a Monday morning. But I finally felt wide awake.

"I'm Heather. And I know who you are."

"Actually," I replied, "you don't. But you will." I turned my smile on Ella and Quinn, who still looked stunned. "I'm going to go be with my friends now. And Shane. Who love *me*." I leaned forward and quietly added, "You two can do whatever the fuck you want."

I raised my head, turned, and walked away. And I smiled at any of my classmates who happened to catch my eye. Some of them even sort've smiled back. Which I took as a good sign they, too, would like the *real* Natalie Carlisle.

The thought gave my steps a very buoyant feel.

Chapter Thirty-Seven

My insides sizzled as Kenickie performed his "Greased Lightning" number while he stood on top of our solid, big car. That looked more like a convertible box on fake tires.

We'd painted the side now facing the school matinee audience as a white piece of crap, and the other as the red, finished side with a gold lightning bolt. Kenickie's car had also been designed to hold his and Liam's weight. The other T-Birds danced around the car.

The Rydell High backdrop, scoreboard, and other props were, for this number, behind the thick curtain. And there were several old tires Shane and his brother had "stolen" from the shop stacked on top of each other on both sides of the stage.

His smooth, pretty powerful singing filled the auditorium. He looked *hot* up there, too, totally owning his big number, in his tight white T-shirt, black jeans, and black high-top Converse. And it hit me, while he sang the catchy chorus, he'd been perfectly cast as Kenickie. Well, except for Kenickie being an asshole. But I had to give Mrs. Chaplin *some* credit.

"He's nailing Kenickie," Meg said around a laugh as she watched him.

"Yeah." This from Warren on my other side. "He's surprisingly good at playing a jerk."

I laughed. Because it was so true.

The instrumental part began, and he jumped off the car and jogged off stage. Then the stage became dark except for flickering lights. Most of the T-Birds stayed on stage and kept dancing to kind've block us from seeing the tech crew turn the car to its Greased Lighting side.

My eyes wandered to Lexi, J.R., and Owen who were sitting with us, too. Kassidy was working backstage, her way of completing her community service hours.

Thank God mine were done. Shane and I had given our sheets to Mrs. Meridian five seconds after walking into school Monday morning.

The instrumental part started to end. I could just see him, in the darkness and flickering lights, jog back onto the stage to finish his number.

My smile tripled in size.

I had him, my friends, and my *permanent* glowing.

And I knew this because he'd told me. In a text.

* * *

"Okay," Shane said from behind me with his right hand covering my eyes. "Don't expect too much. It's looking really rough right now."

I grinned. "Then why are you covering my eyes?"

He slipped his left arm around my waist and hugged me to him. "Because I know how much you love your car."

I rested my head against the spot between his head and shoulder. "Not as much as I love a certain *someone*."

He laughed. "That's right," he said in a serious-but-playful way. "You're the girl who loves me and I love you."

I laughed with him. Because my...spectacle...*that* Monday morning had become the newest joke between us.

"Are you ready?"

I nodded. "Yes. I'd love to see my car now."

He removed his hand from my eyes.

I opened them. And froze. Then did a double take.

"Told you," he said. "The cars don't look like much after being sandblasted."

In truth, it looked like a rusty piece of shit.

I walked closer to my Camaro. To the point I could touch it.

My car, at some point since I last saw it as a chassis, had been put back together, minus its guts. And windows. Just the car's rusty, metal body sitting on the frame.

"But now," he continued as he stood beside me, "we'll start on the bodywork. Fix all the problems you can see."

I smiled. And laughed. Because I didn't see problems. I only saw my beautiful dream car and *everything* it represented.

I squealed, turned. and threw my arms around him.

"Whoa." He laughed. "Way better reaction than I expected."

I brought his head down to mine, gave him a quick kiss, and went back to admiring my car. I then placed my right hand on the...pretty rough roof. "She looks perfect."

"Well, if you think that right now," he teased, "I can't wait to see your reaction when the car's finished." He laughed again. "I've never seen anyone react that way to their car looking like yours does now."

I faced him. "It's not about how it looks right now. It's about what it represents."

He nodded, and every part of me knew he understood.

Something he'd just said, combined with seeing him looking so at ease in his family's shop, caused me to say, "You said '*we'll* start on the bodywork.'" I smiled. "Do you plan on spending more time here once you're done being Kenickie after tonight?"

His face became the color of a tomato. He then ran a hand through his hair and cleared his throat. And I giggled.

"Okay," he said. "Because we agreed to no more secrets, I'll tell you this last secret."

I reached deep into my soul to become serious and said, "I'm listening." But the laughter building inside me wanted to explode with nuclear-level force.

"I've put myself in charge of your Camaro."

My laughter dried up as his confession dangled between us.

I stared at him, blinking, unable to find the right words. Any words, for that matter. Because of all the amazing things Shane had said to me, *this* made my eyes a little wet.

"So, yeah," he continued, finally meeting my gaze. He gave me a warm smile as his face became its normal color. "I'll be here a couple extra days a week, starting Monday. And I'll be here *a lot* this summer." His smile faded. "I talked to my dad about this earlier." He sighed. "But he thinks this decision will change my mind about Marine Biology. His words. Not mine."

Oh.

My eyes cleared and I wrapped my arms around his waist.

He copied my actions, and I searched my mind for something brilliant to say. Something that would make his frustration disappear. Like it had never shown up to begin with.

But all I could find was, "I think your dad just wants you to be a part of this. What your family created."

"I get that," he mumbled. "But working on your Camaro is for *you*."

We shared affectionate smiles.

"And I can still be a part of this place without making it a full-time job." He shrugged. "Like my sister. She works in the office when she's home for her breaks. Then goes back to her life at NYU."

I nodded and tried a playful grin. "I love you even more for putting yourself in charge of my Camaro." That made him smile. "But maybe you shouldn't work *too* hard on my car? And, maybe, your dad will come around? The closer we get to graduation?"

His smile fell. "I doubt it." He raised his eyebrows. "And of course I'm going to work my ass off when it comes to your car." He smiled again. But that smile. "I have big plans for us. In this car," he almost whispered. With a pretty naughty inflection.

My mouth fell open. But my insides were popping. Like those little firecrackers. I also didn't care he'd, once again, smoothly changed the subject.

Just another thing on the already long list to love about him.

"Shane Easton," I said, giving him a pretend stern look, "you keep surprising *me*."

He gave me his pretend stern look. "Natalie Carlisle, I wasn't talking about *just* that." His smile came back. "But that reminds me, we need to talk about a couple things."

I giggled and said, "Like what?"

"Celebrating the end of *Grease*. Tomorrow afternoon?"

I frowned. "Isn't that what tonight is for after the show?"

He tightened his arms around my waist and turned us. To the point my back was facing my Camaro. "The cast parties are cool." He took us a step closer to my car. "But it's because of *Grease* I haven't seen you enough, alone, since you—and loudly—declared I'm your boyfriend."

I fought a smile as he backed me up another step. "Fine. How does...ice skating sound?"

He stopped and dramatically rolled his eyes. "I'm never going to live my wipeout down."

I bit my lower lip before saying, "Never."

He groaned. "I'll have to run that idea by my ass. Can I get back to you?"

I laughed. Pretty loud and hard, too.

"Okay," I managed to say. "What's the second thing we need to talk about?"

He backed me up until I was against my car. And kissed me. Like he'd never kissed me before and never would again.

"Go to prom with me," he then whispered against my lips. "I'm pretty sure" —kiss— "I can talk my dad" —longer kiss— "into letting me borrow the AMX again."

But our mouths fused before I could answer.

I shivered as everything around us became misty.

Oh, what was it about his bad boy side that made the world fade into nothing.

"Yes," I whispered, a bit breathlessly, when we came up for air. "I'll go with you." I paused, then added, "And not just because you're the perfect boy...for me."

He smiled and pressed his forehead to mine. "I'm really loving the real Natalie."

I sighed. "Me, too."

Author's Note

I hope you enjoyed Book Two in the Pacifica Academy Drama Series that will continue with Maddie's story, *Teddy Brewster's Hold On Me*. Each book can stand alone, but it's recommended they're read in series order for maximum enjoyment.

And if you have a moment, please feel free to leave a brief review at wherever you purchased the book. Authors always appreciate and need honest reader reviews.

Acknowledgments

Natalie and Shane's story required so much research on classic muscle cars and the restoration process. Thank you to *Muscle Cars: Kings of the Street from the Golden Era*, *Muscle Cars: An Illustrated Guide* and the Velocity Channel's numerous shows dedicated to restoring vintage cars. And the History Channel ran their *The Cars That Made America* at the perfect time.

Thanks again to The Killion Group for creating another super cute cover.

And to Miles, for inspiring their special connection and answering *all* of my car questions. I couldn't have written Natalie and Shane's story without you.

About the Author

Christine Miles is a full-time writer living in Albuquerque, New Mexico.

An avid reader and writer since elementary school, her passion for literature inspired her to pursue a BA in English and an MA in Creative Writing. She writes YA and Adult Contemporary Romances with sassy, independent heroines and swoony heroes who love them for their strength.

When not writing romances, she loves traveling, binge-watching shows on streaming apps, reading mysteries and thrillers, listening to music, and spending quality time with her family, friends, and dog.

You can find her on Facebook and Instagram. Sign up for her newsletter to get ARC's and updates at www.christine-milesauthor.com.

www.ingramcontent.com/pod-product-compliance
Lightning Source LLC
Chambersburg PA
CBHW061608190726
48288CB00007B/2228